BAD MOOD DRIVE

BAD MOOD DRIVE
English Edition

Alan Douglas

11/17/2010

Crime Fiction Copyright © 2010 by Alan Douglas

BAD MOOD DRIVE © 2010 by Alan Douglas

ISBN: 978 - 1-6140000-3-7

Library of Congress Control Number: 2014916291

eBook Publisher-Los Angeles, CA

Printed in the United States of America

REVIEW by CREATE SPACE

Millionaire Robert Stanley is in Monte Carlo—his yacht Blue Skies in port, a beautiful woman on his lap, and his bodyguard Donald Herman standing nearby, ever vigilant. Stanley's enjoying all the benefits of wealth, little knowing he's about to die.

Stanley's death behind the wheel of his blue Mercedes seems like an accident, but there's no denying many people wanted the man dead. As a businessman, Stanley had been ruthless, gleefully driving competitors into bankruptcy and—it's rumored—suicide. He gained control of his company by turning the board of directors against his own father, an act that cemented his reputation as a merciless egomaniac.

Stanley's behavior at home mirrored his business dealings. Cruel and lascivious, his infidelity drove his wife to suicide. Blamed for her death by his children, Stanley worked to isolate them from each other, leaving them only a small trust from their mother for expenses.

No, Robert Stanley will not be mourned, but was his death murder? And, if so, was he the target of a family plot or organized crime?

A tense thriller from the mind of Alan Douglas, Bad Mood Drive will keep you guessing until its shocking conclusion.

Create Space - Amazon.com Company

KIRKUS REVIEWS

BAD MOOD DRIVE
English Edition
by Alan Douglas
   Getting the largest piece of a wealthy man's inheritance may drive his children to
undertake a few bad deeds, including murder, in the English-language version of Douglas' debut thriller.
   When billionaire Robert Stanley is run down in an automobile accident in Corsica, his three grown children feel they deserve a sizable chunk of his estate. After all, their relationships with their father have been strained for years after his affair with their governess, Rosa, led to their mother's suicide. And they need the money: Judge Thomas Stanley, the oldest brother, is enamored with Connie, who has expensive tastes; fashion designer Carmen is paying off a blackmailer; and polo player Billy has a heroin addiction. But everything changes with the appearance of Jennifer Stanley, Robert's illegitimate daughter with Rosa. Someone wants controlling interest in Stanley Enterprises—not to mention even more money—and is willing to do whatever it takes to get it, even murder. Douglas does an outstanding job establishing the story's characters. Robert, for example, is undoubtedly the villain, callously sending his kids to separate schools when it was clear that they blamed him for their mother's death. But the children are well-developed, particularly Thomas and Carmen, whose self-made careers are the result of showing Robert that they could make something of themselves. The novel is shrouded in mystery and brimming with plot twists: there's the strange family man who watches his son's baseball game before breaking into the office of Robert's attorney and the children exhuming Robert's body (for a DNA test to prove that Jennifer is related) and finding an empty coffin. Likewise, the story is bolstered by a bit of dark humor, like the French police captain who stalls releasing Robert's body to lawyer George so

he can soak up the press' attention for as long as possible. The translation to English from Spanish unfortunately hits some stumbles, with an abundance of typos and odd phrasings, including an explanation of the title: "[Robert] looks at one of the crew member almost angry and this change his mood. He obviously has a very bad mood."

Sturdy characters and an endless batch of surprises make the glaring translation problems relatively easy to overlook.

KIRKUS REVIEWS

1

That's the reality, if you want life to be as it was.

Donald asked, "Did you realize that we're being followed, Mr. Stanley?"

"Yes." He already had noticed of them for the past twenty-four hours.

The two men and the woman were dressed casually, attempting to blend in with the summer tourists strolling along the cobbled streets in the early morning, but it was difficult to remain inconspicuous in a place like Monte Carlo. It is a worldwide well known city with its Casinos, Museums and Gardens.

Robert Stanley had first become aware of them because they were too casual, trying too hard not to look at him. Wherever he turned, one of them was in his background. Robert Stanley was an easy target to follow. He was six feet tall, with white hair lapping over his collar and an aristocratic, almost imperious face. He was accompanied by a strikingly lovely young blonde girl, a pure-black German shepherd, and Donald Herman, a six-foot four-inch bodyguard with a bulging neck and sloping forehead. Hard to lose us, Stanley thought. He knew who had sent them and why, and he was filled with a sense of imminent danger. He had learned long ago to trust his instincts. Instinct and intuition had helped make him one of the wealthiest men in the world.

Forbes magazine estimated the value of Stanley Enterprises at seven billion dollars, while the Fortune 500 appraised it at nine billion. The Wall Street Journal, Barron's, and The Financial Times had all done profiles on Robert Stanley, trying to explain his mystique, his amazing sense of timing, the great ability that had to create the giant Stanley Enterprises. None of them had fully succeeded to give adequate explanation. What they all agree on was that he had a real and substantially big manic energy. He was inexhaustible. His philosophy was simple: A day without making a deal was a day wasted without making money. He was able to eliminate his competitors, his staff, and everyone else who came in contact with him. He was a psychic phenomenon. He was his own man, after all. He was a religious man. He believed in God, and the God he believed in wanted him to be rich and successful, and his enemies dead. Robert Stanley was a public figure, and the press knew everything about him. Robert Stanley was a private figure, and the press knew nothing about him. They had written about his charisma, his lavish life-style, his private plane and his yacht, and his legendary homes in Hawaii, Morocco, Long Island, London, the South of France, and of course his magnificent estate, Bell Air, in West Los Angeles. But the real Robert Stanley remained a mystery.

"Where are we going?" the woman asked.

He was too preoccupied to answer. The couple on the other side of the street was using the cross switch technique, and they had just changed partners again. Along with his sense of danger, Stanley felt a deep anger that they were invading his privacy. They had dared to come to his place, his secret haven from the rest of the world.

Monaco is the second smallest independent state in the world (after the Vatican) and is almost entirely urban. Monte Carlo is not the capital of Monaco but a government district. The country is divided into four areas: Monaco-Ville (the old city), the Condamine (port quarter), Monte-Carlo (business and recreation), and Fontvieille (recreation and light industry). With no natural resources to exploit other than its location and climate, the principality has become a resort for tourists and a tax haven for businesses. Monaco is six times the size of the Vatican and still remains the world's most densely populated independent country.

The nearest airport is the Nice Côte-d'Azur International, which is around 40 kilometers (24.85 miles) away from the city-center in neighboring France. It operates daily flights to nearly all of Europe's main cities, such as London, Paris, Amsterdam, Rome, Brussels, Frankfurt and Zurich. There are regular Rapides Cote D'Azur buses connecting Monte Carlo with both the terminals at Nice Cote-D'Azur airport, and taxis are always available outside the terminal buildings.

Monte Carlo is easily accessed by its land borders from France or Italy by a network of highways, most commonly used of which is the A8 which runs west from Monte Carlo to Nice and Marseilles, and east towards the Italian border.

Monaco-Ville is known as "le rocher" or "the rock." It is still a medieval village at heart and an astonishingly picturesque site. It is made up almost entirely of pedestrian streets and passageways and most previous century houses still remain. There a number of hotels, restaurant and souvenir shops tourists can stay, eat and shop at. Everybody can also visit the Prince's Palace, the Cathedral, the Oceanographic Museum, the City Hall, and the Saint Martin Gardens.

The Palais Princier (Prince's Palace) is in old Monaco-Ville. There are guided tours of the palace each day and usually run around the clock. The Palace also offers a breathtaking panoramic view overlooking the Port and Monte-Carlo. Every day in front of the Palace's main entrance visitors can watch the changing of the guard ceremony performed by the "Carabiniers." "Carabiniers" are not only in charge of the Princes' security but they offer Him a Guard of Honor and on special occasions, are His escorts. The "Compagnie des Carabiniers du Prince" has a military band (Fanfare), which performs at public concerts, official occasions, sports events and international military music festivals.

The Monaco Cathedral was built in 1875 and stands on the site of a 13th century earlier church. It is a Romanesque-Byzantine church dedicated to Saint Nicolas and houses the remains of former Princes of Monaco and Princess Grace.

The church square also contains some of Monaco-Ville's finest restaurants.

The Oceanographic Museum and Aquarium is a world-renowned attraction. Located above sea level, the museum contains stunning collections of marine fauna, numerous specimens of sea creatures (stuffed or in skeleton form), models of Prince Albert's laboratory ships, and craft ware made from the sea's natural products. On the ground floor, exhibitions and film projections are presented daily in the Conference room. In the basement, visitors can take pleasure in watching spectacular shows of marine flora and fauna. With 4,000 species of fish and over 200 families of invertebrates, the aquarium is now an authority on the presentation of the Mediterranean and tropical marine ecosystem. Finally, visitors can have lunch in "La Terrasse" and visit the museum gift shop.

The Jardin Exotique (Exotic Gardens) is one of the many gardens Monaco has to offer. It is also one of Monaco's finest tourist attractions. Several thousand rare plants from around the world are presented in a walking tour that is quite memorable for the views as well as the flora and plants. Due to the rise in altitude, not only are there many displays of desert plants but there are a handful of subtropical flora displays as well. There is also a grotto (cave) that has scheduled guided tours.

The Monaco Opera House or Salle Garnier was built by the famous architect Charles Garnier. The auditorium of the opera house is decorated in red and gold and has frescoes and sculptures all around the auditorium. Looking up to the ceiling of the auditorium, the visitor will be blown away by the superb paintings. The opera house is flamboyant but at the same time very beautiful. There have been some of the most superior international performances of ballet, opera and concerts held in the opera house for more than a century.

The Marlborough Fine Arts Gallery was founded in London by Frank Lloyd and Harry Fischer. A second gallery was opened in Rome, another in New York, and one more in Monaco. The gallery holds a grand collection of post-World War II artists and even paintings by Pablo Picasso, Joan Miró, Jules Brassai, Louise Bourgeois, Dale Chihuly, David Hockney and Henri Matisse.

The Grimaldi Forum is the Monaco convention center.

The Princes car collection has everything, from carriges and old cars, to formula 1 race cars.

The Old Casino in Monte Carlo try your luck in the Grand Casino and gamble alongside the world's richest and often most famous. You'll need your passport to enter (as Monégasque citizens are prohibited from gambling at the casino), and the fees for entry range enormously depending on what room you are going to - often from 30€ right up into the hundreds. You can also visit the casino without gambling, but also for a nominal fee. The dress code inside is extremely strict - men are required to wear coats and ties. The gaming rooms themselves are spectacular, with stained glass, paintings, and sculptures everywhere. There are two other more Americanized casinos in Monte Carlo. Neither of these has an admission fee, and the dress code is more casual.

Monaco's streets host the best known Formula 1 Grand Prix. It is also one of Europe's premier social highlights of the year. The Automobile Club of Monaco organizes this spectacular Formula 1 race each year. The Grand Prix is 77 laps around 263-kilometers of Monte Carlo's narrowest and twisted streets. The main attraction of the Monaco Grand Prix is the proximity of the speeding Formula One cars to the race spectators. The thrill of screaming engines, smoking tires and determined drivers also makes the Monaco Grand Prix one of the most exciting races in the world.

Aquavision: Discover Monaco from the sea during this fascinating boat tour! "Aquavision" is a catamaran-type boat equipped with two windows in the hull for underwater vision, thus allowing the passengers to explore the natural seabed of the coast in an unusual way.

In the summer time, Monte-Carlo is illuminated with dazzling concerts at the exclusive Monte-Carlo Sporting Club. The club has featured such artist as Natalie Cole, Andrea Bocelli, the Beach Boys, Lionel Richie and Julio Iglesias among others. The club also hosts a small casino which includes basic casino games.

Shopping in Monte Carlo is usually quite exclusive. There are plenty of places to melt the credit card alongside Europe's high rollers. The chic clothes shops are in the

Golden Circle, framed by Avenue Monte Carlo, Avenue des Beaux-Arts and Allees Lumieres, where Hermes, Christian Dior, Gucci and Prada all have a presence. The area on and around Place du Casino is home to high-end jewelers such as Bulgari, Cartier and Chopard.

For more shopping in Monte Carlo is the Condamine Market. The market, which can be found in the Place d'Armes, has been in existence since 1880 and is lively and attractive - many hours can be spent simply wandering around, bargaining for souvenirs from the many tiny shops, boutiques and friendly locals. If however you like more modern shopping, just take a short walk along the esplanade to the rue Princess Caroline pedestrian mall.

Monte Carlo is a pretty and interesting in an old-fashioned way, medieval village, weaving its ancient magic on a hilltop in the Alpes Maritimes.It is surrounded by a spectacular and enchanting landscape of hills and valleys covered with flowers, orchards, and pine forests. Monte Carlo itself, has a plenty of artists' studios, galleries, and wonderful antiques shops, is a magnet for tourists from all over the world.

Robert Stanley was one of them. He and his group turned onto the Rue du Portier. Stanley talked to the woman, "Sophia, do you like museums?"

"Yes, my dear." She was very excited to please him. She had never met anyone like Robert Stanley. Wait until I tell my opinion about him. I didn't think there was anything left for me to learn about sex, but my God, he's so creative! He's so fantastic, clever and stimulating. He has the ability to use his imagination to produce new sex ideas and make orgasm happen. He makes me feel tired and exhausted!

They went up the hill to the Chapel of the Visitation Museum, which has been built in baroque style during the 17th century. The Museum collection includes masterpieces by Rubens, Zurbaran, Ribera and the Italian baroque masters. Robert Stanley browsed through the renowned collection of paintings. When he casually glanced around, he saw the woman at the other end of the gallery, carefully studying a painting.

Stanley turned to Sophia. "Hungry?"

"Yes. If you are." Must not be pushy, she thought.

"Good. We'll have lunch at Cafe de Paris, Place du Casino."

Cafe de Paris was one of Stanley's favorite places. The nerve center of Monte Carlo, where people go to see and be seen, buzzing with the feel of old time Monte Carlo, circa early 1900s. It is a meeting point for all of Monte-Carlo. With its new futuristic decor, this casino invites you on a journey through the galaxy. An innovative place where slot machines and systems exclusive in Europe sit side by side and the American table games are out of this world... Stanley and Sophia take a place at a table.

Carl, the black German shepherd, lay at his feet, ever watchful. The dog was Robert Stanley's trademark. Where Stanley went, Carl went with him like as his best friend. It was rumored that at Robert Stanley's command, the animal would tear out a person's throat. No one wanted to test that rumor. Donald sat by himself at a table near the entrance, carefully observing the other patrons as they came and went. Stanley turned to Sophia.

"Shall I order for you, my dear?"

"Yes, please."

Robert Stanley prided himself on being a gourmet. He ordered a green salad and fricassee de lotte for both of them.

As they were being served their main course, Daniela Ramon, who ran the Cafe with her husband, Frank, approached the table and smiled. "Bonjour. Is everything all right, Monsieur Stanley?"

"Wonderful, Madame Ramon."

And it was going to be. Sophia said, "I've never been here before. It's such a lovely place."

Stanley turned his attention to her. Donald had picked her up for him in Monte Carlo a day earlier.

"Mr. Stanley, I brought someone for you."

"Any problem?" Stanley had asked.

Donald had smiled broadly. "None." He had seen her in the lobby of the Louis XV, Hôtel de Paris, Place du Casino. In one of the finest hotels in the world, this Michelin 3 star rated restaurant serves dining perfection amongst luxurious glitterati. Sophia was in Monte Carlo for a few days just to take a short vacation and enjoy the place.

"Excuse me, do you speak English?"

"Yes." She had a lilting Italian accent.

"The man I work for would like you to have dinner with him."

She had been angry and surprised because she feels insulted and unfairly treated. "I'm not a hooker! I'm an actress," she was unbearably arrogant. In fact, she had had a walk-on part in Paul Agati's last film, and a role with two lines of dialogue in a Giuseppe Tornadore film.

"Why should I have dinner with a stranger?"

Donald had taken out a thick pile of hundred-dollar bills. He pushed five of them into her hand. "My friend is very generous. He has a yacht, and he is lonely." He had watched her expression go through a series of changes from anger, to curiosity, to interest.

"As it happens, I'm between pictures." She smiled.

"It would probably do not cause any harm to me if I have dinner with your friend."

"Yes, of cause. He will be pleased."

"Where is he?"

"In Monte Carlo."

Donald had chosen well. Italian. In her late twenties. She was a sensuous and attractive in a sexual way young girl. She has full sensuous lips. She is a beautiful and sensuous. She was sexually exciting and very attractive. "Don't you think she's sexy?" Donald asked. Yes, it is. She is a sexy girl and very attractive one. This type of attraction often occurs amongst individuals. Donald has his own preferences as an individual. These preferences come about as a result of a complex variety of his genetic, psychological, and cultural factors. The sexual attraction is different from one person to another and depends on both - Donald and Sophia. She has catlike face. Full-breasted figure. Now, looking at her across the table, Robert Stanley made a decision.

"Do you like to travel, Sophia?"

"I'm thrill."

"Good. We'll go on a little trip. Excuse me for a moment."

Sophia watched as he walked into the restaurant inside the men's room. Stanley picks up his cellular phone and dialed. "Marine operator, please."

Seconds later, a voice said, "C'est l'operatrice maritime."

"I want to place a call to the yacht Blue Skies. Whiskey bravo lima nine eight zero ..."

The conversation lasted five minutes, and when Stanley was finished, he dialed the airport at Nice. The conversation was shorter this time.

When Stanley was through talking, he spoke to Donald, who rapidly left the restaurant. Then he returned to Sophia. "Are you ready?"

"Yes."

"Let's take a walk." He needed time to work out a plan.

It was a perfect day. The sun had splashed pink clouds across the horizon and rivers of silver light ran through the streets. They walked along the Rue du Portier, past the Eglise, the beautiful twelfth-century church, and stopped at the flower shop. When they came out, one of the three watchers was standing outside, busily studying the church. Donald was also waiting for them.

Robert Stanley handed the flower to Sophia. "Why don't you take this up to the Hotel? I'll be along in a few minutes."

"All right." She smiled and said softly, "Hurry, my dear."

Stanley watched her leave, and then he turned to Donald.

"What did you find out?"

"The woman and one of the men are staying at Rue du Portier, on the road to Nice."

Robert Stanley knew the place. It was one of the streets in Monte Carlo. "And the other one?"

22

"Around the corner." "What do you want me to do with them, sir?"

"Nothing. I'll take care of them."

Robert Stanley's Hôtel de Paris was on Avenue D'ostende, close to the Place du Casino and Port Hercule. When Stanley returned to the Hotel, Sophia was in his bedroom, waiting for him. She was naked.

"What took you so long?" she whispered.

In order to survive, Sophia Loren often picked up money as a call girl between film assignments, and she was used to faking orgasms to please her clients, but with this man, there was no need to pretend. He has insatiable desire, and she found herself climaxing again and again. When they were finally exhausted, Sophia put her arms around him, and murmured happily, "I could stay here forever, my dear."

I wish I could, Stanley thought, cruelly.

They had dinner at the Hôtel de Paris restaurant. The dinner was delicious, and for Stanley the waiter added spice to the meal. When they were finished, they made their way back to the hotel. Stanley walked slowly, to make certain his pursuers followed.

At one A.M., a man standing across the street watched the lights in the hotel being turned off, one by one. At four-thirty in the morning, Robert Stanley went into the bedroom where Sophia slept. He shook her gently.

"Sophia...?"

She opened her eyes and looked up at him, a smile of anticipation on her face, then frowned. He was fully dressed. She sat up. "Is something wrong?"

"No, my dear. Everything is fine. You said you liked to travel. Well, we're going to take a little trip."

She was fully awake and excited now. "At this hour?"

"Yes. We must be very quiet."

"But ..."

"Hurry."

Fifteen minutes later, Robert Stanley, Sophia, Donald, and Carl were moving down with the elevator to the basement garage where a blue Mercedes was parked.

Donald quietly opened the garage door and looked out onto the street. Except for Stanley's white Corniche, parked in front, it seemed deserted. "All clear." Stanley turned to Sophia.

"We're going to play a little game. You and I are going to get in the back of the Mercedes and lie down on the floor."

Her eyes widened. "Why?"

"Some business competitors have been following me," he said very serious and sincere. "I'm about to close a very large deal, and they're trying to find out about it. If they do, it could cost me a lot of money."

"I understand," Sophia said. She had no idea what he was talking about.

Five minutes later, they were driving past the gates of the garage on the road to Nice. A man seated on a bench watched the blue Mercedes as it sped through the gates. At the wheel was Donald Herman and beside him was Carl. The man hastily took out a cellular telephone and began dialing...

"We may have a problem," he told the woman.

"What kind of problem?"

"A blue Mercedes just drove out of the gates. Donald Herman was driving, and the dog was in the car, too."

"And Stanley wasn't in the car?"

"No."

"I don't believe it. His bodyguard never leaves him at night, and that dog never leaves him, ever."

"Is his Corniche still parked in front of the hotel?" asked the other man sent to follow Robert Stanley.

"Yes, but maybe he switched cars."

"Or it could be a trick! Call the airport."

Within minutes, they were talking to the tower.

"Monsieur Stanley's plane? Qui. It arrived an hour ago and has already refueled."

Five minutes later, two members of the surveillance team were on their way to the airport, while the third kept watch on the hotel. As the blue Mercedes passed through Boulevard Princesse Charlotte, Stanley moved onto the seat. "It's all right to sit up, now," he told Sophia. He turned to Donald, "Nice airport. Hurry."

Forty five minutes later, at the Nice airport, a converted Boeing 727 slowly moves down the runway along the ground to the takeoff point. Up in the tower, the flight controller said,

"They certainly are in a hurry to get that plane off the ground. The pilot has asked for a clearance four times."

"Whose plane is it?"

"Robert Stanley's."

"He's probably on his way to make another billion or so."

The controller turned to monitor a Learjet taking off, and then picked up the microphone. "Boeing eight nine five, this is Nice departure control. You are cleared for takeoff. Five left. After departure, turn right to a heading of one four zero."

Robert Stanley's pilot and copilot exchanged a relieved look. The pilot pressed the microphone button.

"Roger. Boeing eight nine five is cleared for takeoff. Will turn right to one four zero."

A moment later, the huge plane thundered down the runway and knifed into the blue sky. The copilot spoke into the microphone again.

"Departure, Boeing eight nine five is climbing out of three thousand for flight level seven zero."

The copilot turned to the pilot.

"Whew! Old Man Stanley was sure anxious for us to get off the ground, wasn't he?"

The pilot shrugged.

"Ours not to reason why, ours but to do and die. How's he doing back there?"

The copilot rose and stepped to the door of the cockpit, and looked into the cabin. "He's resting."

They telephoned the airport tower again from the car.

"Mr. Stanley's plane ... Is it still on the ground?"

"No, monsieur. It has departed."

"Did the pilot file a flight plan?"

"Of course, monsieur."

"To where?"

"The plane is headed for JFK."

"Thank you." He turned to his companion.

"Kennedy. We'll-have people there to meet him."

When the Mercedes passed the outskirts of Monte Carlo, speeding toward the Italian border, Robert Stanley said,

"Donald, there's no chance that we were followed?"

"No, sir. We've lost them."

"Good." Robert Stanley leaned back in his seat and relaxed. There was nothing to worry about. They would be tracking the plane. He reviewed the situation in his mind. It was really a question of what they knew and when they knew it. They were like jackals following the way of a lion, hoping to bring him down. Robert Stanley smiled to himself. They had underestimated the man they were dealing with. Others who had made that mistake had paid dearly for it. Someone would also pay this time. He was Robert Stanley, the confidant of presidents and kings, powerful and rich enough to break the economies of a few small countries. Still...

The 727 was in the skies over. Marseilles. The pilot spoke into the microphone. "Marseilles, Boeing eight nine five is with you, climbing out of flight level one nine zero for flight level two three zero."

"Roger."

The Mercedes reached Monte Carlo shortly after dawn. Robert Stanley had fond memories of the city, but it had changed drastically. He remembered a time when it had been an elegant town with first-class hotels and restaurants, and a casino where black tie was required and where fortunes could be lost or won in an evening. Now it had succumbed to tourism, with loud-mouthed patrons gambling in their shirts.

The Mercedes was approaching the harbor - Port Hercule. Five minutes later, the Mercedes pulled up next to the Blue Skies, a hundred-and-eighty-foot motor yacht. Captain Bargas and the crew of twelve were lined up on deck. The captain hurried down the gangplank to greet the new arrivals.

"Good morning, Signor Stanley," Captain Bargas said. "We'll take your luggage, and ..."

"No luggage. Let's move."

"Yes, sir."

"Wait a minute." Stanley was studying the crew. He looks at one of the crew member almost angry and this change his mood. He obviously has a very bad mood. Most of the similar situations make him to be arrogant. As a result of this bad mood drive Stanley said:

"The man on the end. He's new, isn't he?"

"Yes, sir. Our cabin boy got sick in Capri, and we took on this. He's highly..."

"Get rid of him," Stanley ordered.

The captain looked at him, puzzled. "Get ...?"

"Pay him off. Let's get out of here. Now!"

Captain Bargas nodded. "Right, sir."

Looking around, Robert Stanley was filled with a renewed sense of foreboding. He could almost reach out and touch the danger in the air. He did not want any strangers near him. Captain Bargas and his crew had been with him for years. He could trust them. He turned to look at the girl. Since Donald had picked her up at random, there was no danger there. And as for Donald, his faithful bodyguard had saved his life more than once. Stanley turned to Donald.

"Stay close to me."

"Yes, sir."

Stanley took Sophia's arm. "Let's go aboard, my sweetheart."

Donald Herman stood on deck, watching the crew prepare to cast off. He scanned the harbor, but he saw nothing to be alarmed about. At this time of the morning, there was very little activity. The yacht's huge generators burst into life, and the vessel got under way. The captain approached Robert Stanley "You didn't say where we were heading, Signor Stanley."

"No, I didn't, did I, Captain?" He thought for a moment. "Ajaccio."

"Yes, sir."

"By the way, I want you to maintain strict radio silence."

Captain Bargas frowned at Robert Stanley. "Radio silence? Yes, sir, but what if ...?"

Robert Stanley said, "Don't worry about it. Just do it. And I don't want anyone using the satellite phones."

"Right, sïr. Will we be laying over in Ajaccio?"

"I let you know, Captain."

Robert Stanley took Sophia on a tour of the yacht. It was one of his prized possessions, and he enjoyed showing it off. It was a breathtaking vessel. It had a luxuriously appointed master suite with a sitting room and an office. The office was spacious and comfortably furnished with a couch, several easy chairs, and a desk, behind which was enough equipment to run a small town. On the wall was a large electronic map with a small moving boat showing the current position of the yacht. Sliding glass doors opened from the master suite onto an outside veranda deck furnished with a chaise longue and a table with four chairs. A teak railing ran along the outside. On balmy days, it was Stanley's custom to have breakfast on the veranda. There were six guest staterooms, each with hand painted silk panels, picture windows, and a bath with a Jacuzzi. The large library was done in koa wood. The dining room has a seating capacity for sixteen guests. A fully equipped fitness salon was on the lower deck. The yacht also contained a wine cellar and a theater that was ideal for running films. Robert Stanley had one of the world's greatest libraries of DVD movies, including pornographic. The furnishings throughout the vessel were exquisite, and the paintings would have made any museum proud.

"Well, now you've seen most of it," Stanley told Sophia at the end of the tour. "I'll show you the rest tomorrow."

She was admired. "I've never seen anything like it! It's ... it's like a city!"

Robert Stanley smiled at her enthusiasm. "The steward will show you to your cabin. Make yourself comfortable. I have some work to do."

Robert Stanley returned to his office and checked the electronic map on the wall for the location of the yacht. Blue Skies was in the Ligurian Sea, heading northeast. They won't know where I've gone, Stanley thought. They'll be waiting for me at JFK. When we get to Ajaccio, I'll straighten everything out.

Thirty-five thousand feet in the air, the pilot of the 727 was getting new instructions. "Boeing eight nine five, you are cleared directly to Delta India November upper route forty as filed."

"Roger. Boeing eight nine five is cleared direct upper route forty as filed." He turned to the copilot. "All clear."

The pilot stretched, got up, and walked to the cockpit door. He looked into the cabin. The sky is of the blue of summer day, with large, but not threatening, clouds of a silvery whiteness. Place high up against open sky and moving clouds and it is something else again. Celebration of union of Earth and Sky. Blue, the color of the sky on a sunny day. The sky is clear as glass. It was a murky, pinkish grey; clouds swirled across it exposing higher, greyer banks of cloud.

"How's our passenger doing?" the copilot asked.

"He looks hungry to me."

2

The Ligurian coast is the Italian Riviera, sweeping in a semicircle from the French-Italian border around to Genoa, and then continuing down to the Gulf of La Spezia. The beautiful long ribbon of coast and its sparkling waters contain the storied ports of Ajaccio, Vemazza, and beyond them, Elba, Sardinia, and Corsica. Blue Skies was approaching Ajaccio, which even from a distance was an impressive sight, its hillsides covered with olive trees, pines, cypresses, and palms.

Robert Stanley, Sophia, and Donald were on deck, studying the approaching coastline.

"Have you been to Ajaccio often?" Sophia asked.

"A few times."

"Where is your main home?"

Too personal. "You'll enjoy Ajaccio, Sophia. It's really quite beautiful."

Captain Bargas approached them. "Would you like to have a lunch aboard, Signor Stanley?"

"No, we'll have lunch at the Palazzu U Domu."

"Fantastic. And shall I be prepared to weigh anchor right after lunch?"

"I think not. Let's enjoy the beauty of the place."

Captain Bargas studied him, puzzled. Robert Stanley's mood drive makes him to be in a terrible hurry, or it seems that he has all the time in the world. And the radio to be shut down? Unheard of it! Bull shit. Shit happens. There's nothing that can be done about it.

When Blue Skies dropped anchor in the Quai de la Citadelle, Stanley, Sophia, and Donald took the yacht's launch ashore. The small seaport was charming, with a variety of interesting shops and outdoor trattorie lining the single road that led up to the hills. A dozen or so small fishing boats were pulled up onto the pebbled beach.

Stanley turned to Sophia. "We'll have a lunch at the hotel on top of the hill. There's a lovely view from there." He nodded toward a taxi stopped beyond the docks. "Take a taxi up there, and I'll meet you in a few minutes." He handed her some money.

"Very well, dear."

His eyes followed her as she walked away; then he turned to Donald. "I have to make a call."

But not from the ship, Donald thought. The men went to the two phone booths at the side of the dock. Donald watched as Stanley stepped inside one of them, picked up the receiver, and inserted a token.

"Operator, I would like to place a call to the Union Bank of Switzerland in Geneva."

A woman was approaching the second phone booth. Donald stepped in front of it, blocking her way. "Excuse me," she said. "I ..."

"I'm waiting for a call."

She looked at him in surprise. "Oh." She glanced hopefully at the phone booth Stanley was in.

"I wouldn't wait." Donald said with a grunting sound. "He's going to be on the telephone for a long time."

The woman shrugged and walked away.

"Hello?"

Donald was watching Stanley speaking into the mouthpiece.

"Peter? We have a little problem." Stanley closed the door to the booth. He was speaking very fast, and Donald could not hear what he was saying. At the end of the conversation, Stanley replaced the receiver and opened the door.

"Is everything all right, Mr. Stanley?" Donald asked.

"Let's get some lunch."

The Palazzu U Domu is the crown jewel of Ajaccio, a hotel with a magnificent panoramic view of the emerald bay below. The hotel caters to the very rich, and jealously guards its reputation. Robert Stanley and Sophia had lunch out on the terrace.

"Shall I order for you?" Stanley asked. "They have some specialties here that I think you might enjoy."

"Please," Sophia said.

Stanley ordered the trenette al pesto, the local pasta, veal, and focaccia, the salted bread of the region.

"And bring us a bottle of Schram eighty-eight." He turned to Sophia. "It received a gold medal in the International WINE Challenge in London. I own the vineyard."

She smiled. "You're lucky."

Luck had nothing to do with it. "I believe that man was meant to enjoy the gustatory delights that have been put on the earth." He took her hand in his. "And other delights, too."

"You're an amazing man."

"Thank you."

It excited Stanley to have beautiful women admiring him. This one was young enough to be his daughter and that excited him even more.

When they had finished lunch, Stanley looked at Sophia and smiled. "Let's get back to the yacht."

"Oh, yes!"

Robert Stanley was a changeable lover, passionate and skilled. His enormous ego made him more concerned about satisfying a woman than about satisfying himself. He knew how to excite a woman's erotic zones, and he orchestrated his lovemaking providing pleasure through gratification of the senses and symphony that brought his lovers to heights they had never achieved before. They spent the afternoon in Stanley's suite, and when they were finished making love, Sophia was exhausted. Robert Stanley dressed and went to the bridge to see Captain Bargas.

"Would you like to go on to Sardinia, Signor Stanley?" the captain asked.

"Let's stop off at Elba first."

"Yes, sir. Is everything satisfactory?"

"I hope so," Stanley said. "Everything is satisfactory."

He was feeling aroused again. He went back to Sophia's stateroom. They reached Elba the following afternoon, and anchored at Portoferraio. Elba is a Mediterranean island in Tuscany, Italy. The largest island of the Tuscan Archipelago, Elba is also part of the National Park of the Tuscan and the third largest island in Italy after Sicily and Sardinia. It is located between the Tyrrhenian Sea and Ligurian Sea, about 50 kilometers (30 mi) east of the French island of Corsica.

As the Boeing 727 entered North American airspace, the pilot checked in with ground control.

"New York Center, Boeing eight nine-five is with you, passing flight level two six zero for flight level two four zero."

The voice of New York Center came on. "Roger, you are cleared to one two thousand, direct JFK. Call approach on one two seven point four."

From the back of the plane came a low growl. "Easy, Prince. That's a good boy. Let's get this seat belt around you."

There were four men waiting when the 727 landed. They stood at different vantage points so they could watch the passengers descend from the plane. They waited for half an hour. The only passenger to come out was a black German shepherd.

Portoferraio is the main shopping center of Elba. The streets are lined with elegant, sophisticated shops, and behind the harbor, the eighteenth-century buildings are tucked under the craggy sixteenth-century citadel built by the Duke of Florence.

Robert Stanley had visited the island many times, and in a strange way, he felt at home here.

This was the place where Napoleon Bonaparte was exiled by the Allied governments to Elba following his abdication at Fontainebleau and landed on the island on 4 May 1814.

"We're going to look at Napoleon's villa," he told Sophia. "I'll meet you there." He turned to Donald.

"Take her to the Villa dei Mulini."

"Yes, sir."

Stanley watched Donald and Sophia leave. He looked at his watch. Time was running out. His plane would already have landed at JFKennedy. When they learned that he was not aboard, the manhunt would begin again. It will take them a while to pick up the trail, Stanley thought. By then, everything will have been settled.

He stepped into a phone booth at the end of the dock.

"I want to place a call to London," Stanley told the operator. "Barclay's Bank. One seven one ..."

Half an hour later, he picked up Sophia and brought her back to the harbor.

"You go aboard," Stanley told her. "I have another call to make."

She watched him stride over to the telephone booth beside the dock. Why doesn't he use the telephones on the yacht? Sophia wondered.

Inside the telephone booth, Robert Stanley was saying, "The Sumitomo Bank in Tokyo ..."

Fifteen minutes later, when he returned to the yacht, he was in a fury.

"Are we going to be anchoring here for the night?" Captain Bargas asked.

"Yes," Stanley snapped. "No! Let's head for Sardinia. Now!"

Sardinia is the second largest island in the Mediterranean Sea. The coasts of Sardinia are generally high and rocky, with long, relatively straight stretches of coastline, many outstanding headlands, a few wide, deep bays, rias, and many inlets and with various smaller islands off the coast.

The island has a typical Mediterranean climate. During the year there are approximately 300 days of sunshine, with a major concentration of rainfall in the winter and autumn, some heavy showers in the spring and snowfalls in the highlands.

Porto Cervo is a small town in Sardinia. It's one of the most beautiful places along the Mediterranean coast. The little town of Porto Cervo is a haven for the wealthy, with a large part of the area dotted with villas built by Alan Kimbal.

The first thing Robert Stanley did when they docked was to head for a telephone booth. Donald followed him, standing guard outside the booth.

"I want to place a call to Banca d'Italia in Rome."

The phone booth door closed.

The conversation lasted for almost half an hour. When Stanley came out of the phone booth, he was in serious

41

trouble. Donald wondered what was going on. Stanley and Sophia had lunch at the beach of Porto Cervo. Stanley ordered for them. "We'll start with malloreddus." Flakes of dough made of hard-grain wheat. "Then the porceddu." Little suckling pig, cooked with myrtle and bay leaves. "For a wine, we'll have the Vernaccia, and for dessert, we'll have sebadas." Fried fritters filled with fresh cheese and grated lemon rind, dusted with bitter honey and sugar.

"Bene, signor." The waiter walked away, impressed. As Stanley turned to talk to Sophia, his heart suddenly skipped a beat. Near the entrance to the restaurant two men were seated at a table, studying him. Dressed in dark suits in the summer sun, they were not even bothering to pretend they were tourists. Are they after me or are they innocent strangers? I mustn't let my imagination run away with me, Stanley thought. Sophia was speaking.

"I've never asked you before. What business are you in?"

Stanley studied her. It was refreshing to be with someone who knew nothing about him. "I'm retired," he told her. "I just travel around, enjoying the world."

"And you're all by yourself?" Her voice was filled with sympathy. "You must be very lonely."

It was all he could do not to laugh aloud. "Yes, I am. I'm glad you're here with me."

She put her hand over his. "I, too, dear."

Out of the corner of his eye, Stanley saw the two men leave.

When luncheon was over, Stanley and Sophia and Donald returned to town. Stanley headed for a telephone booth. "I want the Credit Lyonnais in Paris ..."

Watching him, Sophia spoke to Donald. "He's a wonderful man, isn't he?"

"There's no one like him."

"How long have you been with him?"

"Two years," Donald said.

"You're lucky."

"I know." Donald walked over and stood as a guard right outside the telephone booth. He heard Stanley saying,

"Ben? You know why I'm calling ... Yes ... Yes ... You will? ... That's wonderful" His voice was filled with relief. "No not there. Let's meet in Corsica... That's perfect after our meeting, I can return directly home. Thank you, Ben." Stanley put down the receiver. He stood there a moment, smiling, and then dialed a number in Los Angeles. A secretary answered. "Mr. Frank Harold's office."

"This is Robert Stanley. Let me talk to him."

"Oh, Mr. Stanley! I'm sorry, Mr. Frank Harold is on vacation. Can someone else ...?"

"No. I'm on my way back to the States. You tell him I want him in Los Angeles at Bell Air at nine o'clock Monday morning. Tell him to bring a copy of my will and a notary."

"I'll try to..."

"Don't try. Do it, my dear." He put down the receiver and stood there, his mind racing, when he stepped out of the telephone booth, his voice was calm. "I have a little business to take care of, Sophia. Go to the Grand Hotel and wait for me."

"All right," she said flirtatiously. "Don't be too long."

"I won't."

The two men watched her walk away.

"Let's get back to the yacht," Stanley told Donald. "We're leaving."

Donald looked at him in surprise. "What about ...?"

"She can screw her smart ass way back home."

When they returned to the Blue Skies, Robert Stanley went to see Captain Bargas. "We're heading for Corsica," he said "Let's move."

"I just received an updated weather report, Signor Stanley I'm afraid there's a bad storm. It would be better if we waited it out and..."

"I want to leave now, Captain."

Captain Bargas hesitated. "It will be a rough voyage, sir. It's a libeccio...the southwest wind. We'll have heavy seas and squalls."

"I don't care about that." The meeting in Corsica was going to solve all his problems. He turned to Donald. "I want you to arrange for a helicopter to pick up us in Corsica and take to Roma. Use the public telephone on the dock."

"Yes, sir."

Donald Herman walked back to the dock and entered the telephone booth. Twenty minutes later, Blue Skies was under weigh.

3

The person that he loved and adored was David Smith, and he often used the name as his touchstone...

"I don't care what you say about Smith, he's the only politician with real values. Family-that's what it's all about. Without family values, this country would be up the creek even worse than it is. All these young kids are living together without being married, and having babies. It's shocking. No wonder there's so much crime. Physical and sexual assaults against women occur both inside and outside the family. Violence in the home is as much a crime as violence from a stranger, so do not put up with it. If David Smith ever runs for president, he's sure got my vote." It was a shame, he thought, that he couldn't vote because of a stupid law, but, regardless, he was behind Smith all the way.

He had three children: Bob, seven; and two girls: Any and Mary, nine and twelve. They were wonderful children, and his greatest joy was spending what he liked to call quality time with them. His weekends were totally devoted to the children. It's obviously that children have the important function in his life. The children probably appear for him to be a source from which to develop new relationships and the immediate perception. He barbecued for them, played with them, took them to movies and ball games, and helped them with their homework. All the youngsters in the neighborhood adored him. He repaired their bikes and toys, and invited them on picnics with his family. They gave him the nick name of DADDY. On a sunny Saturday morning, he was seated in the bleachers, watching the baseball game. It was a picture perfect day, with warm sunshine and fluffy cumulus clouds dappling the sky. His seven-year-old son, Bob, was at bat, looking very professional and grown up in his Little League uniform. Daddy's two girls and his wife were at his side. It doesn't get any better than this, he thought happily. Why can't all families be like ours?

It was the bottom of the eighth inning; the score was tied, with two outs and the bases loaded. Bob was at the plate, three balls and two strikes against him. Daddy called out, encouragingly, "Get 'em, Bob! Over the fence!"

Bob waited for the pitch. It was fast and low and Bob swung wildly and missed.

The umpire yelled, "Strike three!"

The inning was over. There were groans and cheers from the crowd of parents and family friends. Bob stood there disheartened, watching the teams change sides.

Daddy called out, "It's all right, son. You'll do it next time!" Bob tried to force a smile.

John Blackburn, the team manager, was waiting for Bob.

"You're done! Get the hell out of here! You can't play again" he said.

"But, Mr. Blackburn ..."

"Get out. Get off the field. Now!"

Bob's father watched in hurt amazement as his son left the field. He can't do that, he thought. He has to give Bob another chance. I'll have to speak to Mr. Blackburn and explain. Immediately after that, the cellular phone he carried rang. He let it ring four times before he answered it. Only one person had the number. He knows I hate to be disturbed on weekends, he thought angrily.

Reluctantly, he lifted the antenna, pressed a button, and spoke into the mouthpiece. "Hello?"

The voice at the other end spoke quietly for several minutes. Daddy listened, nodding from time to time. Finally he said, "Yes. I understand. I'll take care of it." He put the phone away.

"Is everything all right, darling?" his wife asked.

"No. I'm afraid it isn't. They want me to work over the weekend. I was planning a nice barbecue for us tomorrow."

His wife took his hand and said lovingly, "Don't worry about it. Your work is more important."

Not as important as my family, he thought stubbornly.

David Smith would understand. His hand began to itch fiercely and he scratched it. Why must he do that? He wondered. I'll have to see a dermatologist one of these days.

John Blackburn was the assistant manager at the local supermarket. A burly man in his fifties, he had agreed to manage the little League team because his son was a ballplayer. His team had lost that afternoon because of young Bob. The supermarket had closed, and John Blackburn was in the parking lot, walking toward his car, when a stranger approached him, carries a package.

"Excuse me, Mr. Blackburn."

"Yes?"

"I wonder if I could talk to you for a moment."

"The store is closed."

"Oh, it's not that. I wanted to talk to you about my son. Bob is very upset that you took him out of the game and told him he couldn't play again."

"Bob is your son? I'm sorry he was even in the game. He'll never be a ballplayer."

Bob's father said earnestly, "You're not being fair, Mr. Blackburn. I know Bob. He's really a fine ballplayer. You'll see. When he plays next Saturday..."

"He isn't going to play next Saturday. He's out."

"But ..."

"No but's. That's it. Now, if there's nothing else ..."

"Oh, there is." Bob's father had unwrapped the package in his hand, revealing a baseball bat. He said pleadingly, "This is the bat that Bob used. You can see that it's chipped, so it isn't fair to punish him because..."

"Look, mister, I don't give a damn about the bat. Your son is out!"

Bob's father sighed unhappily. "You're sure you won't change your mind?"

"No way."

As Blackburn reached for the door handle of his car, Bob's father swung the bat against the rear window and smashing it. Blackburn stared at him in shock. "What ... what the hell are you doing?"

"Warming up," Daddy explained. He raised the bat and swung it again, smashing it against Blackburn's kneecap. John Blackburn screamed and fell to the ground, writhing in pain.

"You're crazy!" He yelled. "Help!"

Bob's father knelt beside him and said softly, "Make one more sound, and I'll break your other kneecap."

Blackburn stared up at him in agony, terrified.

"If my son isn't in the game next Saturday, I'll kill you and I'll kill your son. Do I make myself clear?"

Blackburn looked into the man's eyes and nodded, fighting to keep from screaming with pain.

"Good. Oh, and I wouldn't want this to get out. I've got friends." He looked at his watch. He had just enough time to catch the next flight to Los Angeles. His hand began to itch again.

At seven o'clock Sunday morning, dressed in a vested suit and carrying an expensive leather briefcase, he took the subway to the downtown Los Angeles. He approached the Trust Building entrance. With dozens of tenants in this huge building, there would be no way the guard at the reception desk could identify him.

"Good morning," the man said.

"Good morning, sir. May I help you?"

He sighed. "Even God can't help me. They think I have nothing to do but spend my Sundays doing the work that someone else should have done."

The guard said, sympathetically, "I know the feeling." He pushed a log book forward. "Would you sign in, please?"

He signed in and walked over to the bank of elevators. The office he was looking for was on the fifth floor. He took the elevator to the sixth floor, walked down a flight, and moved down the corridor. The legend on the door read, REYNOLDS & FRANK HAROLD, ATTORNEYS AT LAW. He looked around to make certain the corridor was deserted, then opened his briefcase and took out a small pick and a tension tool. It took him five seconds to open the locked door. He stepped inside and closed the door behind him. The reception room was furnished in old-fashioned conservative taste, as befitted one of Los Angeles's top law firms. The man stood there a moment, orienting himself, and then moved toward the back, to a filing room where records were kept. Inside the room was a bank of steel cabinets with alphabetical labels on the front. He tried the cabinet Divided R-S. It was locked. From his briefcase, he removed a blank key, a file, and a pair of pliers. He pushed the blank key inside the small cabinet lock, gently turning it from side to side. After a moment, he withdrew it and examined the black markings on it. Holding the key with the pair of pliers, he carefully filed off the black spots. He put the key into the lock again, and repeated the procedure. He was humming quietly to himself as he picked the lock, and he smiled as he suddenly realized what he was humming.

"Far Away Places."

I'll take my family on vacation, he thought happily. A real vacation. I'll bet the kids would love Hawaii. The cabinet drawer came open, and he pulled it toward him. It took only a moment to find the folder he wanted. He removed a small Pentax camera from his briefcase and went to work. Ten minutes later he was finished. He took several pieces of kleenex from the briefcase, walked over to the water cooler, and wet them. He returned to the filing room and wiped up the steel shavings on the floor. He locked the file cabinet, made his way out to the corridor, locked the front door to the offices, and left the building.

4

It was glorious weather during the day. Later that evening, Captain Bargas came to Robert Stanley's stateroom.

"Signor Stanley ..."

"Yes?"

The captain pointed to the electronic map on the wall. "I'm afraid the winds are getting worse. The libeccio is centered in the Strait of Bonifacio. I would suggest that we take shelter in a harbor until..." Stanley cut him short. "This is a good ship, and you're a good captain. I'm sure you can handle it."

Captain Bargas hesitated. "As you say, signor. I will do my best."

"I'm sure you will, Captain."

Robert Stanley sat in the office of his suite, planning his strategy. He would meet Ben in Corsica and get everything straightened out. After that, the helicopter would fly him to Roma, and from there he would charter a plane to take him to Los Angeles. Everything is going to be fine, he decided. All I need is forty-eight hours. Just forty-eight hours.

He was awakened at two A.M. by the wild pitching of the yacht and a howling gale outside. Stanley had been in storms before, but this was one of the worst. Captain Bargas had been right. Robert Stanley got out of bed, holding on to the nightstand to steady himself, and made his way to the wall map. The ship was in the Strait of Bonifacio. We should be in Ajaccio in the next few hours, he thought. Once we're there, we'll be safe.

The events that occurred later were a matter of speculation. The next day Robert Stanley was in Ajaccio. He spent the night in Hotel. After breakfast he told Donald Herman:

"I'll go to make one phone call. Stay across the street and watch for me," Donald said.

"O.K., sir. " Ten minutes later Robert Stanley walked toward Donald. All of a sudden a big truck came around the corner with high speed. The driver was not able to stop the truck and Donald Stanley was hit, fall down on the street. Donald run to Robert Stanley, but was too late.
He called for an ambulance and the body was taken to the nearest hospital. What later was found Robert Stanley had terrible head fracture and massive bleeding, which cause his death.

5

Capitaine Frank Duval, chef de police in Corsica, was in a bad mood. The island was overcrowded with plenty of summer tourists who were incapable of holding onto their passports, their wallets, or their children. Complaints had come streaming in all day long to the tiny police headquarters at 2 Cours Napoleon off Rue Sergent Casalonga.

"A man snatched my purse ..."

"My ship sailed without me. My wife is on the board..."

"I bought this watch from someone on the street. It has nothing inside ..."

"The drugstores here don't carry the pills I need ..."

The problems were endless. And now it seemed that the capitaine had a body on his hands. "I have no time for this load of shit now," he shouts it out. "But they're waiting outside," his assistant informed him. "What shall I tell them?"

Capitaine Duval was impatient to get to his girlfriend.

His impulse was ready to say, "Take the body to some other island," but he was, after all, the chief police official on the island.

"Very well." He sighed. "I'll see them briefly."

A moment later, Captain Bargas and Donald Herman were escorted into the office.

"Sit down," Capitaine Duval said, ungraciously. The two men took chairs.

"Tell me, please, exactly what happened."

Captain Bargas said, "I'm not sure exactly. I didn't see it happen ..." He turned to Donald Herman. "He was an eyewitness. Perhaps he could explain it."

Donald took a deep breath. "It was terrible. I work ... worked for the man."

"Doing what, monsieur?"

"Bodyguard, masseur, chauffeur. I run to save him, but there was nothing I could do. I called for help. Ambulance came in. But it was too late. He was killed by auto accident."

"I am very sorry." He could not have cared less. Captain Bargas spoke up. "It was accident but now we would like permission to take the body home."

"That should be no problem." He would still have time to have a drink with his girlfriend before he went home to his wife. "I will have a death certificate and an exit visa for the body prepared at once." He picked up a yellow pad. "The name of the victim?"

"Robert Stanley."

Capitaine Duval was suddenly very still. He looked up. "Robert Stanley?"

"Yes."

"The   Robert   Stanley?"

"Yes."

And Capitaine Duval's future suddenly became much brighter. The gods had dropped blessing in his lap. Robert Stanley was an international legend! The news of his death would be repeated as an echo around the world, and he, Capitaine Duval, was in control of the situation. The immediate question was how to manipulate this event for the maximum benefit to himself. Duval sat there, staring into space, thinking.

"How soon can you release the body?" Captain Bargas asked.

He looked up. "Ah. That's a good question." How much time will it take for the press to arrive? Should I ask the yacht's captain to participate in the interview? No. Why share the glory with him? I will handle this alone.

"There is much to be done," he said regretfully.

"Papers to prepare ..." He sighed. "It could well be a week or more."

Captain Bargas was appalled. "A week or more? But you said..."

"There are certain formalities to be observed," Duval said sternly. "These matters can't be rushed." He picked up the yellow pad again. "Who is the next of his relatives?"

Captain Bargas looked at Donald for help.

"I guess you'd better check with his attorneys in Los Angeles."

"The names?"

"REYNOLDS & FRANK HAROLD ATTORNEYS AT LAW."

6

A sign may be seen above the door with the legend which one can read as REYNOLDS & FRANK HAROLD, the Reynolds had been long deceased. Frank Harold was still very much alive, and at seventy-eight, he was the dynamo that powered the office, with sixty-five attorneys working under him. He was perilously thin, with a full mane of white hair, and he walked with the sternly straight carriage of a military man. At this time, he was pacing back and forth. He always has something on his mind. Trying to feel better by using more never seems to work for a long time. His mind was in a trouble.

He stopped in front of his secretary. "When Mr. Stanley telephoned, didn't he give any indication of what he wanted to see me about so urgently?"

"No, sir. He just said he wanted you to be at his house at nine o'clock Monday morning, and to bring his will and a notary."

"Thank you. Ask Mr. Brown to come in."

George Brown was one of the bright, innovative attorneys in the office. A Harvard Law School graduate in his forties, he was tall and lean, with blond hair, inquisitive blue eyes sparkled with amusement, and an easy, graceful presence. Brown was the troubleshooter for the firm, and Frank Harold's choice to take over one day. If I had had a son, Harold thought, I would have wanted him to be like George. He watched as George Brown walked in.

"You're supposed to be salmon fishing up in Newfoundland," George said.

"Something came up. Sit down, George. We have a problem."

George sighed. "What else is new?"

"It's about Robert Stanley."

Robert Stanley was one of their most prestigious clients. Half a dozen other law firms handled various Stanley Enterprises subsidiaries, but Reynolds & Frank Harold handled his personal affairs. Except for Harold, none of the members of the firm had ever met him, but he was a legend around the office.

"What's Stanley done now?" George asked.

"He's gotten himself dead."

George looked at him, shocked. "He's what?"

"I just received a fax from the police in Corsica. Apparently Stanley crossed the street and was hit by a truck."

"My God!"

"I know you've never met him, but I've represented him for more than thirty years. He was a difficult man."

Harold leaned back in his chair, thinking about the past. "There were really two Robert Stanley's-the public one who could coax the birds off the money tree, and the sonofabitch who took pleasure in destroying people. He was a charmer, but he could turn on you like an animal. He had a split personality-he was both the animal charmer and the animal."

"Sounds fascinating."

"It was about thirty years ago-thirty-one, to be exact when I joined this law firm. Old Man Reynold handled Stanley then. You know how people use the phrase 'larger than life'? Well, Robert Stanley was really larger than life. If he didn't exist, you couldn't have invented him. He was a colossus. He had an amazing energy and ambition. He was a great athlete. He boxed in college and was a ten-goal polo player. But even when he was young, Robert Stanley was impossible. He was the only man I've ever known who was totally without compassion. He was sadistic and unreasonably cruel and unfair towards someone who has harmed him, and he had the instincts of wolf who uses other people's problems and suffering for his own advantage. He loved forcing his competitors into bankruptcy. It was rumored that there was more than a few suicide because of him."

"He sounds like a monster."

"On the one hand, yes. On the other hand, he founded an orphanage in New Guinea and a hospital in Bombay, and he gave millions to charity-anonymously. No one ever knew what to expect next."

"How did he become so wealthy?"

"How's your Greek mythology?"

"I'm a little rusty."

"You know the story of Oedipus?"

George nodded. "He killed his father to get his mother."

"Right. Well, that was Robert Stanley. The only difference is that he killed his father to get his mother's vote."

George was staring at him. "What?"

Harold leaned forward. "In the early thirties, Robert's father had a grocery store here in Los Angeles. It did so well that he opened a second one, and pretty soon he had a small chain of grocery stores. When Robert finished college, his father brought him into the business as a partner and put him on the board of directors. As I said, Robert was ambitious. He had big dreams. Instead of buying meat from packing houses, he wanted the chain to raise its own livestock. He wanted it to buy land and grow its own vegetables, can its own goods. His father disagrees, and they fought a lot.

"Then Robert had his biggest brainstorm of all. He told his father he wanted the company to build a chain of supermarkets that sold everything from automobiles to furniture to life insurance, at a discount, and charge customers a membership fee. Robert's father thought he was crazy, and he turned down the idea. However, Robert didn't intend to let anything get in his way. He decided he had to get rid of the old man. He persuaded his father to take a long vacation, and while he was away, Robert went to work charming the board of directors.

"He was a brilliant salesman and he sold them on his concept. He persuaded his aunt and uncle, who were on the board, to vote for him. He romanced the other members of the board. He took them to lunch, went fox hunting with one, golfing with another. He slept with a board member's wife who had influence over her husband. But it was his mother who held the largest block of stock and had the final vote. Robert persuaded her to give it to him and to vote against her husband."

"That's unbelievable!"

"When Robert's father returned, he learned that his family had voted him out of the company."

"My God!"

"There's more. Robert wasn't satisfied with that. When his father tried to get into his own office, he found that he was barred from the building. And, remember, Robert was only in his thirties then. His nickname around the company was the Iceman. But credit where credit is due, George. He single-handedly built Stanley Enterprises into one of the biggest privately held conglomerates in the world. He expanded the company to include timber, chemicals, communications, electronics, and a staggering amount of real estate. And he wound up with all the stock."

"He must have been an incredible man," George said.

"He was. To men-and to women."

"Was he married?"

Frank Harold sat there for a long time, remembering. When he finally spoke, he said, "Robert Stanley was married to one of the most beautiful women I've ever seen. Emy Trump. They had three children, two boys and a girl. Emy came from a very social family in Bell Air. She adored Robert, and she tried to close her eyes to his cheating, but one day it got to be too much for her. She had a governess for the children, a woman named Rosa Newman. Young and attractive. What made her even more attractive to Robert Stanley was the fact that she refused to go to bed with him. It drove him crazy. He wasn't used to rejection. Well, when Robert Stanley turned on the charm, he was irresistible. He finally got Rosa into bed. He got her pregnant, and she went to see a doctor. Unfortunately, the doctor's son-in-law was a columnist, and he got hold of the story and printed it. There was one hell of a scandal. You know Los Angeles. It was all over the newspapers. I still have clippings about it somewhere."

"Did she get an abortion?"

Harold shook his head. "No. Robert wanted her to have one, but she refused. They had a terrible scene. He told her that he loved her and wanted to marry her. Of course, he had told that to dozens of women. But Emy overheard their conversation, and in the middle of that night she committed suicide."

"That's awful. What happened to the governess?"

"Rosa Newman disappeared. We know that she had a daughter she named Jennifer, at St. Joseph's Hospital in Miami. She sent a note to Stanley, but I don't believe he even bothered to reply. By then, he was involved with someone new. He wasn't interested in Rosa anymore. In general, he didn't give a shit about anybody else."

"Charming ..."

"The real tragedy is what happened later. The children rightfully blamed their father for their mother's suicide. They were ten, twelve, and fourteen at the time. Old enough to feel the pain, but too young to fight their father. They hated him. And Robert's greatest fear was that one day they would do to him what he had done to his own father. So he did everything he could to make sure that never happened. He sent them away to different boarding schools and summer camps, and arranged for his children to see as little of one another as possible. They received no money from him. They lived on the small trust that their mother had left them. All their lives he used the carrot-and-stick approach with them. He held out his fortune as the carrot, and then withdrew it if they displeased him."

"What's happened to the children?"

"Thomas is a judge in the circuit court in San Francisco. William doesn't do anything. He's a playboy. He lives in Bell Air and gambles on golf and polo. A few years ago, he picked up a waitress for a diner, got her pregnant, and to everyone's surprise, married her. Carmen is a successful fashion designer, married to a Frenchman. They live in New York." He stood up.

"George, have you ever been to Corsica?"

"No."

"I'd like you to fly there. They're holding Robert Stanley's body, and the police refuse to release it. I want you to straighten out the matter."

"All right."

"If there's a chance of your leaving today ..."

"All right. I'll work it out."

"Thanks. I appreciate it."

On the Air France commuter flight from Paris to Corsica, George Brown read a travel book about Corsica. He learned that the island was largely mountainous, that its principal port city was Ajaccio, and that it was the birthplace of Napoleon Bonaparte. The book was filled with interesting statistics, but George was totally unprepared for the beauty of the island. As the plane approached Corsica, far below he saw a high solid wall of white rock that resembled the White Cliffs of Dover. It was breathtaking.

The plane landed at Ajaccio airport. Ajaccio is the capital of the French Mediterranean island of Corsica. George took a taxi down the Cours Napoleon, the main street that stretched from Place General-de-Gaulle northward to the train station. He had made arrangements for a plane to stand by to fly Robert Stanley's body back to Paris, where the coffin would be transferred to a plane to Los Angeles. All he needed was to get a release for the body. George had the taxi drop him off at the Prefecture building on Cours Napoleon. He went up one flight of stairs and walked into the reception office. An uniformed sergeant was seated at the desk.

"Bonjour. Puis-je vous aider?"

"Who is in charge here?"

"Capitaine Duval."

"I would like to see him, please."

"And what is it of concern in relationship to?" The sergeant was proud of his English. George took out his business card. "I'm the attorney for Robert Stanley. I've come to take his body back to the States."

The sergeant frowned. "Remain, please." He disappeared into Capitaine Duval's office, carefully closing the door behind him. The office was crowded, filled with reporters from television and news services from all over the globe. All of them seemed to be speaking at the same time.

"Was there any sign of foul play?"

"Have you done an autopsy?"

"Please, gentlemen." Capitaine Duval held up his hand. "Please, gentlemen. Please." He looked around the room at all the reporters hanging on his every word, and he was ecstatic. He had dreamed of moments like this. If I handle this properly, it will mean a big promotion and... The sergeant interrupted his thoughts. "Capitaine..." He whispered in Duval's ear and handed him George Brown's card.

Capitaine Duval studied it and frowned. "I can't see him now," he snapped. "Tell him to come back tomorrow at ten o'clock."

"Yes, sir."

Capitaine Duval watched thoughtfully as the sergeant left the room. He had no intention of letting anyone take away his moment of glory. He turned back to the reporters and smiled. "Now, what were you asking ...?"

In the outer office, the sergeant was saying to Brown: "I am sorry, but Capitaine Duval is very busy immediately. He would like you to expose yourself here tomorrow morning at ten o'clock."

George Brown was disappointed and upset. He looks at the sergeant in dismay.

"Tomorrow morning? That's ridiculous. I don't want to wait that long."

The sergeant raises and then lowers his shoulders in order to show that George doesn't know something or doesn't care about it. "That is of your chosen, monsieur."

George makes an angry, unhappy, and confused expression.

"Very well. I don't have a hotel reservation. Can you recommend a hotel?"

"Mais oui. I am pleased to have recommended Hotel Le Dauphin, eight Avenue de Paris."

George hesitated. "Isn't there some way ...?"

"Ten o'clock tomorrow morning."

George turned and walked out of the office. In Duval's office, the capitaine was happily coping with the barrage of reporters' questions. A television reporter asked, "How can you be sure it was an accident?"

Duval looked into the lens of the camera. "Fortunately, there was an eyewitness to this terrible event. His bodyguard saw it happen and immediately called for help. The ambulance take the body to the hospital, but was too late."

"What did the autopsy show?"

"Corsica is a small island, gentlemen. We are not properly equipped to do a full autopsy. However, our medical examiner reports that the cause of death was head fracture and massive bleeding because of auto accident. There were no signs of foul play."

"Where is the body now?"

"We are keeping it in the cold storage room until authorization is given for it to be taken away."

One of the photographers said, "Do you mind if we take your picture, Capitaine?"

Capitaine Duval hesitated for a moment. "No. Please, gentlemen, do what you must." And the cameras began to flash.

Hotel Le Dauphin was a modest hotel but neat and clean, and his room was satisfactory. George's first move was to telephone Frank Harold.

"I'm afraid this will take longer than I thought," Brown said.

"What's the problem?"

"Red tape. I'm going to see the man in charge tomorrow morning, and I'll get it straightened out. I should be on my way back to Los Angeles by afternoon."

"Very good, George. I'll talk to you tomorrow."

He had lunch at La Fontana on Rue Notre Dame, and with the rest of the day to kill, started exploring the town. Ajaccio was a colorful Mediterranean town that still basked in the glory of having been Napoleon Bonaparte's birthplace. I think Robert Stanley would have identified with this place, George thought.

It was the tourist season in Corsica, and the streets were crowded with visitors chatting away in French, Italian, German, and Japanese.

That evening George had an Italian dinner at Boccaccio and returned to his hotel.

"Any messages?" He asked the room clerk, optimistically.

"No, monsieur."

He lay in bed and his thoughts return to what Frank Harold had told him about Robert Stanley.

"Did she get an abortion?"

"No. Robert wanted her to have one, but she refused. They had a terrible scene. He told her he loved her and wanted to marry her. Of course, he had told that to dozens of women. But Emy overheard their conversation, and in the middle of that night she committed suicide."George wondered how she had done it. He finally fell asleep.

At ten o'clock the following morning, George Brown appeared again at the Prefecture. The sergeant was seated behind the desk.

"Good morning," George said.

"Bonjour, monsieur. Can I help to assist you?" George handed the sergeant another business card. "I'm here to see Capitaine Duval."

"A moment." The sergeant got up, walked into the inner office, and closed the door behind him.

Capitaine Duval, dressed in an impressive new uniform, was being interviewed by an RAI television crew from Italy. He was looking into the camera. "When I took charge of the case, the first thing I did was to make certain that there was no foul play involved in Monsieur Stanley's death."

The interviewer asked, "And you were satisfied that there was none, Capitaine?"

"Completely satisfied. There is no question but that it was an unfortunate accident."

The director said, "Bene. Let us cut to another angle and a closer shot."

The sergeant took the opportunity to hand Capitaine Duval Brown's business card. "He is outside."

"What is the matter with you?" Duval growled.

"Can't you see I'm busy? Have him come back tomorrow." He had just received word that there were a dozen more reporters on their way, some from as far away as Russia and South Africa, "Demain."

"Oui."

"Are you ready, Capitaine?" the director asked. Capitaine Duval smiled. "I'm ready."

The sergeant returned to the outer office. "I am sorry, monsieur. Capitaine Duval is out of business today."

"So am I," George snapped. "Tell him that all he has to do is sign a paper authorizing the release of Mr. Stanley's body, and I'll be on my way. That's not too much to ask, is it?"

"I am afraid, yes. The capitaine has many responsibles, and..."

"Can't someone else give me the authorization?"

"Oh, no, monsieur. Only the capitaine can do the authority."

George Brown stood there, seething.

"When can I see him?"

"I suggest if you try again tomorrow morning."

The phrase try again grated on George's ears. "I'll do that," he said. "By the way, I understand there was an eyewitness to the accident...Mr. Stanley's bodyguard, Donald Herman."

"Yes."

"I would like to talk to him. Could you tell me where he's staying?"

"Australia."

"Is that a hotel?"

"No, monsieur." There was pity in his voice. "It is a country."

George's voice raised an octave. "Are you telling me that the only eyewitness to Stanley's death was allowed by the police to leave here before anyone could interrogate him?"

"Capitaine Duval interrogated him."

George took a deep breath. "Thank you."

"No problems, monsieur."

When George returned to his hotel, he reported back to Frank Harold.

"It looks like I'm going to have to stay another night here."

"What's going on, George?"

"The man in charge seems to be very busy. It's the tourist season. He's probably looking for some lost purses. I should be out of here by tomorrow."

"Stay in touch."

In spite of his irritation, George found the island of Corsica enchanting. It had almost a thousand miles of coastline, with soaring, granite mountains that stayed snow-topped until July. The island had been ruled by the Italians until France took it over, and the combination of the two cultures was fascinating.

During his dinner at the Hotel, he remembered how Frank Harold had described Robert Stanley. "He was the only man I've ever known who was totally without compassion ... sadistic and spiteful... "

Well, Robert Stanley is causing a hell of a lot of trouble even in death, George thought. On his way to his hotel, George stopped at a newsstand to pick up a copy of the International Herald Tribune. The headline read: WHAT WILL HAPPEN TO WHOLE STANLEY EMPIRE? He paid for the newspaper, and as he turned to leave, his eye was caught by the headlines in some of the other foreign papers on the stand. He picked them up and, looked through them, stunned. Every single newspaper had front-page stories about the death of Robert Stanley, and in each one of them, Capitaine Duval was prominently featured, his photograph beaming from the pages. So that's what's keeping him so busy! We'll see about that.

At nine forty-five the following morning, George returned to Capitaine Duval's reception office. The sergeant was not at his desk, and the door to the inner office was slightly open. George pushed it to open and stepped inside.

The capitaine was changing into a new uniform, preparing for his morning press interviews. He looked up as George entered.

"Qu'est-ce que vous faites ici? C'est un bureau privet. Allez-vous-en! "

"I'm with The New York Times," George Brown said.

Instantly, Duval brightened. "Ah, come in, come in. You said your name is ..."

"Jones. Tom Jones."

"Can I offer you something, perhaps? Coffee? Cognac?"

"Nothing, thanks," George said.

"Please, please, sit down." Duval's voice became gloomy, dark, depressing, mournful and very serious.

"You are here, of course, about the terrible tragedy that has happened on our little island. Poor Monsieur Stanley."

"When do you plan to release the body?" George asked.

Capitaine Duval sighed. "Ah, I am afraid not for many, many days. There are a great number of forms to fill out in the case of a man as important as Monsieur Stanley. There are protocols to be followed, you understand..."

"I suppose, I do," George said.

"Perhaps ten days. Perhaps, two weeks." By then the interest of the press will have cooled down.

"Here's my card," George said. He handed Capitaine Duval a card. The capitaine glanced at it, and then took a closer look. "You are an attorney. You are not a reporter?"

"No. I'm Robert Stanley's attorney." George Brown rose. "I want your authorization to release his body."

"Ah, I wish I could give it to you," Capitaine Duval said, regretfully. "Unfortunately, my hands are tied. I do not see how..."

"Tomorrow."

"That is impossible! There is no way ..."

"I suggest that you get in touch with your superiors in Paris. Stanley Enterprises has several very large factories in France. It would be a shame if our board of directors decided to close all of them down and build in other countries."

Capitaine Duval was staring at him. "I ... I have no control over such matters, monsieur."

"But I do," George assured him. "You will see that Mr. Stanley's body is released to me tomorrow, or you're going to find yourself in more trouble than you can possibly imagine." George turned to leave.

"Wait! Monsieur! Perhaps in a few days, I can..."

"I said tomorrow." And George was gone.

Three hours later, George Brown received a telephone call at his hotel.

"Monsieur Brown? Ah, I have wonderful news for you! I have managed to arrange for Mr. Stanley's body to be released to you immediately. I hope you appreciate the trouble ..."

"Thank you. A private plane will leave here at eight o'clock tomorrow morning to take us back. I assume all the proper papers will be in order by then."

"Yes, of course. Do not worry. I will see to..."

"Good." George replaced the receiver.

Capitaine Duval sat there for a long time. Merde!

What bad luck! I could have been a celebrity for at least another week.

When the plane carrying Robert Stanley's body landed at LAX International Airport in Los Angeles, there was a vehicle in which coffins are transported, waiting to meet it. Funeral services were to be held three days later.

George Brown reported back to Frank Harold.

"So the old man is finally home," Harold said.

"It's going to be quite a reunion."

"A reunion?"

"Yes. It should be interesting," he said. "Robert Stanley's children are coming here to celebrate their father's death. Thomas, William, and Carmen."

7

It was Monday night. Judge Thomas Stanley had first seen the story on San Francisco's station WBBW. He had stared at the television set, hypnotized, his adrenaline has increased and his heart starts pounding. There was a picture of the yacht Blue Sky, and a news commentator was saying,"... in Ajaccio, when the tragedy occurred. Donald Herman, Robert Stanley's bodyguard, was an eyewitness to the accident, but was unable to save his employer. Robert Stanley was known in financial circles as one of the intelligent ..."

This was the news he had most wanted to hear. His head was clear enough, for all it was going round. Thomas sat there, watching the shifting images, remembering, remembering...

It was the loud voices that had awakened him in the middle of the night. He was fourteen years old. He had listened to the angry voices for a few minutes, and then crept down the upstairs hall to the staircase. In the foyer below, his mother and father were having a fight. His mother was screaming, and he watched his father slap her across the face.

The picture on the television set shifted. There was a scene of Robert Stanley in the Oval Office of the White House, shaking hands with President Bill Clinton.

" ... One of the cornerstones of the president's new financial task force, Robert Stanley has been an important adviser to ..."

They were playing football in back of the house, and his brother, Billy, threw the ball toward the house. Thomas chased it, and as he picked it up, he heard his father, on the other side of the hedge. "I'm in love with you. You know that!"

He stopped, thrilled that his mother and father were not fighting, and then he heard the voice of their governess, Rosa. "You're married. I want you to leave me alone."

And he suddenly felt sick to his stomach. He loved his mother and he loved Rosa. His father was a horrible stranger.

The picture on the screen flashed to a series of shots of Robert Stanley posing with Margaret Thatcher ... President Mitterrand ... Mikhail Gorbachev ...The announcer was saying, "The legendary tycoon was equally at home with factory workers and world leaders."

He was passing the door to his father's office when he heard Rosa's voice. "I'm leaving." And then his father's voice, "I won't let you leave. You've got to be reasonable, Rosa! This is the only way that you and I can ..."

"I won't listen to you. And I'm keeping the baby!"

Then Rosa had disappeared.

The scene on the television set shifted again. There were old clips of the Stanley family in front of a church, watching a coffin being lifted into a hearse. The commentator was saying, " ... Robert Stanley and the children beside the coffin. ... Mrs. Stanley's suicide was attributed to her failing health. According to police investigators, Robert Stanley ..."

In the middle of the night, he had been shaken awake by his father. "Get up, son. I have some bad news for you."

The fourteen-year-old boy began trembling.

"Your mother had an accident, Thomas." It was a lie. His father had killed her. She had committed suicide because of his father and his affair with Rosa. The newspapers had been filled with the story. It was a scandal that rocked Los Angeles, and the tabloids took full advantage of it. There was no way to keep the news from the Stanley children. Their classmates made their lives hell. In just twenty-four hours, the three young children had lost the two people they loved most. And it was their father who was to blame.

"I don't care if he is our father." Carmen sobbed. "I hate him."

"Me, too!"

"Me, too!"

They thought about running away, but they had nowhere to go. They decided to rebel.

Thomas was delegated to talk to him. "We want a different father. We don't want you."

Robert Stanley had looked at him and said, coldly, "I think we can arrange that."

Three weeks later, they were all shipped off to different boarding schools. As the years went by, the children saw very little of their father. They read about him in newspapers, or watched him on television, escorting beautiful women or chatting with celebrities, but the only time they were with him was on what he called "occasions"- photo opportunities at Christmastime or other holidays to show what a devoted father he was. What the hell of that, the children were sent back to their different schools and camps until the next "occasion."

Thomas sat on the couch. He was completely absorbed by news he was watching. On the television screen was a montage of factories in different parts of the world, with pictures of his father. "... one of the largest privately held conglomerates in the world. Robert Stanley, who created it, was a legend ...The question in the minds of Wall Street experts is what is going to happen to the family owned company now that its founder is gone? Robert Stanley left three children, but it is not known who will inherit the multibillion dollar fortune that Stanley left behind, or who will control the corporation ..."

He was six years old. He loved to move around the house with no clear purpose or direction, usually for a longtime, exploring all the exciting rooms. The only place that was off limits to him was his father's office. Thomas was aware that important meetings went on in there. Impressive-looking men dressed in dark suits were constantly coming and going, meeting with his father. The fact that the office was off limits to Thomas made it irresistible.

One day when his father was away, Thomas decided to go into the office. The huge room was overpowering, awesome. Thomas stood there, looking at the large desk and at the huge leather chair that his father sat in. One day I'm going to sit in that chair, and I'm going to be important like my father. He moved over to the desk and examined it. There were dozens of official-looking papers on it. He moved around to the back of the desk and sat in his father's chair. It felt wonderful. I'm important now, too!

"What the hell are you doing?"

Thomas looked up, startled. His father stood in the doorway, furious.

"Who told you, that you could sit behind that desk?"

The young boy was trembling. "I ... I just wanted to see what it was like. . ."

His father stormed over to him. "Well, you'll never know what it's like! Never! Now get the hell out of here and stay out!"

Thomas ran upstairs, sobbing, and his mother came to his room. She put her arms around him. "Don't cry, darling. It's going to be all right."

"It's ... it's not going to be all right," he sobbed. "He

... he hates me!"

"No. He doesn't hate you."

"All I did was to sit in his chair."

"It's his chair, darling. He doesn't want anyone to sit in it."

He could not stop crying. She held him close and said, "Thomas, when your father and I were, married, he said he wanted me to be part of his company. He gave me one share of stock. It was kind of a family joke. I'm going to give you that share. I'll put it in a trust for you. So now you're part of the company, too. All right?" There were one hundred shares of stock in Stanley Enterprises, and Thomas was now a proud owner of one share.

When Robert Stanley heard what his wife had done, he laughs at her, and talks about it in a way that shows that she was stupid, "What the hell do you think he's going to do with that one share? Take over the company?"

Thomas switched off the television set and sat there, adjusting to the news. He felt a deep sense of satisfaction. Traditionally, sons wanted to be successful to please their fathers. Thomas Stanley had longed to be a success so he could destroy his father.

As a child, he had a recurring dream that his father was charged with murdering his mother, and Thomas was the one who would pass sentence. I sentence you to die in the electric chair! Sometimes the dream would vary, and Thomas would sentence his father to be hanged or poisoned or shot. The dreams became almost real.

The military school he was sent to was in Texas, and it was four years of pure hell. Thomas hated the discipline and the rigid life-style. In his first year at school, he seriously contemplated committing suicide, and the only thing that stopped him was the determination not to give his father "that kind of satisfaction." He killed my mother. He's not going to kill me.

It seemed to Thomas that his instructors were particularly hard on him, and he was sure his father was responsible. Thomas refused to let the school break him. Although he was forced to go home on holidays, his visits with his father grew more and more unpleasant. His brother and sister were also home for holidays, but there was no sense of a family relationship. Their father had destroyed that. They were strangers to one another, waiting for the holidays to be over so they could escape.

Thomas knew that his father was a multibillionaire but that the small allowance that Thomas, Billy, and Carmen had come from their mother's estate. As he grew older, Thomas wondered whether he was entitled to the family fortune. He was sure he and his siblings were being cheated. I need an attorney. That, of course, was out of the question, but his next thought was, I'm going to become an attorney. When Thomas's father heard about his son's plans, he said, "So, you're going to become a lawyer, huh? I suppose you think I'll give you a job with Stanley Enterprises. Well, forget it. I wouldn't let you within a mile of it!"

When Thomas was graduated from law school, he could have practiced in Los Angeles, and because of the family name, he would have been welcomed on the boards of dozens of companies, but he preferred to get far away from his father.

He decided to set up a law practice in San Francisco. In the beginning, it was difficult. He refused to trade on his family name, and clients were scarce. San Francisco politics were run by the Machine, and Thomas very quickly learned that it would be advantageous for a young lawyer to become involved with the powerful central San Francisco Lawyers Association. He was given a job with the district attorney's office. He had a keen mind and was a quick study, and it was not long before he became invaluable to them. He prosecuted felons accused of every conceivable crime, and his record of convictions was phenomenal. He rose rapidly through the ranks, and finally the day came when he received his reward. He was elected San Francisco circuit court judge. He had thought his father finally would be proud of him. He was wrong.

"You? A circuit court judge? For God's sake, I wouldn't let you judge a baking contest!"

Judge Thomas Stanley was a short, slightly overweight man with sharp, calculating eyes and a hard mouth. He had none of his father's charisma or attractiveness. His outstanding feature was a deep, sonorous voice, perfect for pronouncing sentence. Thomas Stanley was a private man who kept his thoughts to himself. He was forty two years old, but he looked much older than his years. He prided himself on having no sense of humor. Life was too grim for levity. His only hobby was chess, and once a week he played at a local club, where he invariably won. Thomas Stanley was a brilliant jurist, held in high esteem by his fellow judges, who often came to him for advice. Very few people were aware that he was one of the Stanley's. He never mentioned his father's name.

The judge's chambers were in the large San Francisco Criminal Court Building at Twenty-sixth and California streets, a fourteen-story stone edifice with steps leading up to the front entrance. It was in a dangerous neighborhood, and a notice outside, stated: BY JUDICIAL ORDER, ALL PERSONS ENTERING THIS BUILDING SHALL SUBMIT TO SEARCH.

This was where Thomas spent his days, hearing cases involving robbery, burglary, rape, shootings, drugs, and murders. Ruthless in his decisions, he became known as the Hanging Judge. All day long he listened to defendants pleading poverty, child abuse, broken homes, and a hundred other excuses. He accepted none of them. A crime was a crime and had to be punished. And in the back of his mind, always, was his father.

Thomas Stanley's fellow judges knew very little about his personal life. They knew that he had had a bitter marriage and was now divorced, and that he lived alone in a small three-bedroom Georgian house on Baker Street close to Buena Vista Park. The area was surrounded by beautiful old homes, because the great fire of 1871 that razed San Francisco had strange. He made no friends in the neighborhood, and his neighbors knew nothing about him. He had a housekeeper who came in two times a week, but Thomas did the shopping himself. He was a methodical man with a fixed routine. On Saturdays, he went to a small shopping mall near his home, or to Mr. G's Fine Foods or Medici's Food. From time to time, at official gatherings, Thomas would meet the wives of his fellow jurists. They sensed that he was lonely, and they offered to introduce him to women friends or invite him to dinner. He always declined.

"I'm busy that evening."

His evenings seemed to be full, but they had no idea what he was doing with them.

"Thomas isn't interested in anything but the law," one of the judges explained to his wife. "And he's just not interested in meeting any women yet. I heard he had a terrible marriage."

He was right.

After his divorce, Thomas had sworn to himself that he would never become emotionally involved again. And then he had met Connie, and everything had suddenly changed. Connie was beautiful, sensitive, and caring-that why Thomas wanted to spend the rest of his life with. Thomas loved Connie, but why should Connie love him? A successful model, Connie had dozens of admirers, most of them wealthy. And Connie liked expensive things.

Thomas had felt that his cause was hopeless. There was no way to compete with others for Connie's affection. But overnight, with the death of his father, everything could change. He could become wealthy beyond his wildest dreams. . He could give Connie the world.

Thomas walked into the chambers of the chief judge.

"Lyn, I'm afraid I have to go to Los Angeles for a few days. Family affairs. I wonder if you would have someone take over my caseload for me."

"Of course. I'll arrange it," the chief judge said.

"Thank you."

That afternoon, Judge Thomas Stanley was on his way to Los Angeles.

8

The weather was cloudy. It was raining in Paris, a warm August rain that sent pedestrians racing along the street for shelter or looking for nonexistent taxis. Inside the auditorium of a large gray building on a corner of the Rue Faubourg St. - Honore, there was panic. A dozen half-naked models were running around in a kind of mass hysteria, while helpers finished setting up chairs and carpenters pounded away at last-minute bits of carpentry. Everyone was screaming and gesticulating wildly, and the noise level was painful.

In the eye of the hurricane, trying to bring order out of chaos, was the maitresse herself, Carmen Stanley Renaux. Four hours before the fashion show was scheduled to begin, everything was falling apart.

Catastrophe: John Fairchild of Washington, D.C. was unexpectedly going to be in Paris, and there was no seat for him.

Tragedy: The speaker system was not working.

Disaster: Lily, one of the top models, was ill.

Emergency: Two of the makeup artists were fighting backstage and were far behind schedule.

Disaster: All the seams on the cigarette skirts were tearing.

In other words, Carmen thought wryly, everything is normal.

Carmen Stanley Renaux could have been mistaken for one of the models herself, and at one time she had been a model. She exuded carefully plotted elegance from her gold chignon to her Chanel pumps. Everything about her-the curve of her aim, the shade of her nail polish, the timbre of her laugh-bespoke well-mannered chic. Her face, if stripped of its careful makeup, was actually plain, but Carmen took pains to see that no one ever realized this, and no one ever did.

She was everywhere at once.

"Who lit that runway, Ray Charles?"

"I want a blue backdrop ..."

"The lining is showing. Fix it!"

"I don't want the models doing their hair and makeup in the holding area. Have Lora find them a dressing room!"

Carmen's venue manager came hurrying up to her.

"Carmen, thirty minutes is too long! Too long! The show should be no more than twenty-five minutes ..."

She stopped what she was doing. "What do you suggest, Paul?"

"We could cut a few of the designs and..."

"No. I'll have the models move faster."

She heard her name called again, and turned.

"Carmen, we can't locate Pam. Do you want Tania to switch to the charcoal gray jacket with the trousers?"

"No. Give that to Daniela. Give the cat suit and tunic to Tania."

"What about the dark gray jersey?"

"Sylvia. And make sure she wears the dark gray stockings."

Carmen looked at the board holding a set of Polaroid pictures of the models in a variety of gowns. When they were set, the pictures would be placed in a precise order. She ran a practiced eye over the board. "Let's change this. I want the beige cardigan out first, then the separates, followed by the strapless silk jersey, then the taffeta evening gown, the afternoon dresses with matching jackets..."

Two of her assistants hurried up to her.

"Carmen, we're having an argument about the seating. Do you want the retailers together, or do you want to mix them with the celebrities?"

The other assistant spoke up. "Or we could mix the celebrities and press together."

Carmen was hardly listening. She had been up for two nights, checking everything to make sure nothing would go wrong. "Work it out yourselves," she said.

She looked around at all the activity and thought about the show that was about to begin, and the famous names from all over the world who would be there to applaud what she had created. I should thank my father for all this. He told me I would never succeed...

She had always known that she wanted to be a designer. From the time she was a little girl, she had had a natural sense of style. Her dolls had the trendiest outfits in town. She would show off her latest creations for her mother's approval. Her mother would hug her and say, "You're very talented, darling. Someday you're going to be a very important designer."

And Carmen was sure of it.

In school, Carmen studied graphic design, structural drawing, spatial conceptions, and color coordination.

"The best way to begin," one of her teachers had advised her, "is to become a model yourself. That way, you will meet all the top designers, and if you keep your eyes open, you will learn from them."

When Carmen had mentioned her dream to her father, he had looked at her and said, "You? A model! You must be joking!"

When Carmen finished school, she returned to Bell Air. Father needs me to run the house, she thought. There were a dozen servants, but no one was really in charge. Since Robert Stanley was away a good deal of the time, the staff was left to its own devices. Carmen tried to organize things. She scheduled the household activities, served as hostess for her father's parties, and did everything she could to make him comfortable. She was longing for his approval. Instead, she suffered a barrage of criticisms.

"Who hired that damned chef? Get rid of him ..."

"I don't like the new dishes you bought. Where the hell is your taste ...?"

"Who told you, that you could redecorate my bedroom? Keep the hell out of there ..."

No matter what Carmen did, it was never good enough.

It was her father's domineering cruelty and bad mood driving that finally drove her out of the house. It had always been a loveless household, and her father had paid no attention to his children, except to try to control and discipline them.

One night, Carmen overheard her father saying to a visitor, "My daughter has a face like a horse. She's going to need a lot of money to hook some poor sucker."

It was the final straw. The following day, Carmen left Los Angeles and headed for New York.

Alone in her hotel room, Carmen thought. All right. Here I am in New York. How do I become a designer? How do I break into the fashion industry? How do I get anyone even to notice me? She remembered her teacher's advice. I'll start as a model. That's the way to begin.

The following morning, Carmen looked through the yellow pages, copied a list of modeling agencies, and began making the rounds. I have to be honest with them, Carmen thought. I'll tell them that I can stay with them only temporarily, until I get started designing.

She walked into the office of the first agency on her list. A middle-aged woman behind a desk said, "May I help you?"

"Yes. I want to be a model."

"So do I, dear. Forget it."

"What?"

"You're too tall."

Carmen gets very upset. "I'd like to see whoever is in charge here."

"You're looking at her. I own this place."

The next half a dozen stops were no more successful.

"You're too short."

"Too thin."

"Too fat."

"Too young."

"Too old."

"Wrong type."

By the end of the week, Carmen was getting desperate. There was one more name on her list.

Paramount Models was the top modeling agency in Manhattan. There was no one at the reception desk. A voice from one of the offices said, "She'll be available next Monday. But you can have her for only one day. She's booked solid for the next three weeks."

Carmen walked over to the office and peered inside. A woman in a tailored suit was talking on the phone.

"Right. I'll see what I can do." Renata Maxwell replaced the receiver and looked up. "Sorry, we aren't looking for your type."

Carmen said desperately, "I can be any type you want me to be. I can be taller or I can be shorter. I can be younger or older, thinner..."

Renata held up her hand. "Hold it."

"All I want is a chance. I really need this ..."

Renata hesitated. There was an appealing eagerness about the girl, and she did have an exquisite figure. She was not beautiful, but possibly with the right makeup …

"Have you had any experience?"

"Yes. I've been wearing clothes all my life."

Renata laughed. "All right. Let me see your portfolio."

Carmen looked at her blankly. "My portfolio?"

Renata sighed. "My dear girl, no self-respecting model walks around without a portfolio. It's your bible. It's what your prospective clients are going to look at."

Renata sighed again. "I want you to get two head shots--one smiling and one serious. Turn around."

"Right." Carmen began to turn.

"Slowly." Renata studied her, "Not bad. I want a photo of you in a bathing suit or lingerie, whatever is the most flattering for your figure."

"I'll get one of each," she said very excited.

Renata had to smile at her earnestness. "All right. You're … er … different, but you might have a shot."
"Thank you."

"Don't thank me too soon. Modeling for fashion magazines isn't as simple as it looks. It's a tough business."

"I'm ready for it."

"We'll see. I'm going to take a chance on you. I'll send you out on some go-sees."

"I'm sorry?"

"A go-see is where clients catch up on all the new models. There will be models from other agencies there, too. It's kind of a cattle call."

"I can handle it."

That had been the beginning. Carmen went on a dozen go-sees before a designer was interested in having her wear his clothes. She was so tense; she almost spoiled her chances by talking too much.

"I really love your dresses, and I think they would look good on me. I mean, they would look good on any woman, of course. They're wonderful! But I think they'll look especially good on me." She was so nervous that she was stammering.

The designer nodded sympathetically. "This is your first job, isn't it?"

"Yes, madam."

She had smiled. "All right. I'll try you. What did you say your name was?"

"Carmen Stanley." She wondered if she would make the connection between her and the Stanley's, but of course, there was no reason for him to.

Renata had been right. Modeling was a tough business. Carmen had to learn to accept constant rejection, go-sees that led nowhere, and weeks without work. When she did work, she was in makeup at six A.M., finished a shoot, went on to the next, and often didn't get through until after midnight.

One evening, after a long day's shoot with half a dozen other models, Carmen looked in a mirror and groaned, "I won't be able to work tomorrow. Look how puffy my eyes are!"

One of the models said, "Put cucumber slices over your eyes. Or you can put some chamomile tea bags in hot water, let them cool, and put them over your eyes for fifteen minutes."

In the morning, the puffiness was gone.

Carmen envied the models who were in constant demand. She would hear Renata arranging their bookings: "I originally gave Stacy a secondary on Mia. Call and tell them that she will be available, so I'm moving them up to a tentative ..."

Carmen quickly learned never to criticize the clothes she was modeling. She became acquainted with some of the top photographers in the business, and had a photo composite made to go with her portfolio. She carried a model's bag filled with necessities-clothes, makeup, a nail-care bag, and jewelry. She learned to blow-dry her hair upside down to give it more body, and to add curl to her hair with heated rollers. There was a lot more to learn. She was a favorite of the photographers, and one of them pulled her aside to give her some advice. "Carmen, always save your smiling shots for the end of the shoot. That way, your mouth will have less creasing."

Carmen was becoming more and more popular. She was not the conventional drop-dead beauty that was the hallmark of most models, but she had something more, a graceful elegance.

"She's got class," one of the advertising agents said. And that summed it up.

She was also lonely. From time to time she went out on dates, but they were meaningless. She was working steadily, but she felt she was no nearer to her goal than she was when she had first arrived in New York. I have to find a way to make contact with the top designers, Carmen thought.

"I have you booked for the next four weeks, "Renata told her. "Everybody loves you."

"Renata ..."

"Yes, Carmen?"

"I don't want to do this anymore."

Renata stared at her, disbelievingly. "What?"

"I want to do runway modeling."

Runway modeling was what most models aspired to.

It was the most exciting and the most lucrative form of modeling.

Renata was dubious. "That's almost impossible. To break into and..."

"I'm going to."

Renata studied her. "You really mean it, don't you?"

"Yes."

Renata nodded. "All right. If you're serious about this, the first thing you have to do is learn to walk the beam."

"What?"

Renata explained.

That afternoon, Carmen bought a six-foot narrow wooden beam, sandpapered it to avoid splinters, and placed it on her floor. The first few times she tried to walk on it, she fell off. This is not going to be easy, Carmen decided. But I'm going to do it.

Each morning she got up early and practiced walking the beam on the balls of her feet. Lead with the pelvis. Feel with the toes. Lower the heel. Day by day her balance improved.

She strode up and back in front of a full-length mirror, with music playing. She learned to walk with a book on her head. She practiced changing rapidly from sneakers and shorts to high heels and an evening gown.

When Carmen felt that she was ready, she went back to Renata.

"I'm sticking my neck out for you, "Renata told her. "Rodriguez is looking for a runway model. I recommended you. He's going to give you a chance."

Carmen was thrilled. Rodriguez was one of the most brilliant designers in the business.

The following week, Carmen arrived at the show. She tried to seem as casual as the other models. Rodriguez handed Carmen the first outfit she was to wear and smiled. "Good luck."

"Thanks."

When Carmen went out on the runway, it was as though she had been doing it all her life. Even the other models were impressed. The show was a big success, and from that time on Carmen was a member of the elite. She started working with the giants of the fashion industry - Yves Saint Laurent, Halston, Christian Dior, Donna Karan, Calvin Klein, Ralph Lauren, and St. John. Carmen was in constant demand, traveling to shows all over the world. In Paris, the haute couture shows took place in January and July. In Milan, the peak months were March, April, May, and June, while in Tokyo, shows peaked in April and October. It was a hectic, busy life, and she loved every minute of it. Carmen kept working and she kept learning. She modeled the clothes of famous designers and thought about the changes she would make if she were the designer. She learned how clothes were supposed to fit, and how fabric was supposed to move and swing around the body. She learned about cuts and drapes and tailoring, and what body parts women wanted to hide, and what parts they wanted to show. She made sketches at home, and the ideas seemed to flow. One day, she took a portfolio of her sketches to the head buyer at B. Martin's. The buyer was impressed. "Who designed these?" she asked.

"I did."

"They're good. They're very good." Two weeks later, Carmen went to work for Dona Karan as an assistant and began to learn the business side of the garment trade. At home, she kept designing clothes. One year later, she had her first fashion show.

It was a disaster. The designs were ordinary and nobody cared. She gave a second show, and no one came. I'm in the wrong profession, Carmen thought.

"Someday you're going to be a very important designer."

What am I doing wrong? Carmen wondered.

The occasion came when she suddenly understand something in the middle of the night. Carmen awakened and lay in bed, thinking, I'm designing dresses for models to wear. I should be designing for real women with real jobs and real families. Smart, but comfortable. Chic, but practical.

It took Carmen about a year to get her next show on, but it was an instant success.

Carmen rarely returned to Bell Air, and when she did, the visits were terrible. Her father had not changed. If anything, he had gotten worse. He still has in his bad mood driving.

"Haven't hooked anybody yet, eh? Probably never will."

It was at a charity ball that Carmen met David Renaux. He worked at the international desk of a New York brokerage house, where he dealt with foreign currencies. Five years younger than Carmen, he was an attractive Frenchman, tall and lean. He was charming and attentive, and Carmen was immediately attracted to him. He asked her to have dinner together. The next evening they go to the near restaurant and that night, Carmen went to bed with him. They were together every night after that.

One evening, David said, "Carmen, I'm madly in love with you, you know."

She said softly, "I've been looking for you all my life, David."

"There is a serious problem. You are a big success. I don't make anywhere near as much money as you. Perhaps one day..."

Carmen had put her finger to his lips. "Stop it. You've given me more than I could ever have hoped for."

On Christmas Day, Carmen took David to Bell Air to meet her father.

"You're going to marry him?" Robert Stanley exploded. "He's a nobody! He's marrying you for the money he thinks you're going to get." If Carmen had needed any further reason to marry David, which would have been it. They got married in Las Vegas the following day. And Carmen's marriage to David gave her happiness she had never known before.

"You mustn't let your father make bull shit of you," he had told Carmen. "All his life, he has used his money as a weapon. We don't need his money."

And Carmen had loved him for that. David was a wonderful husband-kind, considerate, and caring. I have everything, Carmen thought happily. The past is dead. She had succeeded in spite of her father. In a few hours, the fashion world was going to be focused on her talent.

The rain had stopped. It was a good sign.

The show was stunning. At its end, with music playing and flash bulbs popping, Carmen walked out onto the runway, took a bow, and received an ovation. Carmen wished that David could have been in Paris with her to share her triumph, but his brokerage house had refused to give him the time off.

When the crowd had left, Carmen went back to her office, feeling very happy and excited. Her assistant said, "A letter came for you. It was hand-delivered."

Carmen looked at the brown envelope her assistant handed her, and she felt a sudden chill. She knew what it was about before she opened it. The letter read:

Dear Mrs. Renaux,

I regret to inform you that the Wild Animal Protection Association is short of funds again. We will need $100, 000 immediately to cover our expenses. The money should be wired to account number 804072-A at the Credit Suisse bank in Zurich.

There was no signature.

Carmen sat there, staring at it, numb. It's never going to stop. The blackmail is never going to stop. Another assistant came hurrying into the office. "Carmen! I'm so sorry. I just heard some terrible news."

I can't bear any more terrible news, Carmen thought:

"What ... what is it?"

"There was an announcement on Radio-Tele Luxembourg. Your father is ... dead. He died in auto accident." It took Carmen a moment for it to gradually understand and realize the full meaning of these words. Her first thought was, I wonder what would have made him prouder. My success or the fact that I'm a murderer?

9

Anita King had been married to William "Billy" Stanley for two years, but to the residents of Bell Air, she was still referred to as "that waitress." Anita had been waiting on tables at the Grille Chicken restaurant when Billy first met her. Billy Stanley was the golden boy of Bell Air. He lived in the family villa, had classical good looks, was charming and likes to be with other people. He was a target for all the eager debutantes in Bell Air. It was therefore a seismic shock when he suddenly eloped with a twenty five years old waitress who was plain-looking, a high school dropout, and the daughter of a day laborer and a housewife.

It was even more of a shock because everyone had been expecting Billy to marry Nicole Carson, a beautiful, intelligent young heiress to a timber fortune who was madly in love with Billy.

As a rule, the residents of Bell Air preferred to gossip about the affairs of their servants rather than their peers, but in Billy's case, his marriage was so outrageous that they made an exception. The information quickly spread that he had gotten Anita King pregnant and then married her. They were quite sure which was the greater sin.

"For God's sake, I can understand the boy getting her pregnant, but you don't marry a waitress!"

The whole affair was it classic case of deja VU.

Twenty-four years earlier, Bell Air had been rocked by a similar scandal involving the Stanley's. Emy Trump, the daughter of one of the founding families, had committed suicide because her husband had gotten the children's governess pregnant. Billy Stanley made no secret of the fact that he hated his father, and the general feeling was that he had married the waitress out of spite, to show that he was a more honorable man than his father. The only person invited to the wedding was Anita's brother, Harold, who flew in from New York. Harold was two years older than Anita and worked in a bakery in the Bronx. He was tall and emaciated, with a pockmarked face and a heavy Brooklyn accent.

"You're gettin' a great girl," he told Billy after the ceremony.

"I know," Billy said tonelessly.

"You take good care of my sister, huh?"

"I'll do my best."

"Yeah. Cool."

An unmemorable conversation between a baker and the son of one of the wealthiest men in the world. Four weeks after the wedding, Anita lost the baby.

Bell Air is a very exclusive community. It is a haven of privacy-wealthy, self-contained, and protective, with more police per capita than in almost any other place in the world. Its residents pride themselves on being understated. They drive Tauruses or station wagons, and own small sailboats, an eighteen-foot Lightning or a twenty-four-foot Quickstep.

If one was not born to it, one had to earn the right to be a member of this Bell Air community. After the marriage between William Stanley and "that waitress," the burning question was what were the residents going to do about accepting the bride into their society? Mrs. Michele Brickman, the doyen of Bell Air, was the arbiter of all social disputes, and her devout mission in life was to protect her community against parvenus and the nouveau riche. When newcomers arrived at Bell Air and were unfortunate enough to displease Mrs. Brickman, it was her custom to have delivered to them, by her chauffeur, a leather traveling case. It was her way of informing them that they were not welcome in the community.

Her friends delighted in telling the story of the garage mechanic and his wife who had bought a house in Bell Air. Mrs. Brickman had sent them her ritual traveling bag, and when the wife learned its significance, she laughed. She said, "If that old harridan thinks she can drive me out of this place, she's crazy!"

But strange things began to happen. Workmen and repairmen were suddenly unavailable, the grocer was always out of items that she ordered, and it was impossible to become a member of the Jupiter Island Club or even to get a reservation at any of the good local restaurants. And no one spoke to them. Three months after receiving the suitcase, the couple sold their home and moved away.

So it was that when word of Billy's marriage got out, the community held its collective breath. Excommunicating Anita King would also mean excommunicating her popular husband. There were bets being quietly made.

For the first few weeks, there were no invitations to dinners or to any of the usual community functions. But the residents liked Billy and, after all, his grandmother on his mother's side had been one of the founders of Bell Air: Gradually, people started inviting him and Anita to their homes. They were excited to see what his bride was like.

"The old girl must have something special or Billy never would have married her."

They were in for a big disappointment. Anita was dull and graceless, she had no personality, and she dressed badly. She was not attractive or fashionable: dowdy was the word that came to people's minds. Billy's friends were unable to understand the reason what actually was driven him to make a stupid decision. He was intelligent enough not to make his mind based on his bad mood drive. "What the hell does he see in her? He could have married anyone."

One of the first invitations was from Nicole Carson. She had been devastated by the news of Billy's marriage, but she was too proud to reveal it. When her closest friend had tried to console her by saying, "Forget it, Nicole! You'll get over him," Nicole had replied, "I'll live with it, but I'll never get over him."

Billy tried hard to make a success of the marriage. He knew he had made a mistake, and he did not want to punish Anita for it. He tried desperately to be a good husband. The problem was that Anita had nothing in common with him or with any of his friends. The only person Anita seemed comfortable with was her brother, and she and Harold spoke on the telephone every day.

"I miss him," Anita complained to Billy.

"Would you like to have him come down and stay with us for a few days?"

"He can't." And she looked at her husband and said spitefully, "He's got a job."

At parties, Billy attempted to bring Anita into the conversations, but it was quickly apparent that she had nothing to contribute. She sat in comers, tongue-tied, nervously, licking her lips, obviously uncomfortable. Billy's friends were aware that even though he was staying at the Stanley villa, he was estranged from his father and that he was living off the small annuity that his mother had left him. His passion was polo and he rode the ponies owned by friends. In the world of polo, players are ranked by goals, with ten goals being the best. Billy was nine goals, and he had ridden with Mariano Aguerre from Buenos Aires, Wicky el Effendi from Texas, Andres Diniz from Brazil, and dozens of other top goals. There were only about twelve ten-goal players in the world, and Billy's driving ambition was to join the group.

"You know why, don't you?" one of his friends remarked. "His father was ten goals."

Because Nicole Carson knew that Billy could not afford to buy his own polo ponies, she purchased a string for him to ride. When friends asked why, she said, "I want to make him happy in any way I can."

When newcomers asked what Billy did for a living, people just raise their shoulders and then drop them to show that they do not know or care about it. In reality, he was living a second hand life, making money playing skins at golf, betting on polo matches, borrowing other people's ponies and racing yachts, and on occasion, other people's wives.

The marriage with Anita was deteriorating rapidly, but Billy refused to admit it.

"Anita," he would say, "when we go to parties, please try to join in the conversation."

"Why should I? Your friends all think they're too good for me."

"Well, they're not," Billy assured her.

Once a week, the Bell Air Literary Circle met at the country club for a discussion of the latest books, followed by a luncheon. On this particular day, as the ladies were dining, the steward approached Mrs. Brickman. "Mrs. William Stanley is outside. She would like to join you."

A hush fell over the table.

"Show her in," Mrs. Brickman said.

A moment later, Anita walked into the dining room. She had washed her hair and pressed her best dress. She stood there, nervously looking at the group.

Mrs. Brickman gave her a nod, then said pleasantly, "Mrs. Stanley."

Anita smiled eagerly, "Yes, ma'am."

"We won't need you. We already have a waitress."

And Mrs. Brickman turned back to her lunch.

When Billy heard the story, he was furious. "How dare she do that to you!" He took her in his arms. "Next time, ask me before you do a thing like that, Anita. You have to be invited to that luncheon."

"I didn't know," she said sullenly.

"It's all right. Tonight we're having dinner at the Blakes', and I want..."

"I won't go!"

"But we've accepted their invitation."

"You go."

"I don't want to go without ..."

"I'm not going."

Billy went alone, and after that, he began going to every party without Anita.

He would come home at all hours, and Anita was sure he had been with other women. The accident changed everything. It happened during a polo match. Billy was playing the Number-Three position, and a member of the opposing team, trying to stroke the ball in close quarters, accidentally hit the legs of the pony that Billy was riding. The pony went down and rolled on top of him. In the pileup that followed, a second pony kicked Billy. At the emergency room of the hospital, the doctors diagnosed a broken leg, three fractured ribs, and a punctured lung.

Over the next two weeks, there were three separate operations, and Billy was in excruciating pain. The doctors gave him morphine to ease it. Anita came to visit him every day. Harold flew in from New York to console his sister.

His physical pain was unbearable, and the only relief Billy had was from the drugs the doctors kept prescribing for him. It was shortly after Billy got home that he seemed to change. He began to have violent mood swings. Very bad mood. One minute he was his usual ebullient self, and the next minute he would go into a sudden rage or a deep depression. At dinner, laughing and telling jokes, Billy would suddenly become angry and abusive toward Anita and storm out. In the middle of a sentence he would drift off into a deep reverie. He became forgetful. He would make dates and not show up; he would invite people to his home and not be there when they arrived. Everyone was concerned about him. Soon, he became abusive to Anita in public. Bringing a cup of coffee to a friend one morning, Anita spilled some, and Billy sneered, "Once a waitress, always a waitress."

Anita also began to show signs of physical abuse, and when people asked her what happened, she would make excuses.

"I bumped into a door" or "I fell down," and she would make light of it. The community was outraged. Now it was Anita they were feeling sorry for. But when Billy's erratic behavior offended someone, Anita would defend her husband.

"Billy is under a lot of stress," Anita would insist.

"He isn't himself." She would not allow anyone to say anything against him.

It was Dr. Thompson who finally brought it out into the open. He asked Anita to come see him in his office one day.

She was nervous. "Is something wrong, doctor?"

He studied her a moment. She had a bruise on her cheek, and her eye was swollen.

"Anita, are you aware that Billy is doing drugs?"

Her eyes flashed with indignation. "No! I don't believe it!" She stood up. "I won't listen to this!"

"Sit down, Anita. It's about time you faced the truth. It's becoming obvious to everyone else. Surely you've noticed his behavior. One minute he's on top of the world, talking about how wonderful everything is, and the next minute he's suicidal."

Anita sat there, watching him, her face pale.

"He's addicted."

Her lips tightened. "No," she said stubbornly. "He's not."

"He is. You've got to be realistic. Don't you want to help him?"

"Of course, I do!" She was wringing her hands. "I'd do anything to help him. Anything."

"All right. Then let's start. I want you to help me get Billy into a rehabilitation center. I've asked him to come in and see me."

Anita looked at him for a long time, and then nodded.

"I'll talk to him," she said quietly.

That afternoon, when Billy walked into Dr. Thompson's office, he was in a euphoric mood. "You wanted to see me, doc? It's about Anita, isn't it?"

"No. It's about you, Billy."

Billy looked at him in surprise. "Me? What's my problem?"

"I think you know what your problem is."

"What are you talking about?"

"If you go on like this, you're going to destroy your life and Anita's life. What are you taking, Billy?"

"Taking?"

"You heard me."

There was a long silence.

"I want to help you."

Billy sat there, staring at the floor. When he finally spoke, his voice was hoarse. "You're right. I've ... I've tried to kid myself, but I can't do this any longer."

"What are you on?"

"Heroin. ".

"My God!"

"Believe me, I've tried to stop, but I ... I can't."

"You need help, and there are places where you can get it."

Billy said wearily, "I hope to God you're right."

"I want you to go to the Harbor Group Clinic in Jupiter. Will you try it?"

There was a brief hesitation. "Yes."

"Who's supplying you with the heroin?" Dr. Thompson asked.

Billy shook his head. "I can't tell you that."

"Very well. I'll make arrangements for you at the clinic."

The following morning, Dr. Thompson was seated in the office of the chief of police.

"Someone is supplying him with heroin," Dr. Thompson said, "but he won't tell me who."

Chief of Police Murphy looked at Dr. Thompson and nodded. "I think I know who."

There were several possible suspects. Bell Air was a small enclave, and everyone knew everyone else's business. A liquor store had opened recently on Bridge Road that made deliveries to their Bell Air customers at all hours of the day and night.

A doctor at a local clinic had been fined for over prescribing drugs. A gymnasium had opened a year earlier, on the other side of the waterway, and it was rumored that the trainer took steroids and had other drugs available for his good customers. But Chief of Police Murphy had another suspect in mind.

Tim Brooks had served as a gardener for many of the homes in Bell Air for years. He had studied horticulture and loved spending his days creating beautiful gardens. The gardens and lawns he tended were the loveliest in Bell Air. He was a quiet man who kept to himself, and the people he worked for knew very little about him. He seemed to be too well educated to be a gardener, and people were curious about his past. Murphy sent for him.

"If this is about my driver's license, I renewed it," Brooks said.

"Sit down," Murphy ordered.

"Is there some kind of problem?"

"Yeah. You're an educated man, right?"

"Yes."

The chief of police leaned back in his chair. "So how come you're a gardener?"

"I happen to love nature."

"What else do you happen to love?"

"I don't understand."

"How long have you been gardening?"

Brooks looked at him, puzzled. "Have any of my customers been complaining?"

"Just answer the question."

"About fifteen years."

"You have a nice house and a boat?"

"Yes."

"How can you afford all that on what you make as a gardener?"

Baker said, "It's not that big a house, and it's not that big a boat."

"Maybe you make a little money on the side."

"What do you ...?"

"You work for some people in Miami, don't you?"

"Yes."

"There's a lot of Italians there. Do you ever do them some little favors?"

"What kind of favors?"

"Like pushing drugs."

Baker looked at him, horrified. "My God! Of course not."

Murphy leaned forward. "Let me tell you something, Baker. I've been keeping an eye on you. I've had a talk with a few of the people you work for. They don't want you or your Mafia friends here anymore. Is that clear?"

Brooks squeezed his eyes shut for a second, then opened them.

"Very clear."

"Good. I'll expect you out of here by tomorrow. I don't want to see your face again."

Billy Stanley went into the Harbor Group Clinic for three weeks, and when he came out, he was the old Billy-charming, gracious, and delightful to be with. He went back to playing polo, riding Nicole Carson's ponies.

Sunday was the Palm Beach Polo & Country Club's eighteenth anniversary, and South Shore Boulevard was heavy with traffic as three thousand fans converged on the polo grounds. They rushed to fill the box seats on the west side of the field and the bleachers at the opposite end. Some of the finest players in the world were going to be in the day's game.

Anita was in a box seat next to Nicole Carson, as Nicole's guest.

"Billy told me that this is your first polo match, Anita. Why haven't you been to one before?"

Anita licked her lips. "I ... I guess I've always been too nervous to watch Billy play. I don't want him to get hurt again. It's a very dangerous sport, isn't it?"

Nicole said thoughtfully, "When you get eight players, each weighing about one hundred and seventy-five pounds, and their nine-hundred-pound ponies racing at each other over three hundred yards at forty miles an hour-yes, accidents can happen."

Anita shouted out. "I couldn't stand it if anything happened to Billy again. I really couldn't. I go crazy worrying about him."

Nicole Carson said gently, "Don't worry. He's one of the best. He studied under Hary Brown, you know."

Anita was looking at her blankly. "Who?"

"He's a ten-goal player. One of the legends of polo."

"Oh."

There was a murmur from the crowd as the ponies moved across the field.

"What's happening?" Anita asked.

"They just finished a practice session before the game. They're ready to begin now."

On the field, the two teams were starting to line up under the hot Florida sun, getting ready for the umpire's throw-in. Billy looked wonderful, tan and fit and lithe-- ready to do battle. Anita waved and blew him a kiss.

Both teams were lined up now, side by side. The players held their mallets down for the throw-in.

"There are usually six periods of play, called chukkers, "Nicole Carson explained to Anita. "Each chukker lasts seven minutes. The chukker ends when the bell rings. Then there's a short rest. They change ponies every period. The team that scores the most goals wins."

"Right."

Nicole wondered just how much Anita understood. On the field, the players' eyes were fixed on the umpire, anticipating when the ball would be tossed. The umpire looked around at the crowd, and then suddenly bowled the white plastic ball between the two rows of players. The game had begun. The action was swift. Billy made the first play, getting possession of the ball and hitting an offside forehand. The ball sped toward a player on the opposing team. The player galloped down the field after it. Billy rode up to him and hooked his mallet to spoil his shot.

"Why did Billy do that?" Anita asked.

Nicole Carson explained. "When your opponent gets the ball, it's legal to hook his mallet so he can't score or pass. Billy will use an offside stroke next to control the ball."

The action was happening so fast that it was almost impossible to follow.

There were cries of "Center ..."

"Boards."

"Leave it."

And the players were racing down the field at full speed. The ponies-usually pure or three-quarter Thoroughbreds-were responsible for 75 percent of their riders' successes. The ponies had to be fast, and have what players call polo sense, being able to anticipate their rider's every move.

Billy was brilliant during the first three chukkers, scoring two goals in each one and being cheered on by the roaring crowd. His mallet seemed to be everywhere. It was the old Billy Stanley, riding like the wind, fearless. By the end of the fifth chukker, Billy's team was well ahead. The players went off the field for the break.

As Billy passed Anita and Nicole, sitting in the front row, he smiled at both of them.

Anita turned to Nicole Carson, excitedly. "Isn't he wonderful?"

She looked over at Anita. "Yes. In every way."

Billy's teammates were congratulating him. "Right

on the David, old boy! You were fabulous!"

"Great plays!"

"Thanks."

"We're going out there and rub their noses in it some more. They haven't got a chance!"

Billy grinned. "No problem."

He watched his teammates move out to the field, and he suddenly felt exhausted. I pushed myself too hard, he thought. I wasn't really ready to go back to the game yet. I'm not going to be able to keep this up. If I go out there, I'll make a fool of myself. He began to panic, and his heart started to pound. What I need is a little pick me-up. No! I won't do that. I can't. I promised. But the team is waiting for me. I'll do it just this once, and never again. I swear to God, this is the last time. He went to his car and reached into the glove compartment.

When Billy returned to the field, he was humming to himself, and his eyes were unnaturally bright. He waved to the crowd, and joined his waiting team. I don't even need a team, he thought. I could beat those bastards single-handedly. I'm the best damned player in the world. He was giggling to himself.

The accident occurred during the sixth chukker, although some of the spectators were to insist later that it was no accident.

The ponies were bunched together, racing toward the goal, and Billy had control of the ball. Out of the comer of his eye he saw one of the opposing players closing in on him. Using a tail shot, he sent the ball to the rear of the pony. It was picked up by Richard Smith, the best player on the opposing team, who began racing toward the goal. Billy was after him at full speed. He tried to hook Smith's mallet and missed. The ponies were getting closer to the goal. Billy kept desperately trying to get possession of the ball, and failed each time. As Smith neared the goal, Billy deliberately swerved his pony to crash into Smith and rides him off the ball. Smith and his pony went tumbling to the ground. The crowd rose to its feet, screaming. The umpire angrily blew the whistle and held up a hand.

The first rule in polo is that when a player has possession of the ball and is heading toward the goal, it is illegal to cut across the line in which the player is traveling. Any player who crosses that line creates a dangerous situation and commits a foul. Play stopped. The umpire approached Billy, anger in his voice.

"That was a deliberate foul, Mr. Stanley!"

Billy grinned. "It wasn't my fault! His damned pony..."

"The opponents will receive a penalty goal."

The chukker turned into a disaster. Billy committed two more blatant violations within three minutes of each other. The penalties resulted in two more goals for the other team. In each case the opponents were awarded a free penalty shot on an unguarded goal. In the last thirty seconds of the game, the opposing team scored the winning goal. What had been an assured victory, had turned into a rout.

In the box, Nicole Carson was stunned by the sudden turn of events.

Anita said timidly, "It didn't go well, did it?"

Nicole turned to her. "No, Anita. I'm afraid it didn't."

A steward approached the box. "Miss Carson, may I have a word with you?"

Nicole Carson turned to Anita. "Excuse me a moment."

Anita watched them walk away.

After the game, Billy's team was very quiet. Billy was too ashamed to look at the others. Nicole Carson hurried over to Billy.

"Billy, I'm afraid I have some terrible, terrible news." She put a hand on his shoulder, "Your father is dead."

Billy looked up at her and shook his head from side to side. He began to sob. "I'm ... I'm responsible. It's m ... my fault."

"No. You mustn't blame yourself. It isn't your fault."

"Yes, it is," Billy cried. "Don't you understand? If it weren't for my penalties, we would have won the game."

10

Jennifer Stanley had never known her father, and now he was dead, reduced to a black headline in the Miami Star: TYCOON Robert Stanley DIE IN AUTO ACCIDENT! She sat there, staring at his photograph on the front page of the newspaper, filled with conflicting emotions. Do I hate him because of the way he treated my mother, or do I love him because he's my father? Do I feel guilty because I never tried to get in touch with him, or do I feel angry because he never tried to find me? It doesn't matter anymore, she thought. He's gone.

Her father had been dead to her all her life, and now he had died again, cheating her out of something she had no words for. Inexplicably, she felt an overwhelming sense of loss. Stupid! Jennifer thought. How can I miss someone I never knew? She looked at the newspaper photograph again. Do I have anything of him in me?

Jennifer stared into the mirror on the wall. The eyes. I have the same deep gray eyes.

Jennifer went into her bedroom closet, removed a battered cardboard box, and from it lifted a leather-bound scrapbook. She sat on the edge of her bed and opened the scrapbook. For the next two hours, she pored over its familiar contents. There were countless photographs of her mother in her governess's uniform, with Robert Stanley and Mrs. Stanley and their three young children. Most of the pictures had been taken on their yacht, at Bell Air, or at the Bell Air villa.

Jennifer picked up the yellowed newspaper clippings recounting the scandal that had happened so many years before in Los Angeles. The faded headlines were lurid:

LOVE NEST ON BELL AIR

BILLIONAIRE ROBERT STANLEY IN

SCANDAL TYCOON'S WIFE COMMITS

SUICIDE GOVERNESS ROSA NEWMAN

DISAPPEARS

There were dozens of gossip columns filled with an indirect remark about this event, usually suggesting something bad or rude. Jennifer sat there for a long time, lost in the past.

She had been born at St. Joseph's Hospital in Miami. Her earliest memories were of living in dreary walk up apartments and constantly moving from city to city. There were times when there was no money at all, and little to eat. Her mother was continually ill, and it had been difficult for her to find steady work. The young girl quickly learned never to ask for toys or new dresses.

Jennifer started school when she was five, and her classmates would mock her because she wore the same dress and scruffy shoes every day. When the other children teased her, Jennifer fought them. She was a rebel, and she was always being brought up before the principal. Her teachers didn't know what to do with her. She was in constant trouble. She might have been expelled except for one thing: She was the brightest student in her class.

Her mother had told Jennifer that her father was dead, and she had accepted that. But when Jennifer was twelve years old, she stumbled across a picture album filled with photographs of her mother with a group of strangers.

"Who are these people?" Jennifer asked. And Jennifer's mother decided that the time had come. "Sit down, my darling." She took Jennifer's hand and held it tightly. There was no way to break the news tactfully. "That is your father, and your half-sister, and your two half-brothers."
Jennifer was looking at her, puzzled.
"I don't understand."

The truth had finally come out, shattering Jennifer's peace of mind. Her father was alive! And she had a half-sister and two half-brothers. It was too much to comprehend. "Why ... why did you lie to me?"

"You were too young to understand. Your father and I ... had an affair. He was married, and I ... I had to leave, to have you."

"I hate him!" Jennifer said.

"You mustn't hate him."

"How could he have done this to you?" she demanded.

"What happened was my fault as much as his." Each word was agony. "Your father was a very attractive man, and I was young and foolish. I knew that nothing could ever come of our affair. He told me he loved me ... but he was married and had a family. And ... and then I became pregnant." It was difficult for her to go on. "A reporter got hold of the story and it was in all the newspapers. I ran away. I intended for you and me to go back to him, but his wife killed herself, and I ... I could never face him or the children again. It was my fault, you see. So don't blame him."

But there was a part of the story Rosa never revealed to her daughter. When the baby was born, the clerk at the hospital said, "We're filling out the birth certificate. The baby's name is Jennifer Newman?"

Rosa had started to say yes, and then she thought fiercely, No! She's Robert Stanley's daughter. She's entitled to his name, and his support.

"My daughter's name is Jennifer Stanley."

She had written to Robert Stanley, telling him about Jennifer, but she had never received a reply.

Jennifer was fascinated by the idea that she had a family she had not known about, and also by the fact that they were famous enough to be written about in the press. She went to the public library and looked up everything she could find about Robert Stanley. There were dozens of articles about him. He was a billionaire, and he lived in another world, a world that Jennifer and her mother were totally excluded from.

One day, when one of Jennifer's classmates teased her about being poor, Jennifer said defiantly, "I'm not poor! My father is one of the richest men in the world. We have a yacht and an airplane, and a dozen beautiful homes."

Her teacher heard her. "Jennifer, come up here."

Jennifer approached the teacher's desk. "You must not tell a lie like that."

"It's not a lie," Jennifer retorted. "My father is a billionaire! He knows presidents and kings!"

The teacher looked at the young girl standing before her in her shabby Blackburn dress and said, "Jennifer, that's not true."

"It is!" Jennifer said stubbornly.

She was sent to the principal's office. She never mentioned her father at school again. Jennifer learned that the reason she and her mother kept moving from city to city was because of the news media. Robert Stanley was constantly in the press, and the gossip newspapers and magazines kept digging up the old scandal. Investigative reporters would eventually discover who Rosa Newman was and where she lived, and she would have to take Jennifer and flying. Jennifer read every newspaper story that appeared about Robert Stanley, and each time, she was tempted to telephone him. She-wanted to believe that during all those years he had been desperately searching for her mother. I'll call and say, "This is your daughter. If you want to see us ..."

And he would come to them and fall in love all over again, and marry her mother, and they would all live happily together.

Jennifer Stanley grew into a beautiful young woman. She had lustrous dark hair, a laughing, generous mouth, the luminous gray eyes of her father, and a gently curved figure. But when she smiled, people forgot about everything else but that smile.

Because they were forced to move so often, Jennifer went to schools in five different states. During the summers she worked as a clerk in a department store, behind the counter in a drugstore, and as a receptionist. She was always fiercely independent.

They were living in Miami, Florida, when Jennifer finished college on a scholarship. She was not sure what she wanted to do with her life. Friends, impressed by her beauty, suggested that she become a movie actress.

"You'd be a star overnight!"

Jennifer had dismissed the idea with a casual, "Who wants to get up that early every morning?"

But the real reason she was not interested was because she wanted, above all, her privacy. It seemed to Jennifer that all their lives, she and her mother had been hounded by the press because of what had happened so many years earlier. Jennifer's dream of one day uniting her mother and father ended the day her mother died. Jennifer felt an overpowering sense of loss. My father has to know, Jennifer thought. Mother was a part of his life. She looked up the telephone number of his business headquarters in Los Angeles. A receptionist answered.

"Good morning, Stanley Enterprises." Jennifer hesitated.

"Stanley Enterprises. Hello? May I help you?"

Slowly Jennifer replaced the receiver. Mother wouldn't have wanted me to make this call. She was alone now. She had no one.

Jennifer buried her mother at Memorial Park Cemetery in Miami. There were no other mourners. Jennifer stood at the graveside and thought, it isn't fair, Mama. You made one mistake and paid for it with the rest of your life. I wish I could have taken some of your pain away. I love you very much, Mama. I'll always love you. All she had left of her mother's years on earth was a collection of old photographs and clippings.

With her mother gone, Jennifer's thoughts turned to the Stanley family. They were rich. She could go to them for help. Never, she decided. Not after the way Robert Stanley treated my mother. But she had to earn a living. She was faced with a career decision. She thought that she is both amused and disappointed; maybe I'll become a brain surgeon. Or a painter? Opera singer?

Physicist? Astronaut?

She settled for a secretarial course at night school at Miami Florida Community College. The day after Jennifer finished the course, she visited an employment agency. There were a dozen applicants waiting to see the employment counselor. Sitting next to Jennifer was an attractive woman her age.

"Hi! I'm Susan Crawford."

"Jennifer Stanley."

"I've got to get a job today." Susan moaned. "I've been kicked out of my apartment."

Jennifer heard her name called.

"Good luck!" Susan said.

"Thanks."

Jennifer walked into the office of the employment counselor.

"Sit down, please."

"Thank you."

"I see from your application that you have a college education and summer work experience. And you have a high recommendation from the secretarial school." She looked at the dossier on her desk. "You take short- hand at ninety words per minute, and type at sixty words per minute?"

"Yes, ma'am."

"I might have just the thing for you. There's a small firm of architects that's looking for a secretary. The salary isn't very large, I'm afraid ..."

"That's okay," Jennifer said quickly.

"Very well. I'm going to send you over there." She handed Jennifer a slip of paper with a typed name and address on it. "They'll interview you at noon tomorrow."

Jennifer smiled happily. "Thank you." She was filled with a sense of excitement. When Jennifer came out of the office, Susan's name was being called.

"I hope you get something," Jennifer said.

"Thanks!"

On an impulse, Jennifer decided to stay and wait. Ten minutes later, when Susan came out of the inner office, she was smiling widely.

"I got an interview! She telephoned, and I'm going to the American Mutual Insurance Company tomorrow for a receptionist job. How did you do?"

"I'll know tomorrow, too."

"I'm sure we'll make it. Why don't we have lunch together and celebrate?"

"Fine."

At lunch they talked, and their friendship clicked instantly.

"I looked at an apartment in Overland Park," Susan said. "It's a two-bedroom and bath, with a kitchen and living room. It's really nice. I can't afford it alone, but if the two of us ..."

Jennifer smiled. "I'd like that." She crossed her fingers.

"If I get the job."

"You'll get it!" Susan assured her.

On the way to the offices of John, Mark & Thomson, Jennifer thought, this could be my big opportunity. This could lead anywhere. I mean, this isn't just a job. I'll be working for architects. Dreamers who build and shape the city's skyline, who create beauty and magic out of stone and steel and glass. Maybe I'll study architecture myself, so that I can help them and be a part of that dream.

The office was in a dingy old commercial building on west site of the city. Jennifer took the elevator to the third floor, got off, and stopped at a scarred door divided JOHN, MARK & THOMSON ARCHITECTS. She took a deep breath to calm herself and entered. Three men were waiting for her in the reception room, examining her as she walked in the door.

"You're here for the secretarial job?"

"Yes, sir."

"I'm John." The bald one.

"Mark." The ponytail.

"Thomson." The potbelly.

They all appeared to be somewhere in their forties.

"We understand this is your first secretarial job," John said.

"Yes, it is," Jennifer replied. Then quickly she added, "But I'm a fast learner. I'll work very hard." She decided not to mention her idea about going to school to study architecture yet. She would wait until they got to know her better.

"All right, we'll try you out," Mark said, "and see how it goes."

Jennifer felt a sense of exhilaration. "Oh, thank you! You won't be..."

"About the salary," Thomson said. "I'm afraid we can't pay very much at the beginning."

"That's all right," Jennifer said. "I... "

"Three hundred a week," John told her.

They were right. It was not much money. Jennifer made a quick decision. "I'll take it."

They looked at one another and exchanged smiles.

"Great!" John said. "Let me show you around."

The tour took only a few seconds. There was the little reception room and three small offices that looked as though they had been furnished by the Salvation Army. The lavatory was down the hall. They were all architects, but John was the businessman, Mark was the salesman, and Thomson handled construction.

"You'll be working for all of us," John told her.

"Fine." Jennifer knew she was going to make herself indispensable to them.

John looked at his watch. "It's twelve-thirty. How about some lunch?"

Jennifer felt a little thrill. She was part of the team now. They're inviting me to lunch.

He turned to Jennifer.

"There's a delicatessen down the block. I'll have a corned beef sandwich on rye with mustard, potato salad, and Danish."

"Oh." So much for "They're inviting me to lunch."

Thomson said, "I'll have pastrami and some chicken soup."

"Yes, sir."

Mark spoke up. "I'll have the pot roast platter and a soft drink."

"Oh, make sure the corned beef is lean," John told her.

"Lean corned beef."

Thomson said, "Make sure that the soup is hot."

"Right. Soup hot."

Mark said, "Make my soft drink a diet cola."

"Diet cola."

"Here's some money." John handed her a twenty-dollar bill. Ten minutes later, Jennifer was in the delicatessen, talking to the man behind the counter. "I want one lean corned beef sandwich on rye with mustard, potato salad, and Danish. A pastrami sandwich and very hot chicken soup. And a pot roasts platter and diet cola."

The man nodded. "You work for John, Mark, and Thomson, huh?"

Jennifer and Susan moved into the apartment in Overland Park the following week. The apartment consisted of two small bedrooms, a living room with furniture that had seen too many tenants, a small kitchen with dining area, and a bathroom. They'll never confuse this place with The Ritz, Jennifer thought.

"We'll take turns at cooking," Susan suggested.

"Fine."

Susan prepared the first meal, and it was delicious. The next night was Jennifer's turn. Susan took one bite of the dish that Jennifer had made and said, "Jennifer, I don't have a lot of life insurance. Why don't I do the cooking and you do the cleaning?"

The two roommates got along well. On weekends, they would go to see movies at the Glenwood 4, and shop at the Bannister Mall. They bought their clothes at the Super Flea Discount House. One night a week they went out to an inexpensive restaurant for dinner-Stephenson's Old Apple Farm or the Cafe Max for Mediterranean specialties. When they could afford it, they would drop in at Charlie to hear jazz.

Jennifer enjoyed working for John, Mark & Thomson. To say that the firm was not doing well was an understatement. Clients were scarce. Jennifer felt that she wasn't doing much to help build the skyline of the city, but she enjoyed being around her three bosses. They were like a surrogate family, and each one confided his problems to Jennifer. She was capable and efficient, and she very quickly reorganized the office.

Jennifer decided to do something about the lack of clients. But what? She soon had the answer. There was an item in the Miami Star about a luncheon for a new executive women's organization. The chairperson was Sylvia Bradford.

The following day, at noon, Jennifer said to John, "I may be a little late coming back from lunch."

He smiled. "No problem, Jennifer." He thought how lucky they were to have her. Jennifer arrived at the Plaza Inn and went to the room where the luncheon was being given. The woman seated at the table near the door said, "May I help you?"

"Yes. I'm here for the Executive Women's luncheon."

"Your name?"

"Jennifer Stanley."

The woman looked at the list in front of her. "I'm afraid I don't see you're..."

Jennifer smiled. "Isn't that just like Sylvia? I'll have to have a talk with her. I'm the executive secretary with John, Eastman, and Thomson."

The woman looked uncertain. "Well ..."

"Don't worry about it. I'll just go in and find Sylvia."

In the banquet room was a group of well-dressed women chatting among themselves. Jennifer approached one of them. "Which one is Sylvia Bradford?"

"She's over there." She indicated a tall, striking looking woman in her forties.

Jennifer went up to her. "Hi. I'm Jennifer Stanley."

"Hello."

"I'm with John, Eastman, and Thomson. I'm sure you've heard of them."

"Well, I ..."

"They're the fastest growing architectural firm in Miami."

"I see."

"I don't have a lot of time to spare, but I would like to contribute whatever I can to the organization."

"Well, that's very kind of you, Miss ...?"

"Stanley."

That was the beginning.

The Executive Women's organization represented most of the top firms in Miami, and in no time at all, Jennifer was networking with them. She had lunch with one or more of the individual members at least once a week.

"Our company is going to put up a new building in Olathe."

And Jennifer would immediately report back to her bosses.

"Mr. Hanley wants to build a summer home in Tonganoxie."

And before anyone else found out about it, John, Mark & Thomson had the jobs. Mark called Jennifer in one day and said, "You deserve a raise, Jennifer. You're doing a great job. You're one hell of a secretary!"

"Would you do me a favor?" Jennifer asked.

"Sure."

"Call me an executive secretary. It will help my credibility."

From time to time, Jennifer would read newspaper articles about her father, or watch him being interviewed on television. She never mentioned him to Susan or to any of her employers.

When Jennifer was younger, one of her daydreams had been that, like Dorothy, she would one day be whisked away from Florida to some beautiful, magical place. It would be a place filled with yachts and private planes and palaces. But now, with the news of her father's death, that dream was ended forever. Well I got the Miami part right, she thought that she is both amused and disappointed. I have no family left. But I do, Jennifer corrected herself. I have two half-brothers and a half-sister. They're my family. Should I go visit them? Good idea? Bad idea? I wonder how we would feel about one another.

Her decision turned out to be a matter of life or death.

11

They were strangers, two men and a girl. They stayed in the house, staring at the front door. It was a glorious, deep brown. They were silent and full of secrets. People believed they knew things that could never be shared; mysteries too deep and powerful for outsiders to understand. It was the gathering of a clan of strangers. It had been years since they had been seen or communicated with one another.

Judge Thomas Stanley arrived in Los Angeles by plane. Carmen Stanley Renaux flew in from Paris. David Renaux took the train from New York. Billy Stanley and Anita drove up from Bell Air. The heirs had been notified that the funeral services would take place at King's Chapel. The street outside the church was barricaded, and there were policemen to hold back the crowd that had gathered to watch the dignitaries arrive. The vice president of the United States was there, as well as senators and ambassadors and statesmen from as far away as Turkey and Saudi Arabia. During his lifetime, Robert Stanley had cast a large shadow, and all seven hundred seats in the chapel would be occupied.

Thomas, Billy and Carmen, with their spouses, met inside the vestry. It was an awkward meeting. They were alien to one another, and the only thing they had in common was the body of the man in the hearse outside the church.

"This is my husband, David," Carmen said.

"This is my wife, Anita. Anita, my sister, Carmen, and my brother, Thomas."

There were polite exchanges of hellos. They stood there, uncomfortably studying one another, until an usher carne up to the group.

"Excuse me," he said in a hushed voice. "The services are about to begin. Would you follow me, please?"

He led them to a reserved pew at the front of the chapel. They took their seats and waited, each preoccupied with his or her own thoughts.

As concern to Thomas, he felt strange to be back in Los Angeles. The only good memories he had of it were when his mother and Rosa were alive. When he was eleven, Thomas had seen a print of the famous Goya painting Saturn Devouring His Son, and he had always identified it with his father.

And now, Thomas, looking over at his father's coffin as it was carried into the church by the pallbearers, thought, Saturn is dead. Thomas has very bad mood driving.

"I know your dirty little secrets."

147

The minister stepped into the chapel's historic wine glass-shaped pulpit.

"Jesus said unto her, I am the resurrection and the life: he that believeth in me, though he were dead, yet shall he live: and whosoever liveth and believeth in me shall never die."

Billy was feeling exhilarated. He had taken a hit of heroin before coming to the church, and it had not worn off yet. He glanced over at his brother and sister. Thomas has put on weight. He looks like a judge. Carmen has turned into a beauty, but she seems to be under a strain. I wonder if it's because Father died. No. She hated him as much as I did. He looked at his wife, seated next to him. I'm sorry I didn't get to show her off to the old man. He would have died of a heart attack.

The minister was speaking.

"Like as a father pitieth his children, so the Lord pitieth them that fear him. For he knoweth our frame; he remembereth that we are dust."

Carmen was not listening to the service. She was thinking about the red dress. Her father had telephoned her in New York one afternoon.

"So you've become a big-shot designer, have you? Well, let's see how good you are. I'm taking my new girlfriend to a charity ball Saturday night. She's your size. I want you to design a dress for her. "

"By Saturday? I can't, Father. I ..."

"You'll do it."

And she had designed the ugliest dress she could conceive of. It had a large black bow in front and yards of ribbons and lace. It was a monstrosity. She had sent it to her father, and he had telephoned her again.

"I got the dress. By the way, my girlfriend can't make it Saturday, so you're going to be my date, and you're going to wear that dress. "

"No!"

And then the terrible phrase: "You don't want to disappoint me, do you?"

And she had gone, not daring to change the dress, and had spent the most humiliating evening of her life.

"For we brought nothing into this world, and it is certain we can carry nothing out.

"The Lord gave, and the Lord hath taken away; blessed be the name of the Lord!"

Anita Stanley was uncomfortable. She was awed by the splendor of the huge church and the elegant-looking people in it. She had never been to Los Angeles before, and to her it meant the world of Stanley's, with all its pomp and glory. These people were so much better than she was. She took her husband's hand.

"All flesh is grass, and all the goodliness thereof is as the flower of the field ... The grass withereth, the flower fadeth; but the word of our God shall stand forever."

David was thinking about the blackmail letter that his wife had received. It had been worded very carefully, very cleverly. It would be impossible to find out who was behind it. He looked at Carmen, seated next to him, pale and tense. How much more can she take? He wondered. He moved closer to her.

" ... Unto God's gracious mercy and protection we commit you. The Lord blesses you and keeps you. The Lord makes his face to shine upon you and be gracious unto you. The Lord lifts up the light of his countenance upon you and gives you peace, now and forever. Amen."

With the service finished, the minister announced, "The burial services will be private-family members only."

Thomas looked at the coffin and thought about the body inside. Last night, before the casket was sealed, he had gone straight from Los Angeles LAX International Airport to the viewing at the funeral home. He wanted to see his father dead. Billy watched as the coffin was carried out of the church past the staring mourners and he smiled: Give the people what they want.

The graveside ceremony at the old Mount Sinai Memorial Park in Los Angeles was brief. The family watched Robert Stanley's body being lowered to its final resting place, and as the dirt was being thrown onto the casket, the minister said, "There's no need for you to stay any longer if you don't wish to."

Billy nodded. "Right." The effect of the heroin was beginning to wear off, and he was starting to feel jittery.

"Let's get the hell out of here."

David said, "Where are we going?"

Thomas turned to the group. "We're staying at Bell Air.

It's all been arranged. We'll stay there until the estate is settled."

A few minutes later, they were in limousines on their way to the house.

Los Angeles had a strict social hierarchy. The nouveau riche lived on Wilshire Boulevard, and the social climbers on downtown. Less-affluent old families lived on Main Street. Back Bay was the city's newest and most prestigious address, but Beverly Hills was still the citadel for Los Angeles' oldest and wealthiest families. It was a rich mixture of Victorian town houses and brownstones, old churches, and chic shopping areas.

Bell Air, the Stanley estate, was a beautiful old Victorian house that stood amid three acres of land on the Hill. The house that the Stanley children had grown up in was filled with unpleasant memories. When the limousines arrived in front of the house, the passengers got out and stared up at the old mansion.

"I can't believe Father isn't going to be inside, waiting for us," Carmen said.

Billy grinned. "He's too busy trying to run things in hell."

Thomas took a deep breath. "Let's go."

As they approached the front door, it opened, and Damon, the butler, stood there. He was in his seventies, a dignified, capable servant who had worked at Bell Air for more than thirty years. He had watched the children grow up, and had lived through all the scandals.

Damon's face lit up as he saw the group. "Good afternoon!"

Carmen gave him a warm hug. "Damon, it's so good to see you again."

"It's been a long time, Miss Carmen."

"It's Mrs. Renaux now. This is my husband, David."

"How do you do, sir?"

"My wife has told me a great deal about you."

"Nothing too terrible I hope, sir."

"On the contrary. She has only fond memories of you."

"Thank you, sir." Damon turned to Thomas. "Good afternoon, Judge Stanley."

"Hello, Damon."

"It's a pleasure to see you, sir."

"Thank you. You're looking very well."

"So are you, sir. I'm so sorry about what has happened."

"Thank you. Are you set up here to take care of all of us?"

"Oh, yes. I think we can make everyone comfortable."

"Am I in my old room?"

Damon smiled. "That's right." He turned to Billy.

"I'm pleased to see you, Mr. William. I want to..."

Billy grabbed Anita's arm. "Come on," he said curtly. "I want to get freshened up."

The others watched as Billy pushed past them and took Anita upstairs.

The rest of the group walked into the huge drawing room. The room was dominated by a pair of massive Louis XIV armoires. Scattered around the room were a gilt wood console table with a molded marble top, and an array of exquisite period chairs and couches. An ormolu chandelier hung from the high ceiling. On the walls were dark medieval paintings.

Damon turned to Thomas. "Judge Stanley, I have a message for you. Mr. Frank Harold would like you to call him when it would be convenient to arrange a meeting with the family."

"Who is Frank Harold?" David asked.

Carmen replied. "He's the family attorney. Father has been with him forever but we've never met him."

"I presume he wants to discuss the disposition of the estate," Thomas said. He turned to the others. "If it's all right with all of you, I'll arrange for him to meet us here tomorrow morning."

"That will be fine," Carmen said.

"The chef is preparing dinner," Damon told them.

"Will eight o'clock be satisfactory?"

"Yes," Thomas said. "Thank you."

"Evelyn and Maryanne will show you to your rooms."

Thomas turned to his sister and her husband. "We'll meet down here at eight, shall we?"

As Billy and Anita entered their bedroom upstairs, Anita asked, "Are you all right?"

"I'm fine," Billy snapped. "Leave me alone."

She watched him go into the bathroom and slam the door shut. She stood there, waiting.

Ten minutes later, Billy came out. He was smiling.

"Hi, baby."

"Hi."

"Well, how do you like the old house?"

"It's ... it's enormous."

"It's a monstrosity." He walked over to the bed and put his arms around Anita. "This is my old room. These walls were covered with sports posters-the Bruins, the Celtics, the Red Sox. I wanted to be an athlete. I had big dreams. In my senior year in boarding school, I was captain of the football team. I got offers of admission from half a dozen college coaches."

"Which one did you take?"

He shook his head. "None of them. My father said they were only interested in the Stanley name, that they just wanted money from him. He sent me to an engineering school where they didn't play football." He was silent for a moment. Then he mumbled, "I could'a been a contenda ...″

She looked at him puzzled. "What?"

He looked up. "Didn't you ever see on the Waterfront?"

"No."

"It was a line that Marlon Brando said. It means we both got screwed."

"Your father must have been tough."

Billy gave a short, derisive laugh. "That's the nicest thing anyone has ever said about him. I remember when I was just a kid, I fell off a horse. I wanted to get back on and ride again. My father wouldn't let me. 'You'll never be a rider,' he said. 'You're too clumsy.' "Billy looked up at her. "That's why I became a nine-goal polo player."

They came together at the dinner table, strangers to one another, seated in an uncomfortable silence, their only connection, childhood traumas.

Carmen looked around the room. Terrible memories mingled with an appreciation for its beauty. The dining table was classical French, an early Louis XV, surrounded by Directoire walnut chairs. In one corner was a blue-and-cream painted French provincial corner armoire. On the walls were drawings by Watteau and Fragonard.

Carmen turned to Thomas. "I read about your decision in the Fiorello case. He deserved what you gave him."

"It must be exciting being a judge," Anita said.

"Sometimes it is."

"What kind of cases do you handle?" David inquired.

"Criminal cases-rapes, drugs, murder."

Carmen turned pale and started to say something, and David grabbed her hand and squeezed it as a warning. Thomas said politely to Carmen, "You've become a successful designer."

Carmen was finding it hard to breathe.

"Yes."

"She's fantastic," David said.

"And David, what do you do?"

"I'm with a brokerage house."

"Oh, you're one of those young Wall Street millionaires."

"Well, not exactly, Judge. I'm really just getting started."

Thomas gave David a patronizing look. "I guess it's lucky you have a successful wife."

Carmen blushed and whispered in David's ear, "Pay no attention. Remember I love you."

Billy was beginning to feel the effect of the drug. He turned to look at his wife. "Anita could use some decent clothes," he said. "But she doesn't care how she looks. Do you, angel?"

Anita sat there, embarrassed, not knowing what to say.

"Maybe a little waitress costumes?" Billy suggested.

Anita said, "Excuse me." She got up from the table and fled upstairs.

They were all staring at Billy. He grinned. "She's oversensitive. So, we're having a discussion about the will tomorrow, eh?"

"That's right," Thomas said.

"I'll make you a bet the old man didn't leave us one dime."

David said, "But there's so much money in the estate ..."

Billy snorted. "You didn't know our father. He probably left us his old jackets and a box of cigars. He liked to use his money to control us. His favorite line was 'You don't want to disappoint me, do you?' And we all behaved like good little children because, as you said, there was so much money. Well, I'll bet the old man found a way to take it with him." Thomas said, "We'll know tomorrow, won't we?"

Early the following morning, Frank Harold and George Brown arrived. Damon escorted them into the library. "I'll inform the family that you're here," he said.

"Thank you." They watched him leave.

The library was huge and opened onto a garden through two large French doors. The room was paneled in dark-stained oak, and the walls were lined with bookcases filled with handsome leather-bound volumes. There was a scattering of comfortable chairs and Italian reading lamps. In one corner stood a customized beveled-glass and ormolu-mounted mahogany cabinet that displayed Robert Stanley's enviable gun collection. Special drawers had been designed beneath the display case to house the ammunition.

"It's going to be an interesting morning," George said. "I wonder how they're going to react."

"We'll find out soon enough."

Carmen and David came into the room first. Frank Harold said,

"Good morning. I'm Frank Harold. This is my associate, George Brown."

"I'm Carmen Renaux, and this is my husband, David."

The men shook hands.

Billy and Anita entered the room.

Carmen said, "Billy, this is Mr. Frank Harold and Mr. Brown."

Billy nodded. "Hi. Did you bring the cash with you?"

"Well, we really ..."

"I'm only kidding! This is my wife, Anita." Billy looked at George. "Did the old man leave me anything or ..."

Thomas entered the room. "Good morning."

"Judge Stanley?"

"Yes."

"I'm Frank Harold, and this is George Brown, my associate. It was George who arranged to have your father's body brought back from Corsica."

Thomas turned to George. "I appreciate that. We're not sure what happened exactly. The press has had so many different versions of the story. Was there foul play involved?"

"No. It seems to have been an accident. Your father's yacht was caught in a terrible storm off the coast of Corsica. Later on, according to a deposition from Donald Herman, his bodyguard, your father die in auto accident."

"What a horrible way to die." Carmen trembled.

"Did you talk to this Herman in person?" Thomas asked.

"Unfortunately, no. By the time I arrived in Corsica, he had left."

Harold said, "The captain of the yacht had advised your father not to sail into that storm, but for some reason, he was in a hurry to return here. He had arranged for a helicopter to bring him back. There was some kind of urgent problem."

Thomas asked, "Do you know what the problem was?"

"No. I cut short my vacation to meet him back here. I don't know what..."

Billy interrupted. "That's all very interesting, but it's ancient history, isn't it? Let's talk about the will. Did he leave us anything or not?" His hands were twitching.

"Why don't we sit down?" Thomas suggested.

They took chairs. Frank Harold sat at the desk, facing them. He opened a briefcase and started to take out some papers.

Billy was ready to explode. "Well? For God's sake, did he or didn't he?"

Carmen said, "Billy ..."

"I know the answer," Billy said angrily. "He didn't leave us a damn cent."

Harold looked into the faces of the children of Robert Stanley. "As a matter of fact," he said, "each of you will share equally in the estate."

George could feel the sudden euphoria that swept through the room.

Billy was staring at Harold, openmouthed. "What? Are you serious?" He jumped to his feet.

"That's fantastic!" He turned to the others. "Did you hear that? The old bastard finally came through!" He looked at Frank Harold. "How much money are we talking about?"

"I don't have the exact figure. According to the latest issue of Forbes magazine, Stanley Enterprises is worth six billion dollars. Most of it is invested in various 'corporations, but there is roughly four hundred million dollars available in liquid assets."

Carmen was listening, stunned. "That's more than a hundred million dollars for each of us. I can't believe it!" I'm free, she thought. I can pay them off and be rid of them forever. She looked at David, her face shining, and squeezed his hand.

"Congratulations," David said. He knew more than the others what the money would mean.

Frank Harold spoke up. "As you know, ninety-nine percent of the shares in Stanley Enterprises were held by your father. So those shares will be divided equally among you. Also, now that his father is deceased, Judge Stanley owns outright that other one percent that had been held in trust. Of course, there will be certain formalities. Furthermore, I should inform you that there is a possibility of another heir being involved."

"Another heir?" Thomas asked.

"Your father's will specifically provide that the estate is to be divided equally among his issue."

Anita looked puzzled. "What ... what do you mean by issue?"

Thomas spoke up. "Natural-born descendants and legally adopted descendants."

Harold nodded. "That is correct. Any descendant born out of wedlock is deemed a descendant of the mother and the father, whose protection is established under the law of the jurisdiction."

162

"What are you saying?" Billy asked impatiently.

"I'm saying that there may be another claimant."

Carmen looked at him. "Who?"

Frank Harold hesitated. There was no way to be tactful. "I'm sure that you are all aware of the fact that, a number of years ago, your father sired a child by a governess who worked here."

"Rosa Newman," Thomas said.

"Yes. Her daughter was born at St. Joseph's Hospital in Miami. She named her Jennifer."

The room was thick with silence.

"Hey!" Billy exclaimed. "That was twenty-five years ago."

"Twenty-six, to be exact."

Carmen asked, "Does anyone know where she is?"

Frank Harold could hear Robert Stanley's voice.

"She wrote to tell me that it was a girl. Well, if she thinks she's going to get a dime out of me, she can go to hell." "No," Harold said slowly. "No one knows where she is."

"Then what the hell are we talking about?" Billy demanded. "I just wanted all of you to be aware that if she does appear, she will be entitled to an equal share of the estate."

"I don't think we have anything to worry about,"

Billy said confidently. "She probably never even knew who her father was."

Thomas turned to Frank Harold. "You say you don't know the exact amount of the estate. May I ask why not?"

"Because our firm handles only your father's personal affairs. His corporate affairs are represented by two other law firms. I've been in touch with them and have asked them to prepare financial statements as soon as possible."

"What kind of time frame are we talking about?"

Carmen asked anxiously. "We will need $100, 000 immediately to cover our expenses."

"Probably two to three months."

David saw the consternation on his wife's face. He turned to Harold. "Isn't there some way to hurry things along?"

George Brown answered. "I'm afraid not. The will has to go through probate court, and their calendar is rather heavy right now."

"What is a probate court?" Anita asked

"Probate is from the past participle of probate-to proving. It's the act of..."

"She didn't ask you for a damned English lesson!"

Billy exploded. "Why can't we just wrap things up now?"

Thomas turned to his brother. "The law doesn't work that way. When there's a death, the will has to be filed in the probate court. There has to be an appraisal of all assets- real estate, closely held corporations, cash, jewelry-then an inventory has to be prepared and filed in the court. Taxes have to be taken care of, and specific bequests paid. After that, a petition is filed for permission to distribute the balance of the estate to the beneficiaries. "

Billy shouts it. "What the hell. I've waited almost forty years to be a millionaire. I guess I can wait another month or two."

Frank Harold stood up. "Aside from your father's bequests to you, there are some minor gifts, but they don't affect the bulk of the estate." Harold looked around the room. "Well, if there's nothing else ..."

Thomas rose. "I think not. Thank you, Mr. Frank Harold, Mr. Brown. If there are any problems, we'll be in touch."

Harold nodded to the group. "Ladies and gentlemen." He turned and went toward the door, George Brown following him. Outside, in the driveway, Frank Harold turned to George. "Well, now you've met the family. What do you think?"

"It was more like a celebration than a mourning. I'm puzzled by something, Frank. If their father hated them as much as they seem to hate him, why did he leave them all that money?"

Frank Harold trembled. "That's something we'll never know. Maybe that's why he was coming to see me, to leave the money to someone else."

None of the group was able to sleep that night, each lost in his or her own thoughts.

Thomas was thinking. It's happened. It's really happened! I can afford to give Connie the world. Anything!

Everything!

Carmen was thinking, As soon as I get the money, I'll find a way to buy them off permanently, and I'll make sure they never bother me again.

Billy was thinking, I'm going to have the best string of polo ponies in the world. No more borrowing other people's ponies. I'm going to be ten goals! He glanced over at Anita, sliding at his side. The first thing I'll do is get rid of this stupid bitch. Then he thought, No, I can't do that...He got out of bed and went into the bathroom. When he came out, he was feeling wonderful.

The atmosphere at breakfast the next morning was exuberant.

"Well," Billy said happily, "I suppose all of you have been making plans."

David shrugged. "How does one plan for something like this? It is an unbelievable amount of money."

Thomas looked up. "It's certainly going to change all our lives."

Billy nodded. "The bastard should have given it to us while he was alive, so we could have enjoyed it then. If it's not impolite to hate the dead, I have to tell you something..."

Carmen said reproachfully, "Billy ..."

"Well, let's not be hypocrites. We all despised him, and he deserved us. Just look what he tried to..."

Damon came into the room. He stood there, apologetically. "Excuse me," he said. "There is a Miss Jennifer Stanley at the door."

12

"Jennifer Stanley?"

They stared at one another, frozen.

"The hell she is!" Billy exploded.

Thomas said quickly, "I suggest we adjourn to the library." He turned to Damon. "Would you send the young lady in there, please?"

"Yes, sir."

She stood in the doorway, looking at each of them, obviously ill at ease. "I ... I probably shouldn't have come," she said.

"You're damn right!" Billy said. "Who the hell are you?"

"I'm Jennifer Stanley." She was almost stammering in her nervousness.

"No. I mean who are you really?"

She started to say something, and then shook her head. "I ... My mother was Rosa Newman. Robert Stanley was my father."

The group looked at one another.

"Do you have any proof of that?" Thomas asked. She swallowed. "I don't think I have any real proof."

"Of course you don't," Billy snapped. "How do you have the nerve to..."

Carmen interrupted. "This is rather a shock to all of us, as you can imagine. If what you're saying is true, then you're ... you're our half-sister."

Jennifer nodded. "You're Carmen." She turned to Thomas.

"You're Thomas." She turned to Billy. "And you're William. They call you Billy."

"As People magazine could have told you," Billy said sarcastically.

Thomas spoke up. "I'm sure you can understand our position, Miss ... er .... Without some positive proof, there's no way we could possibly accept ..."

"I understand." She looked around nervously. "I don't know why I came here."

"Oh, I think you do," Billy said. "It's called money."

"I'm not interested in the money," she said indignantly. "The truth is that I ... I came here hoping to meet my family."

Carmen was studying her. "Where is your mother?"

"She passed away. When I read that our father died ..."

"You decided to look us up," Billy said mockingly.

Thomas spoke. "You say you have no legal proof of who you are."

"Legal? I ... I suppose not. I didn't even think about that. But there are things I couldn't possibly know about unless I had heard them from my mother."

"For example?" David said.

She stopped to think. "I remember my mother used to talk about a greenhouse in back. She loved plants and flowers, and she would spend hours there ..."

Billy spoke up. "Photographs of that greenhouse were in a lot of magazines."

"What else did your mother tell you?" Thomas asked.

"Oh, there were so many things! She loved to talk about all of you and the good times you used to have." She thought for a moment. "There was the day she took you on the swan boats when you were very young. One of you almost fell overboard. I don't remember which one."

Billy and Carmen looked over at Thomas.

"I was the one," he said.

"She took you shopping at Filene's. One of you got lost, and everyone was in a panic."

Carmen said slowly, "I got lost that day."

"Yes? What else?" Thomas asked.

"She took you to the Union Oyster House and you tasted your first oyster and got sick."

"I remember that."

They stared at each other, silent.

She looked at Billy. "You and Mother went to the Charlestown Navy Yard to see the USS Constitution, and you wouldn't leave. She had to drag you away."

She turned to Carmen. "And in the Public Garden one day, you picked some flowers and were almost arrested."

Carmen swallowed. "That's right."

They were all listening to her intently now, fascinated.

"One day, Mother took all of you to the natural history museum, and you were terrified of the mastadon and sea serpent skeletons."

Carmen said slowly, "None of us slept that night." Jennifer turned to Billy. "One Christmas, she took you skating. You fell down and broke a tooth. When you were seven years old, you fell out of a tree and had to have your leg stitched up. You had a scar."

Billy said reluctantly, "I still do."

She turned to the others. "One of you was bitten by a dog. I forgot which one. My mother rushed you to the emergency room at Cedars Sinai Hospital."

Thomas nodded. "I had to have shots against rabies." Her words were coming out in a torrent now.

"Billy, when you were eight years old, you ran away. You were going to Hollywood to become an actor. Our father was furious with you. He made you go to your room without dinner. Mother sneaked some food up to your room."

Billy nodded, silent.

"I ... I don't know what else I can tell you. I ..."

She suddenly remembered something. "I have a photograph in my purse." She opened her purse and took it out. She handed the picture to Carmen.

They all gathered around to look at it. It was a picture of the three of them when they were children, standing next to an attractive young woman in a governess's uniform.

"Mother gave me that."

Thomas asked, "Did she leave you anything else?"

She shook her head. "No. I'm sorry. She didn't want anything around that reminded her of Robert Stanley."

"Except you, of course," Billy said.

She turned to him, defiantly. "I don't care whether you believe me or not. You don't understand ...I ... I was so hoping..." She broke off.

Thomas spoke. "As my sister said, your sudden appearance is rather a shock for us. I mean ... someone appearing out of nowhere and claiming to be a member of the family ... you can see our problem. I think we need a little time to discuss this."

"Of course, I understand."

"Where are you staying?"

"At the Beverly Hills Hotel."

"Why don't you go back there? We'll have a car take you. And we'll be in touch shortly."

She nodded. "All right." She looked at each of them for a moment, and then said softly, "No matter what you think, you're my family."

"I'll walk you to the door," Carmen said.

She smiled. "That's all right. I can find my own way. I feel as if I know every inch of this house."

They watched her turn and walk out of the room.

Carmen said, "Well! It ... it looks as though we have a sister."

"I don't believe it," Billy retorted.

"It seems to me ...," David began.

They were all talking at once. Thomas raised a hand.

"This isn't getting us anywhere. Let's look at this logically. In a sense, this person is on trial here and we're her jurors. It's up to us to determine her innocence or guilt.

In a jury trial, the decision must be unanimous. We must all agree."

Billy nodded. "Right."

Thomas said, "Then I would like to cast the first vote. I think the lady is a fraud."

"A fraud? How can she be?" Carmen demanded.

"She couldn't possibly know all those intimate details about us if she weren't real."

Thomas turned to her. "Carmen, how many servants worked in this house when we were children?"

Carmen looked at him, puzzled. "Why?"

"Dozens, right? And some of them would have known everything this young lady told us. Over the years, there have been maids, chauffeurs, butlers, chefs. Anyone of them could have given her that photograph as well."

"You mean ... she could be in league with someone?"

"One or more," Thomas said. "Let's not forget that there's an enormous amount of money involved."

"She says she doesn't want the money." David reminded them.

Billy nodded. "Sure, that's what she says." He looked at Thomas. "But how do we prove she's a fake? There's no way that..."

"There is a way," Thomas said thoughtfully.

They all turned to him.

"How?" David asked.

"I'll have the answer for you tomorrow."

Frank Harold said slowly, "Are you saying that Jennifer Stanley has appeared after all these years?"

"A woman who claims she's Jennifer Stanley has appeared." Thomas corrected him.

"And you don't believe her?" George asked.

"Absolutely not. The only so-called proofs of her identity that she offered were some incidents from our childhood that at least a dozen former employees could have been aware of and an old photograph that really doesn't prove a thing. She could be in league with any one of them. I intend to prove she's a fraud."

Thomas gets angry. "How do you propose to do that?"

"It's very simple. I want a DNA test done."

George Brown was surprised. "That would mean exhuming your father's body."

"Yes." Thomas turned to Frank Harold. "Will that be a problem?"

"Under the circumstances, I could probably obtain an exhumation order. Has she agreed to this test?"

"I haven't asked her yet. If she refuses, it's an affirmation that she's afraid of the results." He hesitated. "I have to confess that I don't like doing this. But I think it's the only way we can determine the truth."

Harold was thoughtful for a moment. "Very well." He turned to George. "Will you handle this?"

"Of course." He looked at Thomas. "You're probably familiar with the procedure. The next of kin-in this case, any of the deceased's children-has to apply to the coroner's office for an exhumation permit. You'll have to tell them the reason for the request. If it's approved, the coroner's office will contact the funeral home and give them permission to go ahead. Someone from the coroner's office has to be present at the exhumation."

"How long will this take?" Thomas asked.

"I'd say three or four days to get an approval. Today is Wednesday. We should be able to exhume the body on Monday."

"Good." Thomas hesitated. "We're going to need a DNA expert, someone who will be convincing in a courtroom, if it ever goes that far. I was hoping you might know someone."

George said, "I know just the man. His name is Paul Weissman. He's here in Los Angeles. He's given expert testimony in trials all over the country. I'll call him."

"I'd appreciate it. The sooner we get this over with, the better it will be for all of us."

At ten o'clock the following morning, Thomas walked into the Bell Air library, where Billy, Anita, Carmen, and David were waiting. At Thomas's side was a stranger.

"I want you to meet Paul Weissman," Thomas said.

"Who is he?" Billy asked.

"He's our DNA expert."

Carmen looked at Thomas. "What in the world do we... need a DNA expert for?"

Thomas said, "To prove that this stranger, who so conveniently appeared out of nowhere, is an imposter. I have no intention of letting her get away with this."

"You're going to dig the old man up?" Billy asked.

"That's right. I have our attorneys working on the exhumation order now. If the woman is our half-sister, the DNA will prove it. If she's not, it will prove that, too."

David said, "I'm afraid I don't understand about this DNA."

Paul Weissman cleared his throat. "Simply put, deoxyribonucleic acid-or DNA-is the molecule of heredity. It contains each individual's unique genetic code. It can be extracted from traces of blood, semen, saliva, hair roots, and even bone. Traces of it can last in a corpse for more than fifty years."

"I see. So it is really quite simple," David said. Paul Weissman frowned. "Believe me, it is not. There are two

177

types of DNA testing. A per test, which takes three days to get results, and the more complex RFLP test, which takes six to eight weeks. For our purposes, the simpler test will be sufficient."

"How do you do the test?" Carmen asked.

"There are several steps. First, the sample is collected and the DNA is cut into fragments. The fragments are sorted by length by placing them on a bed of gel and applying an electric current. The DNA, which is negatively charged, moves toward the positive and, several hours later, the fragments have arranged themselves by length." He was just getting warmed up. "Alkaline chemicals are used to split the DNA fragments apart, and then the fragments are transferred to a nylon sheet, which is immersed in a bath and radioactive probes..."

The eyes of his listeners were beginning to glaze over.

"How accurate is this test?" Billy interrupted.

"It's one hundred percent accurate in determining if the man is not the father. If the test is positive, it's ninety-nine point nine percent accurate."

Billy turned to his brother. "Thomas, you're a judge. Let's say for the sake of argument that she really is Robert Stanley's child. Her mother and our father were never married. Why should she be entitled to anything?"

"Under the law," Thomas explained, "if our father's paternity is established, she would be entitled to an equal share with the rest of us."

"Then I say let's go ahead with the damned DNA test and expose her!"

Thomas, Billy, Carmen, David, and Jennifer were seated at a table in the dining-room restaurant at the Tremont House.

Anita remained behind at Bell Air. "All this talk about digging up a body gives me the creeps," she had said.

Now the group was facing the woman claiming to be Jennifer Stanley.

"I don't understand what you're asking me to do."

"It's really very simple," Thomas informed her. "A doctor will take a skin sample from you to compare with our father's. If the DNA molecules match, it's positive proof that you're really his daughter. On the other hand, if you're not willing to take the test ..."

"I ... I don't like it." Billy closed in. "Why not?"

"I don't know." She shuddered. "The idea of digging up my father's body to ... to ..."

"To prove who you are."

She looked into each of their faces. "I wish all of you would..."

"Yes?"

"There's no way I can convince you, is there?"

"Yes," Thomas said. "Agree to take this test."

There was a long silence.

"All right. I'll do it."

The exhumation order had been more difficult to obtain than anyone had anticipated. Frank Harold had spoken to the coroner personally.

"No! For God's sake, Frank! I can't do that! Do you know what a stink that would cause? I mean, we aren't dealing with John Doe here; we're dealing with Robert Stanley. If this ever leaked out, the media would have a field day!"

"Marvin, this is important. Millions of dollars are at stake here. So you make sure it doesn't leak out."

"Isn't there some other way you can ...?"

"I'm afraid not. The woman is very convincing."

"But the family is not convinced."

"No."

"Do you think she's a fraud, Frank?"

"Frankly, I don't know. But my opinion doesn't matter. In fact, none of our opinions matters. A court will demand proof, and the DNA test will provide that."

The coroner shook his head. "I knew old Robert Stanley. He would have hated this. I really shouldn't let ..."

"But you will."

The coroner sighed. "I suppose so. Would you do me a favor?"

"Of course."

"Keep this quiet. Let's not have a media circus."

"You have my word. Top secret. I'll have just the family there."

"When do you want to do this?"

"We would like to do it on Monday."

The coroner sighed again. "All right. I'll call the funeral home. You owe me one, Frank."

"I won't forget this."

At nine o'clock Monday morning, the entrance to the section of Mount Sinai Memorial Park where Robert Stanley's body was buried was temporarily closed off "for maintenance repairs." No one was allowed into the grounds. Billy, Anita, Thomas, Carmen, David, Jennifer, Frank Harold, George Brown, and Dr. Coleman, a representative from the coroner's office, stood at the site of Robert Stanley's grave, watching four employees of the cemetery raise his coffin. Paul Weissman waited off to the side.

When the coffin reached ground level, the foreman turned to the group. "What do you want us to do now?"

"Open it, please," Harold said. He turned to Paul Weissman. "How long will this take?"

"No more than a minute. I'll just get a quick skin sample."

"All right," Harold said. He nodded to the foreman. "Go ahead."

The foreman and his assistants began to unseal the coffin.

"I don't want to see this," Carmen said. "Do we have to?"

"Yes!" Billy told her. "We really do."

They all watched, fascinated, as the lid of the coffin was slowly removed and pushed to one side.

They stood there, staring down.

"Oh, my God!" Carmen exclaimed. The coffin was empty.

13

Back at Bell Air, Thomas had just gotten off the phone. "Harold says there won't be any media leaks. The cemetery certainly doesn't want that kind of bad publicity. The coroner has ordered Dr. Coleman to keep his mouth shut, and Paul Weissman can be trusted not to talk."

Billy wasn't paying any attention. "I don't know how the bitch did it!" he said. "But she isn't going to get away with it!" He glared at the others. "I suppose you don't think she arranged it?"

Thomas said slowly, "I'm afraid I have to agree with you, Billy. No one else possibly could have had a reason for doing this. The woman is clever and resourceful, and she's obviously not working alone. I'm not sure exactly what we're up against."

"What are we going to do now?" Carmen asked. Thomas trembled. "Frankly, I don't know. I wish I did. I'm sure she plans to go to court to contest the will."

"Does she have a chance of winning?" Anita asked timidly.

"I'm afraid she does. She's very persuasive. She had some of us convinced."

"There must be something we can do," David exclaimed. "What about bringing the police in on this?"

"Harold says they're already looking into the disappearance of the body, and they've come to a dead end. No pun intended," Thomas said. "What's more, the police want this kept quiet, or they'll have every weir do in town turning up a body."

"We can ask them to investigate this phony!" Thomas shook his head. "This is not a police matter.

"It's a private" He stopped for a moment, and then said thoughtfully, "You know ..."

"What?"

"We could hire a private investigator to try to expose her."

"That's not a bad idea. Do you know one?"

"No, not locally. But we could ask Harold to find someone. Or ... "He hesitated." I've never met him, but I've heard about a private detective the district attorney in San Francisco uses a great deal. He has an excellent reputation."

David spoke up. "Why don't we find out if we can hire him?"

Thomas looked around. "That's up to the rest of you."

"What can we lose?" Carmen asked.

"He could be expensive," Thomas warned.

Billy snorted. "Expensive? We're talking about millions of dollars."

Thomas nodded. "Of course. You're right."

"What's his name?"

Thomas frowned. "I can't remember. Simpson ... Simmons ... No, that's not it. It sounds something like that. I can call the district attorney's office in San Francisco."

The group watched as Thomas picked up the telephone on the console and dialed a number. Two minutes later, he was speaking to an assistant district attorney. "This is Judge Thomas Stanley. I understand that your office retains a private detective from time to time who does excellent work for you. His name is something like Simmons or..."

The voice on the other end said, "Oh, you must mean Fredy Tillman."

"Tillman! Yes, that's it." Thomas looked at the others and smiled. "I wonder if you could give me his telephone number so I can contact him directly."

After he wrote down the telephone number, Thomas replaced the receiver.

He turned to the group, and said, "Well, then, if we all agree, I'll try to reach him."

Everyone nodded.

The following afternoon, Damon came into the drawing room, where the group was waiting. "Mr. Tillman is here."

He was a man in his forties, with a pale complexion and the solid build of a boxer. He had a broken nose and bright, inquisitive eyes. He looked from Thomas to David to Billy, questioningly. "Judge Stanley?"

Thomas nodded. "I'm Judge Stanley."

"Fredy Tillman," he said.

"Please have a seat, Mr. Tillman."

"Thank you." He sat down. "You're the one who telephoned, right?"

"Yes."

"To be honest, I don't know what I can do for you.

I don't have any official connections here."

"This is purely unofficial," Thomas assured him. "We merely want to trace the background of a young woman."

"You told me on the phone she claims to be your half-sister, and there's no way of running a DNA test."

"That's right," Billy said.

He looked at the group. "And you don't believe she's your half-sister?"

There was a moment's hesitation.

186

"We don't," Thomas told him. "On the other hand, it's just possible that she is telling the truth. What we want to hire you to do is provide irrefutable evidence that she is either genuine or a fraud."

"Fair enough. It will cost you a thousand dollars a day and expenses."

Thomas said, "A thousand ...?"

"We'll pay it." Billy cut in.

"I'll need all the information you have on this woman." Carmen said, "There doesn't seem to be very much."

Thomas spoke up. "She has no proof of any kind. She came in with a lot of stories that she says her mother told her about our childhood, and..."

He held up a hand. "Hold it. Who was her mother?"

"Her purported mother was a governess we had as children named Rosa Newman."

"What happened to her?"

They looked at one another uncomfortably. Billy spoke up. "She had an affair with our father and got pregnant. She ran away and had a baby girl." He added to. "She disappeared."

"I see. And this woman claims to be her child?"

"That's right."

"That's not a lot to go on." He sat there, thinking.

Finally, he looked up. "All right. I'll see what I can do."

"That's all we ask," Thomas said.

The first move he made was to go to the Los Angeles Public Library and read all the microfiche about the twenty-six year-old scandal involving Robert Stanley, the governess, and Mrs. Stanley's suicide. There was enough material for a novel.

His next step was to visit Frank Harold.

"My name is Fredy Tillman. I'm..."

"I know who you are, Mr. Tillman. Judge Stanley asked me to cooperate with you. What can I do for you?"

"I want to trace Robert Stanley's illegitimate daughter. She'd be about twenty-six, right?"

"Yes. She was born August 9, 1969, at St. Joseph's Hospital in Miami, Florida. Her mother named her Jennifer." He said. "They disappeared. I'm afraid that's all the information we have."

"It's a beginning," he said. "It's a beginning."

Mrs. Downey, the superintendent at St. Joseph's Hospital in Miami, was a gray-haired woman in her sixties.

"Yes of course, I remember," she said. "How could I ever forget it? There was a terrible scandal. There were stories in all the newspapers. The reporters here found out who she was, and they wouldn't leave the poor girl alone."

"Where did she go when she and the baby left here?"

"I don't know. She left no forwarding address."

"Did she pay her bill in full before she left, Mrs. Downey?"

"As a matter of fact ... she didn't."

"How do you happen to remember that?"

"Because it was so sad. I remember she sat in that very chair you're sitting in, and she told me that she could pay only part of her bill, but she promised to send me the money for the rest of it. Well, that was against hospital rules, of course, but I felt so sorry for her, she was so ill when she left here, and I said yes."

"And did she send you the rest of the money?"

"She certainly did. About two months later. Now I recall. She had gotten a job at some secretarial service."

"You wouldn't happen to remember where that was, would you?"

"No. Goodness, that was about twenty-five years ago, Mr. Tillman."

"Mrs. Downey, do you keep all your patients' records on file?"

"Of course." She looked up at him. "Do you want me to go through the records?"

He smiled pleasantly. "If you wouldn't mind."

"Will it help Rosa?"

"It could mean a great deal to her."

"If you'll excuse me." Mrs. Downey left the office. She returned fifteen minutes later, holding a paper in her hand. "Here it is. Rosa Newman. The return address is The Elite Typing Service. Omaha, Nebraska."

The Elite Typing Service was run by a Mr. Greg Braxton, a man in his sixties.

"We hire so many temporary employees." He protested. "How do you expect me to remember someone who worked here that long ago?"

"This was a rather special case. She was a single woman in her late twenties, in poor health. She had just had a baby and..."

"Rosa!"

"That's right. Why do you remember her?"

"Well, I like to associate things, Mr. Tillman. Do you know what mnemonics is?"

"Yes."

"Well, that's what I use. I associate words. There was a movie out called Rosa's Baby. So when Rosa came in and told me she had a baby, I put the two things together and..."

"How long was Rosa Newman with you?"

"Oh, about a year, I guess. Then the press found out who she was, somehow, and they wouldn't leave her alone. She left town in the middle of the night to get away from them."

"Mr. Braxton, do you have any idea where Rosa Newman went when she left here?"

"Florida, I think. She wanted a warmer climate. I recommended her to an agency I knew there."

"May I have the name of that agency?"

"Certainly. It's the Gale Agency. I can remember it because I associate it with the big storms they have down in Florida every year."

Ten days after his meeting with the Stanley family, he returned to Los Angeles. He had called ahead, and the family was waiting for him. They were seated in a semicircle, facing him as he entered the drawing room at Bell Air.

"You said you had some news for us, Mr. Tillman," Thomas said.

"That's right." He opened a briefcase and pulled out some papers. "This has been a most interesting case," he said. "When I began..."

"Cut to the chase," Billy said impatiently. "Is she a fraud or not?"

He looked up. "If you don't mind, Mr. Stanley, I would like to present this in my own way."

Thomas gave Billy a warning look. "That's fair enough. Please go ahead."

They watched him consult his notes. "The Stanley governess, Rosa Newman, had a female child sired by Robert Stanley. She and the child went to Omaha, Nebraska, where she went to work for The Elite Typing Service. Her employer told me that she had difficulty with the weather."

"Next, I traced her and her daughter to Florida, where she worked for the Gale Agency. They moved around a great deal. I followed the trail to San Francisco, where they were living up to ten years ago. That was the end of the trail. After that, they disappeared." He looked up.

"That's it, Tillman?" Billy demanded. "You lost the trail ten years ago?"

"No, that is not it." He reached into his briefcase and took out another paper. "The daughter, Jennifer, applied for a driver's license when she was seventeen."

"What good is that?" David asked.

"In the state of California, drivers are required to have their fingerprints taken." He held up a card. "These are the real Jennifer Stanley's fingerprints."

Thomas said, excitedly, "I see! If they match..."

Billy interrupted. "Then she would really be our sister."

He nodded. "That's right. I brought a portable fingerprint kit with me, in case you want to check her out now. Is she here?"

Thomas said, "She's at a local hotel. I've been talking to her every morning, trying to persuade her to stay here until we get this resolved."

"We've got her!" Billy said. "Let's get over there!"

Half an hour later, the group was entering a hotel room at the Beverly Hills Hotel. As they walked in, she was packing a suitcase.

"Where are you going?" Carmen asked.

She turned to face them. "Home. It was a mistake for me to come here in the first place."

Thomas said, "You can't blame us for ...?"

She turned on him, furious. "Ever since I arrived, I've been met with nothing but suspicion. You think I came here to take some money away from you: Well, I didn't. I came because I wanted to find my family. I ... Never mind." She returned to her packing.

Thomas said, "This is Fredy Tillman. He's a private detective."

She looked up. "Now what? Am I being arrested?"

"No, ma'am. Jennifer Stanley obtained a driver's license in San Francisco when she was seventeen years old."

She stopped. "That's right, I did. Is that against the law?"
"No, ma'am. The point is..."

"The point is"-Thomas interrupted-"that Jennifer Stanley's fingerprints are on that license."

She looked at them. "I don't understand. What ...?"

Billy spoke up. "We want to check them against your fingerprints."

Her lips tightened. "No! I won't allow it!"

"Are you saying that you won't let us take your fingerprints?"

"That's right."

"Why not?" David asked.

Her body was rigid. "Because all of you make me feel like I'm some kind of criminal. Well, I've had enough! I want you to leave me alone."

Carmen said gently, "This is your chance to prove who you really are. We've been as upset by all this as you have. We would like to settle it."

She stood there, looking into their faces, one by one. Finally, she said wearily, "All right. Let's get this over with."

"Good."

"Mr. Tillman," Thomas said.

"Right." He took out a small fingerprint kit and set it up on the table. He opened the ink pad. "Now, if you'll just step over here, please."

The others watched as she walked over to the table.

He picked up her hand and, one by one, pressed her fingertips onto the pad. Next, he pressed them onto a piece of white paper. "There. That wasn't so bad, was it?" He placed the license bureau's card next to the fresh fingerprints.

The group walked over to the table and looked down at the two sets of prints. They were identical. Billy was the first to speak. "They're ... the ... same."

Carmen was looking at her with a mixture of feelings.

"You really are our sister, aren't you?"

She was smiling through her tears. "That's what I've been trying to tell you."

Everybody was suddenly talking at once.

"It's incredible ...!"

"After all these years ..."

"Why didn't your mother ever come back?"

"I'm sorry we gave you such a hard time"

Her smile lit up the room. "It's all right. Everything's all right now."

Billy picked up the fingerprint card and looked at it with respect. "My God! This is a billion-dollar card." He put the card in his pocket. "I'm going to have it bronzed."

Thomas turned to the group. "This calls for a real' celebration! I suggest we all go back to Bell Air." He turned to her and smiled. "We'll give you a welcome home party. Let's get you checked out of here."

She looked around at them, and her eyes were shining.

"It's like a dream come true. I finally have a family!"

Half an hour later, they were back at Bell Air, and she was settling into her new room. The others were downstairs, talking excitedly.

"She must feel as though she's just been through the Inquisition," Thomas said.

"She has," Anita replied. "I don't know how she stood it."

Carmen said, "I wonder how she's going to adjust to her new life."

"The same way we're all going to adjust," Billy said agreeably. "With a lot of champagne and caviar."

Thomas rose. "I, for one, am glad it's finally settled. Let me go up and see if she needs any help."

He went upstairs and walked along the corridor to her room. He knocked at her door and called loudly, "Jennifer?"

"It's open. Come in."

He stood in the doorway, and they stared silently at each other. And then Thomas carefully closed the door, held out his hands, and broke into a slow grin.

When he spoke, he said, "We did it, Mary! We did it! "

14

Thomas had plotted it with the overwhelming sense to win the game as a chess master. Only this had been the most lucrative chess game in history, with stakes of billions of dollars-and he had won! He was filled with a sense of absolute power. Is this how you felt when you closed a big deal, Father? Well, this is a bigger deal than you ever made. I've planned the crime of the century, and I've gotten away with it. That's was his mood drive. In a sense, it had all started with Connie. Beautiful, wonderful Connie. The person he loved most in the world. They had met in the bar. Connie was tall and blonde, and she was the most beautiful girl Thomas had ever seen.

Their meeting had started with, "May I buy you a drink?"

Connie had looked him over and nodded. "That would be nice."

After the second drink, Thomas had said, "Why don't we have a drink over at my place?"

Connie had smiled. "I'm expensive."

"How expensive?"

"Five hundred dollars for the night."

Thomas had not hesitated. "Let's go."

They spent the night at Thomas's home. Connie was warm and sensitive and caring, and Thomas felt closeness to her that he had never had with any other human being. He was flooded with emotions he had not known existed. By morning, Thomas was madly in love. In the past, he had picked up young girls at the Theater and several other girls hangouts in San Francisco, but now he knew that all that was going to change. From now on, he wanted only Connie.

In the morning, while Thomas was preparing breakfast, he said, "What would you like to do tonight?"

Connie looked at him in surprise. "Sorry. I have a date tonight."

Thomas felt as though he had been hit in the stomach.

"But, Connie, I thought that you and I ..."

"Thomas, dear, I'm a very valuable piece of merchandise. I go to the highest bidder. I like you, but I'm afraid you really can't afford me."

"I can give you anything you want," Thomas said. Connie smiled lazily. "Really? Well, what I want is a trip to St.-Tropez on a beautiful white yacht. Can you afford that?"

"Connie, I'm richer than all your friends put together."

"Oh? I thought you said you are a judge."

"Well, I am, yes, but I'm going to be rich. I mean ... very rich."

Connie put his arm around him. "Don't fret, Thomas. I'm free a week from Thursday. Those eggs look delicious."

That was the beginning. Money had been important to Thomas before, but now it became an obsession. He needed it for Connie. He could not get him out of his mind. The thought of him making love with other girl was unbearable. I've got to have her for my own.

From the age of twelve, Thomas had known that he was strong man. One day, his father had caught him fondling and kissing a girl from his school, and Thomas had borne the full brunt of his father's fury. "I can't believe I have a son who's an idiot! Now that I know your dirty little secret, I'm going to keep a close eye on you."

Thomas's marriage was a cosmic joke, perpetrated by a god with a macabre sense of humor.

"There's someone I want you to meet," Robert Stanley said.

It was Christmas and Thomas was at Bell Air for the holidays. Carmen and Billy had already made their departures and Thomas was planning his when the bombshell dropped.

"You're going to get married."

"Married? That's out of the question! I don't ..."

"Listen to me. People are beginning to talk about you, and I can't have that. It's bad for my reputation. If you get married, that will shut them up."

Thomas was defiant. "I don't care what people say. This is my life."

"And I want it to be a rich life for you, Thomas. I'm getting older. Pretty soon ..." He said.

The carrot and the stick.

Nancy Schmidt was a plain-looking woman, from a middle-class family, whose flaming desire in life was to "better" herself. She was so impressed by Robert Stanley's name that she would probably have married his son if he were pumping gas instead of being a judge. Robert Stanley had taken Nancy to bed once. When someone asked him why, Stanley replied, "Because she was there."

She quickly bored him, and he decided she would be perfect for Thomas. What Robert Stanley wanted, Robert Stanley got. The wedding took place two months later. It was a small wedding-one hundred and fifty people-and the bride and groom went to Jamaica for their honeymoon. It was a fiasco.

On their wedding night, Nancy said, "What kind of man have I married, for God's sake? What have you got a dick for?"

Thomas tried to reason with her. "We don't need sex. We can live separate lives. We'll stay together, but we'll each have our own ... friends."

"You're damned right, we will!"

Nancy took out her vengeance on him by becoming a black-belt shopper. She bought everything at the most expensive stores in the city, and took shopping trips to New York.

"I can't afford your extravagances on my income." Thomas protested. .

"Then get a raise. I'm your wife. I'm entitled to be supported."

Thomas went to his father and explained the situation. Robert Stanley grinned. "Women can be damned expensive, can't they? You'll just have to handle it."

"But, Father, I need some..."

"Someday you'll have all the money in the world." Thomas tried to explain it to Nancy, but she had no intentions of waiting until "someday." She sensed that that "someday" might never come. When Nancy had squeezed what she could out of Thomas, she sued for divorce, settled for what was left of his bank account, and disappeared.

When Robert Stanley heard the news, he said, "Once idiot, always an idiot."

And that was the end of it.

His father went out of his way to demean Thomas. One day, when Thomas was on the bench, in the middle of a trial, his bailiff came up to him and whispered, "Excuse me, Your Honor..."

Thomas had turned to him, impatiently. "Yes?"

"There's a phone call for you."

"What? What's the matter with you? I'm in the middle of..."

"It's your father, Your Honor. He says it's very urgent and he must talk to you immediately."

Thomas was furious. His father had no right to interrupt him. He was tempted to ignore the call. But on the other hand, if it was that urgent...

Thomas stood up. "Court is recessed for fifteen minutes."

Thomas hurried into his chambers and picked up the telephone. "Father?"

"I hope I'm not disturbing you, Thomas." There was malice in his voice.

"As a matter of fact, you are. I'm in the middle of a trial and..."

"Well, give him a traffic ticket and forget it."

"Father ..."

"I need your help with a serious problem."

"What kind of problem?"

"My chef is stealing from me."

Thomas could not believe what he was hearing. He was so angry he could hardly speak. "You called me off the bench because ...?"

"You're the law, aren't you? Well, he's breaking the law. I want you to come back to Los Angeles and check out my whole staff. They're robbing me blind!"

It was all Thomas could do to keep from exploding.

"Father ..."

"You just can't trust those damn employment agencies."

"I'm in the middle of a trial. I can't possibly go back to Los Angeles now."

There was a moment of silence. "What did you say?"

"I said ..."

"You aren't going to disappoint me again, are you, Thomas? Maybe I should talk to Harold about some changes in my will."

And there was the carrot again. The money. His share of the billions of dollars waiting for him when his father died.

Thomas cleared his throat. "If you could send your plane for me ..."

"Hell, no! If you play your cards right, Judge, that plane will belong to you one day. Just think about that. Meanwhile, fly commercial like everyone else. But I want you to get your ass back here!" The line went dead.

Thomas sat there, filled with humiliation. My father has done this to me all my life. The hell with him! I won't go. I won't go.

Thomas flew to Los Angeles that evening. Robert Stanley employed a staff of twenty-two. There was a phalanx of secretaries, butlers, housekeepers, maids, chefs, chauffeurs, gardeners, and a bodyguard.

"Thieves, every damned one of them," Robert Stanley complained to Thomas.

"If you're so worried, why don't you hire a private detective or go to the police?"

"Because I have you," Robert Stanley said. "You're a judge, right? Well, you judge them for me."

It was pure spitefulness. Thomas looked around the huge house with its exquisite furniture and paintings, and he thought of the dreary little house he lived in. This is what I deserve to have, he thought. And one day, I'll have it. Thomas talked to the butler, Damon, and other senior members of the staff. He interviewed the servants, one by one, and checked their resumes. Most of the employees were fairly new because Robert Stanley was an impossible man to work for. The staff turnover at the house was extraordinary. Some of them lasted only a day or two. A few new employees were guilty of petty pilfering, and one was an alcoholic, but other than that, Thomas could see no problem.

Except for Donald Herman. Donald Herman had been hired by his father as a bodyguard and masseur. Sitting on the bench had made Thomas a good judge of character, and there was something about Donald that Thomas instantly mistrusted. He was the most recent employee. Robert Stanley's former bodyguard had quit-Thomas could imagine why-and he had recommended Herman.

The man was huge, with a barrel chest and large, muscular arms. He spoke English with a thick Russian accent. "You want to see me?"

"Yes." Thomas gestured to a chair. "Sit down." He had looked at the man's employment record, and it had told him very little, except that Donald had come from Russia recently. "You were born in Russia?"

"Yes." He was watching Thomas suspiciously.

"What part?"

"Smolensk."

"Why did you leave Russia to come to America?"

Herman asked. "There is more opportunity here."

Opportunity for what? Thomas wondered. There was something evasive about the man's manner. They spoke for twenty minutes, and at the end of that time, Thomas was convinced that Donald Herman was concealing something. Thomas telephoned Phillip Mason, an acquaintance of his with the FBI.

"Fred, I want you to do me a favor."

"Sure. If I'm ever in San Francisco, will you fix my traffic tickets?"

"I'm serious."

"Shoot."

"I want you to check on a Russian who came over here six months ago."

"Wait a minute. You're talking CIA, aren't you?"

"Maybe, but I don't know anyone at CIA."

"Neither do I."

"Fred, if you could do this for me, I would really be grateful."

Thomas heard a sigh.

"Okay. What's his name?"

"Donald Herman."

"I'll tell you what I'll do. I know someone at the Russian Embassy in D.C. I'll see if he has any information on Herman. If not, I'm afraid I can't help you."

"I'd appreciate it."

That evening, Thomas had dinner with his father. Subconsciously, Thomas had hoped that his father would have aged, would have become more fragile, more vulnerable with time. Instead, Robert Stanley looked hale and hearty, in his prime. He's going to live forever, Thomas thought desperately. He'll outlive all of us.

The conversation at dinner was completely one sided.

"I just closed a deal to buy the power company in Hawaii…"

"I'm flying over to Amsterdam next week to straighten out some GAIT complications ..."

"The secretary of state has invited me to accompany him to China ..."

Thomas scarcely got in a word. At the end of the meal, his father rose. "How are you coming along with the servant problem?"

"I'm still checking them out, Father."

"Well, don't take forever," his father growled, and walked out of the room.

The following morning, Thomas received a call from Phillip Mason at the FBI.

"Thomas?"

"Yes."

"You picked a real beauty."

"Oh?"

"Donald Herman was a hit man for polgoprudnenskaya."

"What the hell is that?"

"I'll explain. There are eight criminal groups that have taken over in Moscow. They all fight among themselves, but the two most powerful groups are the Chechens and the polgoprudnenskaya. Your friend Herman worked for the second group. Three months ago, they handed him a contract on one of the leaders of the Chechens. Instead of carrying out the contract, Herman went to him to make a better deal. The polgoprudnenskaya found out about it and put out a contract on Herman. Gangs have a quaint custom over there. First they cut the hand, then they let it bleed for a while, and then they shoot."

"My God!"

"Herman got himself smuggled out of Russia, but they're still looking for him. And looking hard."

"That's incredible," Thomas said.

"That's not all. He's also wanted by the state police for a few murders. If you know where he is, they'd love to have that information."

Thomas was thoughtful for a moment. He could not afford to get involved in this. It could mean giving testimony and wasting a lot of time.

"I have no idea. I was just checking him out for a Russian friend. Thanks, Phillip."

Thomas found Donald Herman in his room, reading a hard-core porno magazine. Donald rose as Thomas walked into the room.

"I want you to pack your things and get out of here." Donald stared at him. "What's the matter?"

"I'm giving you a choice. You're either out of here by this afternoon, or I'll tell the Russian police where you are."

Donald's face turned pale.

"Do you understand?"

"Yes. I understand."

Thomas went to see his father. He's going to be pleased, he thought. I've done him a real favor. He found him in the study.

"I checked on all the staff," Thomas said, "and ..."

"I'm impressed. Did you find any little girl to take to bed with you?"

Thomas's face turned red. "Father ..."

"You're a sonofabitch, Thomas, and you'll always be. I don't know how the hell anything like you came from my loins. Go on back to San Francisco with your friends."

Thomas stood there, fighting to control himself.

"Right," he said stiffly. He started to leave.

"Is there anything about the staff you found out that I should know?"

Thomas turned and studied his father a moment. "No," he said slowly. "Nothing."

When Thomas went to Herman's room, he was packing.

"I'm going," Herman said gloomily.

"Don't. I've changed my mind."

Donald looked up, puzzled. "What?"

"I don't want you to leave. I want you to stay on as my father's bodyguard."

"What about ... you know, the other thing?"

"We're going to forget about that."

Donald was watching him, suspiciously. "Why? What do you want me to do?"

211

"I'd like you to be my eyes and ears here. I need someone to keep an eye on my father, and let me know what goes on."

"Why should I?"

"Because if you do as I say, I'm not going to turn you over to the Russians. And because I'm going to make you a rich man."

Donald Herman studied him a moment. A slow grin lit his face. "I'll stay."

It was the opening gambit. The first pawn had been moved.

That had been two years earlier. From time to time, Donald had passed on information to Thomas. It was mostly unimportant gossip about Robert Stanley's latest romance or bits of business that Donald had overheard. Thomas had begun to think he had made a mistake, that he should have turned Donald in to the police. And then the fateful telephone call had come from Sardinia, and the gamble had paid off.

"I'm with your father on his yacht. He just called his attorney. He's meeting him in Los Angeles on Monday to change his will. "

Thomas thought of all the humiliations his father had heaped on him through the years, and he was filled with a terrible rage. If he changes his will I've taken all those years of abuse for nothing. I'm not going to let him get away with this! There is only one way to stop him.

"Donald, I want you to call me again on Saturday."

"Right." Thomas replaced the receiver and sat there, thinking. It was time to bring in the knight.

15

In the Circuit Court of San Francisco, there was a constant ebb and flow of defendants accused of arson, rape, drug dealing, murder, and a variety of other illegal and unsavory activities. In the course of a month, Judge Thomas Stanley dealt with at least half a dozen murder cases. The majority never went to trial since the attorneys for the defendant would offer to plea bargain, and because the court calendars and prisons were so overcrowded, the State would usually agree. The two sides would then strike a deal and go to Judge Stanley for his approval.

The case of Henry Brooks was an exception. Henry Brooks was a man with good intentions and bad luck. When he was fifteen, his older brother had talked him into helping him rob a grocery store. Henry had tried to dissuade him, and when he couldn't, he went along with him. Henry was caught, and his brother escaped. Two years later, when Henry Brooks got out of reform school, he was determined never to get in trouble with the law again. One month later, he accompanied a friend to a jewelry store.

"I want to pick out a ring for my girlfriend."

Once inside the store, his friend pulled out a gun and yelled, "This is a holdup!"

In the ensuing excitement, a clerk was shot to death. Henry Brooks was caught and arrested for armed robbery. His friend escaped.

While Brooks was in prison, Phyllis Gibson, a social worker who had read about his case and felt sorry for him, went to visit him. It was love at first sight, and when Brooks was released from prison, he and Phyllis were married. Over the next eight years, they had four lovely children.

Henry Brooks adored his family. Because of his prison record, he had a difficult time finding jobs, and to support his family, he reluctantly went to work for his brother, carrying out various acts of arson, robbery, and assault. Unfortunately for Brooks, he was caught flagrante delicto in the commission of a burglary. He was arrested, held in jail, and tried in Judge Thomas Stanley's court.

It was time for sentencing. Brooks was a second offender with a bad juvenile record, and it was such a clear-cut case that the assistant district attorneys were making bets on how many years Judge Stanley would give Brooks. "He'll throw the book at him!" one of them said. "I'll bet he gives him twenty years. Stanley's not called the Hanging Judge for nothing."

Henry Brooks, who felt deep in his heart that he was innocent, was acting as his own attorney. He stood before the bench, dressed in his best suit, and said, "Your Honor, I know I made a mistake, but we're all human, aren't we? I have a wonderful wife and four children. I wish you could meet them, Your Honor-they're great. What I did, I did for them."

Thomas Stanley sat on the bench, listening, and his face impassive. He was waiting for Henry Brooks to finish so he could pass sentence. Does this fool really think he's going to get off with that stupid sob story?

Henry Brooks was finishing. "... and so you see, Your Honor, even though I did the wrong thing, I did it for the right reason: family. I don't have to tell you how important that is. If I go to prison, my wife and children will starve. I know I made a mistake, but I'm willing to make up for it. I'll do anything you want me to do, Your Honor... "

And that was the phrase that caught Thomas Stanley's attention. He looked at the defendant before him with a new interest. "Anything you want me to do." Thomas suddenly had the same instinct he had had about Donald Herman. Here was a man who might be very useful one day.

To the prosecutor's utter astonishment, Thomas said, "Mr. Brooks, there are extenuating circumstances in this case. Because of them and because of your family, I am going to put you on probation for five years. I will expect you to perform six hundred hours of public service. Come into my chambers, and we will discuss it."

In the privacy of his chambers, Thomas said, "You know, I could still send you to prison for a long, long time."

Henry Brooks turned pale. "But, Your Honor! You said..."

Thomas leaned forward. "Do you know the most impressive thing about you?"

Henry Brooks sat there, trying to think what was impressive about him. "No, Your Honor."

"Your feelings about your family," Thomas said piously. "I really admire that." Henry Brooks brightened. "Thank you, sir. They're the most important thing in the world to me. I..."

"Then you wouldn't want to lose them, would you? If I sent you to prison, your children would grow up without you; your wife would probably find another man. Do you see what I'm getting at?"

Henry Brooks was shocked. "N ... No, Your Honor. Not exactly."

"I'm saving your family for you, Brooks. I would think you'd be grateful."

Henry Brooks said passionately, "Oh, I am, Your Honor! I can't tell you how grateful I am."

"Perhaps you can prove it to me in the future. I may be calling on you to do some little errands for me."

"Anything!"

"Good. I'm placing you on probation, and if I should find anything in your behavior that displeases me ..."

"You just tell me what you want," Brooks begged.

"I'll let you know when the time comes. Meanwhile, this will be strictly confidential between the two of us."

Henry Brooks put his hand over his heart. "I would die before I'd tell anyone."

"You're right," Thomas assured him.

It was a short time after that when Thomas received the phone call from Donald Herman. "Your father just called his attorney. He's meeting him in Los Angeles on Monday to change his will."

Thomas knew that he had to see that will. It was time to call Henry Brooks.

"... the name of the firm is REYNOLDS & FRANK HAROLD ATTORNEYS AT LAW. Make a copy of the will and bring it to me."

"No problem. I'll take care of it, Your Honor."

Twelve hours later, Thomas had a copy of the will in his hands. He read it and was filled with a sense of high spirits and good mood. He and Billy and Carmen were the sole heirs. And on Monday Father is planning to change the will. The bastard is going to take it away from us! Thomas thought bitterly. After all we've gone through ... those billions belong to us. He's made us earn them! There was only one way to stop him.

When Donald's second phone call came, Thomas said,

"I want you to kill him. Tonight."

There was a long silence. "But if I'm caught..."

"Don't get caught. You'll be at sea. A lot of things can happen there."

"All right. When it's over ...?"

"The money and a plane ticket to Australia will be waiting for you."

And then later, the last wonderful phone call.

"I did it. It was auto accident."

16

The last chess composition created a lot of problems. Thomas had been thinking about his father's will, and he felt outraged that Billy and Carmen were getting an equal share of the estate with him. They don't deserve it. If it had not been for me, they both would have been cut out of the will completely. They would have had nothing. It's not fair, but what can I do about it?

He had the one share of stock that his mother had given him long ago, and he remembered his father's words: "What the hell do you think he's going to do with that one share? Take over the company?"

Together, Thomas thought, Billy and Carmen have two thirds of Father's Stanley Enterprises stock. How can I get control with only my one extra share? And then the answer came to him, and it was so clever that it stunned him.

"I should inform you that there is a possibility of another heir being involved ... Your father's will specifically provide that the estate is to be divided equally among his issue... Your father sired a child by a governess who worked here..."

If Jennifer showed up, there would be four of us, Thomas thought. And if I could control her share, I would then have fifty percent of Father's stock plus the one percent I already own. I could take over Stanley Enterprises. I could sit in my father's chair. His next thought was, Rosa is dead, and she probably never told her daughter who her father was. Why does it have to be the real Jennifer Stanley?

The answer was Mary Perkins. He had first encountered her two months earlier, as court was called into session. The bailiff had turned to the spectators in the courtroom. "Oyez, oyez. The Circuit Court of San Francisco is now in session, the Honorable Judge Thomas Stanley presiding. All rise."

Thomas walked in from of his chambers and sat down at the bench. He looked down at the docket. The first case was State of California v. Mary Perkins. The charges were assault and attempted murder. The prosecuting attorney rose. "Your Honor, the defendant is a dangerous person who should be kept off the streets of San Francisco. The State will prove that the defendant has a long criminal history. She has been convicted for shoplifting, larceny, and is a known prostitute. She was one of a stable of women working for a notorious pimp named Rafael. In January of this year, they got into an altercation and the defendant willfully and cold-bloodedly shot him and his companion."

"Did either victim die?" Thomas asked.

"No, Your Honor. They were hospitalized with serious injuries. The gun in Mary Perkins's possession was an illegal weapon."

Thomas turned to look at the defendant, and he felt a sense of surprise. She did not fit the image of what he had just heard about her. She was a well-dressed, attractive young woman in her late twenties, and there was a quiet elegance about her that completely belied the charges against her. That just goes to prove, Thomas thought ironically, you never know... He listened to the arguments from both sides, but his eyes were drawn to the defendant. There was something about her that reminded him of his sister. When the summations were finished, the case went to the jury, and in less than four hours they returned with a verdict of guilty on all counts.

Thomas looked down at the defendant and said, "The court cannot find any extenuating circumstances in this case. You are herewith sentenced to five years at Dwight Correctional Center... Next case."

And it was not until Mary Perkins was being led away that Thomas realized what it was about her that reminded him so much of Carmen. She had the same dark gray eyes. The Stanley eyes.

Thomas did' not think about Mary Perkins again until the phone call from Donald.

The beginning chess game had been successfully completed. Thomas had planned each move carefully in his mind. He used the classical queen's gambit: Decline opening, moving the queen pawn two squares. It was time to move into the middle game.

Thomas went to visit Mary Perkins at the women's prison.

"Do you remember me?" Thomas asked.

She stared at him. "How could I forget you? You're the one who sent me to this place."

"How are you getting along?" Thomas asked.

She grimaced. "You must be kidding! It's a hell hole here."

"How would you like to get out?"

"How would I ...? Are you serious?"

"I'm very serious. I can arrange it."

"Well, that ... that's great! Thanks. But what do I have to do for it?"

"Well, there is something I want you to do for me."

She looked at him, flirtatiously. "Sure. That's no problem."

"That's not what I had in mind."

She said, cautiously, "What did you have in mind, Judge?"

"I want you to help me play a little joke on someone."

"What kind of joke?"

"I want you to impersonate someone."

"Impersonate someone? I wouldn't know how to..."

"There's twenty-five thousand dollars in it for you."

Her expression changed. "Sure," she said quickly. "I can impersonate anyone. Who did you have in mind?"

Thomas leaned forward and began to talk.

Thomas had Mary Perkins released into his custody. As he explained to Lynda Powell, the chief judge, "I learned that she's a very talented artist, and she's eager to live a normal, decent life. I think it's important that we rehabilitate that type of person whenever we can, don't you?"

Lynda was impressed and surprised. "Absolutely, Thomas. That's a wonderful thing you're doing."

Thomas moved Mary into his home and spent five full days briefing her on the Stanley family.

"What are the names of your brothers?"

"Thomas and Woodruff."

"William."

"That's right-William."

"What do we call him?"

"Billy."

"Do you have a sister?"

"Yes. Carmen. She's a designer."

"Is she married?"

"She's married to a Frenchman. His name is ... David Renoir."

"Renaux."

"Renaux."

"What was your mother's name?"

"Rosa Newman. She was a governess to the Stanley's children."

"Why did she leave?"

"She got knocked up by ..."

"Mary!" Thomas admonished her.

"I mean, she became pregnant by Robert Stanley."

"What happened to Mrs. Stanley?"

"She committed suicide."

"What did your mother tell you about the Stanley children?"

Mary stopped to think for a minute.

"Well?"

"There was the time you fell out of the swan boat."

"I didn't fall out!" Thomas said. "I almost fell out."

"Right. Billy almost got arrested for picking flowers in the Public Garden."

"That was Carmen ..."

He was ruthless. They went over the scenario again and again, late into the nights, until Mary was exhausted.

"Carmen was bitten by a dog."

"I was bitten by the dog."

She rubbed her eyes. "I can't think straight anymore. I'm so tired. I need some sleep."

"You can sleep later!"

"How long is this going to go on?" she asked defiantly.

"Until I think you're ready. Now let's go through it again."

And on it went, over and over, until Mary became letter perfect. When the day finally arrived that she knew the answer to every question Thomas asked, he was satisfied.

"You're ready," he said. He handed her some legal documents.

"What's this?"

"It's just a technicality," Thomas said casually.

What he had her sign was a paper giving her share of the Stanley estate to a corporation controlled by a second corporation, which in turn was controlled by an offshore subsidiary of which Thomas Stanley was the sole owner. There was no way they could trace the transaction back to Thomas. Thomas handed Mary five thousand dollars in cash.

"You'll get the balance when the job is done," he told her. "If you convince them that you're Jennifer Stanley."

From the moment Mary had appeared at Bell Air, Thomas had played the devil's advocate. It was the classic anti positional chess move.

"I'm sure you can understand our position, Miss. Without some positive proof, there's no way."

"I think the lady is a fraud... "

"How many servants worked in this house when we were children? ... Dozens, right? And some of them would have known everything this young lady told us . . . Any one of them could have given her that photograph... Let's not forget that there's an enormous amount of money involved."

His crowning move had been when he had demanded a DNA test. He had called Henry Brooks and given him his new instructions: "Dig up Robert Stanley's body and dispose of it."

And then his inspiration of calling in a private detective. With the family present, he had telephoned the district attorney's office in San Francisco.

"This is Judge Thomas Stanley. I understand that your office retains a private detective from time to time who does excellent work for you. His name is something like Simmons or..."

"Oh, you must mean Fredy Tillman."

"Tillman! Yes, that's it. I wonder if you could give me his telephone number so I can contact him directly."

Instead, he had summoned Henry Brooks and introduced him as Fredy Tillman.

At first Thomas had planned for Henry Brooks merely to pretend to go through the motions of checking on Jennifer Stanley, but then he decided it would make a more impressive report if Brooks really pursued it. The family had accepted Brooks' findings without question.

Thomas's plan had gone off without a hitch. Mary Perkins had played her part perfectly, and the fingerprints had been the crowning touch. Everyone was convinced that she was the real Jennifer Stanley.

"I, for one, am glad it's finally settled. Let me go up and see if she needs any help. "

He went upstairs and walked along the corridor to her room. He knocked at her door and called loudly,

"Jennifer?"

"It's open. Come in."

He stood in the doorway, and they stared silently at each other. And then Thomas carefully closed the door, held out his hands, and broke into a slow grin.

When he spoke, he said, "We did it, Mary! We did it!"

17

In the offices of REYNOLDS & FRANK HAROLD, George Brown and Frank Harold were having coffee.

"As the great bard once said, 'Something is rotten in the state of Denmark. "

"What's bothering you?" Harold asked.

George sighed. "I'm not sure. It's the Stanley family. They puzzle me."

Frank Harold snorted. "Join the club."

"I keep coming back to the same question, Frank, but I can't find the answer to it."

"What's the question?"

"The family was anxious to exhume Robert Stanley's body so they could check his DNA against the woman's. So I think we have to assume that the only possible motive for getting rid of the body would be to ensure that the woman's DNA could not be checked against Robert Stanley's. The only one who could have anything to gain from that would be the woman herself, if she were a fraud."

"Yes."

"And yet this private detective, Fredy Tillman. I checked with the district attorney's office in San Francisco, and he has a great reputation--came up with fingerprints that prove she is the real Jennifer Stanley. My question is, who the hell dug up Robert Stanley's body and why?"

"That's a billion-dollar question. If ..."

The intercom buzzed. A secretary's voice came over the box. "Mr. Brown, there's a call for you on two."

George Brown picked up the telephone on the desk.

"Hello ..."

The voice on the other end of the line said, "Mr. Brown, this is Judge Stanley. I would appreciate it if you could drop by Bell Air this morning."

George Brown glanced at Harold. "Right. In about an hour?"

"That will be fine. Thank you."

George replaced the receiver. "My presence is requested at the Stanley house."

"I wonder what they want."

"Ten to one, they want to speed up the probate so they can get their hands on all that beautiful money."

"Connie? It's Thomas. How are you?"

"Fine, thanks."

"I really miss you."

There was a slight pause. "I miss you, too, Thomas."

The words thrilled him. "Connie, I have some really exciting news. I can't discuss it over the phone, but it's something that's going to make you very happy. When you and I..."

"Thomas, I have to go. Someone's waiting for me."

"But ..."

The line went dead.

Thomas sat there a moment. Then he thought, she wouldn't have said she missed me if she didn't mean it. With the exception of Billy and Anita, the family was gathered in the drawing room at Bell Air. George studied their faces. Judge Stanley seemed very relaxed. George glanced at Carmen. She seemed unnaturally tense. Her husband had come up from New York the day before for the meeting. George looked over at David. The Frenchman was good-looking, a few years younger than his wife.

And then there was Jennifer. She seemed to be taking her acceptance into the family very calmly. I would have expected someone who had just inherited a billion dollars or so to be a little more excited, George thought.

He glanced at their faces again, wondering if one of them was responsible for having Robert Stanley's body stolen, and if so, which one? And why?

Thomas was speaking. "Mr. Brown, I'm familiar with the probate laws in California, but I don't know how much they differ from the laws in Massachusetts. We were wondering whether there wasn't some way to expedite the procedure."

George smiled to himself. I should have made Frank take that bet. He turned to Thomas. "We're already working on it, Judge Stanley." Thomas said pointedly, "The Stanley name might be useful in speeding things up." He's right about that, George thought. He nodded. "I'll do everything I can. If it's at all possible to..."

There were voices from the staircase.

"Just shut up, you stupid bitch! I don't want to hear another word. Do you understand?"

Billy and Anita came down the stairs and into the room. Anita's face was badly swollen, and she had a black eye. Billy was grinning, and his eyes were bright.

"Hello, everybody. I hope the party's not over."

The group was looking at Anita in shock. Carmen rose. "What happened to you?"

"Nothing… I bumped into a door."

Billy took a seat. Anita sat next to him. Billy patted her hand and asked solicitously, "Are you all right, my dear?"

Anita nodded, not trusting herself to speak.

"Good." Billy turned to the others. "Now, what did I miss?"

Thomas looked at him disapprovingly. "I just asked Mr. Brown if he could expedite the probating of the will."

Billy grinned. "That would be nice." He turned to Anita. "You'd like some new clothes, wouldn't you, darling?"

"I don't need any new clothes," she said timidly.

"That's right. You don't go anywhere, do you?" He turned to the others. "Anita is very shy. She doesn't have anything to talk about, do you?"

Anita got up and ran out of the room.

"I'll see if she's all right," Carmen said. She rose and hurried after her.

My God! George thought. If Billy behaves like this in front of others, what must it be like when he and his wife are alone?

Billy turned to George. "How long have you been with Harold's law firm?"

"Five years."

"How they could stand working for my father, I'll never know."

George said carefully, "I understand your father was ... could be difficult."

Billy snorted. "Difficult? He was a two-legged monster. Did you know he had nicknames for all of us? Mine was Charlie. He named me after Charlie McCarthy, a dummy that a ventriloquist named Edgar Bergen had. He called my sister Pony, because he said she had a face like a horse. Thomas was called ..."

George said, uncomfortably, "I really don't think you should..."

Billy shouted out. "It's all right. A billion dollars heals a lot of wounds."

George rose. "Well, if there's nothing else, I think I had better be going." He could not wait to get outside, into the fresh air.

Carmen found Anita in the bathroom, putting a cold cloth to her swollen cheek.

"Anita? Are you all right?"

Anita turned. "I'm fine. Thank you. I ... I'm sorry about what happened down there."

"You're apologizing? You should be furious. How long has he been beating you?"

"He doesn't beat me," Anita said stubbornly. "I bumped into a door."

Carmen moved closer to her. "Anita, why do you put up with this? You don't have to, you know."

There was a pause. "Yes, I do."

Carmen looked at her, puzzled. "Why?"

She turned. "Because I love him." She went on, the words pouring out. "He loves me, too. Believe me, he doesn't always act like this. The thing is, he sometimes he's not himself."

"You mean, when he's on drugs."

"No!"

"Anita... "

"No!"

"Anita ... "

Anita hesitated. "I suppose so."

"When did it start?"

"Right ... right after we got married." Anita's voice was ragged. "It started because of a polo game. Billy fell off his pony and was badly hurt. While he was in the hospital, they gave him drugs to help with the pain. They got him started." She looked at Carmen, pleadingly. "So you see, it wasn't his fault, was it? After Billy got out of the hospital, he ... he kept on using drugs. Whenever I tried to get him to quit, he would ... beat me."

"Anita, for God's sake! He needs help! Don't you see that? You can't do this alone. He's a drug addict. What does he take? Cocaine?"

"No." There was a small silence. "Heroin."

"My God! Can't you make him get some help?"

"I've tried." Her voice was a whisper. "You don't know how I've tried! He's gone to three rehabilitation hospitals." She shook her head. "He's all right for a while, and then ... he starts again. He ... he can't help it."

Carmen put her arms around Anita. "I'm so sorry," she said.

Anita forced a smile. "I'm sure Billy will be all right. He's trying hard. He really is." Her face lit up.

"When we were first married, he was so much fun to be with. We used to laugh all the time. He would bring me little presents and..." Her eyes filled with tears. "I love him so much"

"If there's anything I can do ..."

"Thank you," Anita whispered. "I appreciate that."

Carmen squeezed her hand. "We'll talk again."

Carmen started down the stairs to join the others. She was thinking, when we were children, before Mother died, we made such wonderful plans. "You're going to be a famous designer, and I'm going to be the world's greatest athlete!" And the sad part of it, Carmen thought, is that he could have been. And now this.

Carmen was not sure if she felt more sorry for Billy or for Anita.

As Carmen reached the bottom of the stairs, Damon approached her, carrying a tray with a letter on it. "Excuse me, Miss Carmen. A messenger just delivered this for you." He handed her the envelope.

Carmen looked at it in surprise. "Who ...?" She nodded. "Thank you, Damon."

Carmen opened the envelope, and as she began to read the letter, she turned pale. "No!" she said, under her breath. Her heart was pounding, and she felt a wave of dizziness. She stood there, bracing herself against a table, trying to catch her breath.

After a moment, she turned and walked into the drawing room, her face pale.

"David ..." Carmen forced herself to appear calm.

"May I see you for a moment?"

He looked at her, concerned. "Yes, certainly."

Thomas asked Carmen, "Are you all right?"

She forced a smile. "I'm fine, thank you." She took David's hand and led him upstairs. When they entered the bedroom, Carmen closed the door.

David said, "What is it?"

Carmen handed him the envelope. The letter read:

Dear Mrs. Renaux,

Congratulations! Our Wild Animal Protection Association was delighted to read of your good fortune. We know how interested you are in the work we are doing, and we are counting on your further support. Therefore, we would appreciate it if you would deposit one million U.S. dollars in our numbered bank account in Zurich within the next ten days. We look forward to hearing from you shortly.

As in the other letters, all the E's were broken.

"The bastards!" David exploded.

"How did they know I was here?" Carmen asked.

David said bitterly, "All they had to do was pick up a newspaper." He read the letter again and shook his head. "They aren't going to quit. We have to go to the police."

"No!" Carmen cried. "We can't! It's too late! Don't you see? It would be the end of everything. Everything!"

David took her in his arms and held her tightly. "All right. We'll find a way."

But Carmen knew that there was no way.

It had happened a few months earlier, on what had started out to be a glorious spring day. Carmen had gone to a friend's birthday party in Ridgefield, Connecticut. It had been a wonderful party, and Carmen had chatted with old friends. She had had a glass of champagne. In the middle of a conversation, she had suddenly looked at her watch. "Oh, no! I had no idea it was so late. David is waiting for me."

There were hasty good-byes, and Carmen had gotten into her car and driven off. Driving back to New York, she had decided to take a winding country road over to I-684. She was traveling at almost fifty miles per hour as she rounded a sharp curve and spotted a car parked on the right side of the road. Carmen automatically swerved to the left. At that moment, a woman carrying a handful of freshly picked flowers started to cross the narrow road. Carmen tried frantically to avoid her, but it was too late.

Everything seemed to happen in a blur. She heard a sickening thud as she hit the woman with her left front fender. Carmen brought the car to a screeching stop, her whole body trembling violently. She ran back to where the woman was lying in the road, covered with blood.

Carmen stood there, frozen. Finally, she bent down and turned the woman over, and looked into her sightless eyes. "Oh, my God!" Carmen whispered. She felt the bile rising in her throat. She looked up, desperate, not knowing what to do. She swung around in a panic. There were no cars in sight. She's dead, Carmen thought. I can't help her. This was not my fault, but they'll accuse me of reckless drunk driving. My blood will show alcohol. I'll go to prison!

She took one last look at the body of the woman, and then hurried back to her car. The left front fender was dented, and there were blood spots on it. I've got to put the car away in a garage, Carmen thought. The police will be searching for it. She got into the car and drove off.

For the rest of the drive into New York, she kept looking into the rearview mirror, expecting to see flashing red lights and to hear the sound of a siren. She drove into the garage on Ninety-sixth Street where she kept her car. Scott, the owner of the garage, was talking to Red, his mechanic. Carmen got out of the car.

"Evenin', Mrs. Renaux," Scott said.

"Go ... Good evening." She was fighting to keep her teeth from chattering.

"Put it away for the night?"

"Yes ... yes, please."

Red was looking at the fender. "You got a bad dent here, Mrs. Renaux. Looks like there's blood on it."

The two men were looking at her. Carmen took a deep breath. "Yes. I ... I hit a deer on the highway."

"You're lucky it didn't do more damage," Scott said.

"A friend of mine hit a deer, and it ruined his car." He grinned. "Didn't do much for the deer either."

"If you'll just put it away," Carmen said tightly.

"Sure."

Carmen walked over to the garage door, and then looked back. The two men were staring at the fender. When Carmen got home and told David about the terrible thing that had happened, he took her in his arms and said, "Oh, my God! Darling, how could ...?"

Carmen was sobbing. "I ... I couldn't help it. She started across the road right in front of me. She ... she had been picking flowers and..."

"S' sh! I'm sure it wasn't your fault. It was an accident. We've got to report this to the police."

"I know. You're right. I ... I should have stayed there and waited for them to come. I just ... panicked, David. Now it's a hit-and-run. But there wasn't anything I could do for her. She was dead. You should have seen her face. It was awful."

He held her for a long time, until she quieted down.

When Carmen spoke, she said tentatively, "David ... do we have to go to the police?"

He frowned. "What do you mean?"

She was fighting hysteria. "Well, it's over, isn't it?

Nothing can bring her back. What good would it do for them to punish me? I didn't mean to do it. Why couldn't we just pretend it never happened?"

"Carmen, if they ever traced..."

"How can they? There was no one around."

"What about your car? Was it damaged?"

"There's a dent. I told the garage attendant I hit a deer." She was fighting for control. "David, no one saw the accident ... Do you know what would happen to me if they arrested me and sent me to prison? I'd lose my business, everything I've built up all these years, and for what? For something that's already done! It's over!" She began to sob again.

He held her close. "S'sh! We'll see. We'll see."

The morning papers gave the story a big play. What gave it added drama was the fact that the dead woman had been on her way to Manhattan to be married. The New York Times covered it as a straight news story, but the Daily News and Newsday played it up as a heart-tugging drama.

Carmen bought a copy of each newspaper, and she became more and more horrified at what she had done. Her mind was filled with all the terrible ifs.

If I hadn't gone to Connecticut for my friend's birthday...

If I had stayed home that day...

If I hadn't had anything to drink…

If the woman had picked the flowers a few seconds earlier or a few seconds later...

I'm responsible for murdering another human being! Carmen thought of the terrible grief she had caused the woman's family, and her fiancé's family, and she felt sick to her stomach again.

According to the newspapers, the police were asking for information from anyone who might have a clue about the hit-and-run.

They have no way of finding me, Carmen thought. All I have to do is act as if nothing happened.

When Carmen went to the garage to pick up her car the next morning, Red was there.

"I wiped the blood off the car," he said. "Do you want me to fix the dent?"

Of course! I should have thought of it sooner. "Yes, please."

Red was looking at her strangely. Or was it her imagination?

"Scott and I talked about it last night," he said. "It's funny, you know. A deer should have done a lot more damage."

Carmen's heart began to beat wildly. Her mouth was suddenly so dry she could hardly speak. "It was a ... a small deer."

Red nodded laconically. "Must have been real small."

Carmen could feel his eyes on her as she drove out of the garage. When Carmen walked into her office, her secretary, Cristina, took one look at her and said, "What happened to you?"

Carmen froze. "What ... what do you mean?"

"You look shaky. Let me get you some coffee."

"Thanks."

Carmen walked over to the mirror. Her face looked pale and drawn. They're going to know just by looking at me! Cristina came into the office with a cup of hot coffee.

"Here. This will make you feel better." She looked at Carmen curiously. "Is everything all right?"

"I ... I had a little accident yesterday," Carmen said.

"Oh? Was anyone hurt?"

In her mind, she could see the face of the dead woman. "No. I ... I hit a deer."

"What about your car?"

"It's being repaired."

"I'll call your insurance company."

"Oh, no, Cristina, please don't."

Carmen saw the surprised look in Cristina's eyes.

It was two days later that the first letter came:

Dear Mrs. Renaux,

I'm the chairman of the Wild Animal Protection Association, which is in desperate need. I'm sure that you would like to help us out. The organization needs money to preserve wild animals. We are especially interested in deer. You can wire $50,000 to account number 804072-A at the Credit Suisse bank in Zurich. I would strongly suggest that the money be there within the next five days.

It was unsigned. All the E's in the letter were broken. Enclosed in the envelope was a newspaper clipping about the accident. Carmen read the letter twice. The threat was unmistakable. She agonized over what to do. David was right, she thought. I should have gone to the police. But now everything was worse. She was a fugitive. If they found her now, it would mean prison and disgrace, as well as the end of her business.

At lunchtime, she went to her bank. "I want to wire fifty thousand dollars to Switzerland . . ."

When Carmen got home that evening, she showed the letter to David.

He was stunned. "My God!" he said. "Who could have sent this?"

"Nobody ... nobody knows." She was trembling.

"Carmen, someone knows."

Her body was twitching. "There was no one around, David! I..."

"Wait a minute. Let's try to figure this out. Exactly what happened when you returned to town?"

"Nothing. I ... I put the car in the garage, and..."

She stopped. "You got a bad dent here, Mrs. Renaux. Looks like there's blood on it."

David saw the expression on her face. "What?"

She said slowly, "The owner of the garage and his mechanic were there. They saw the blood on the fender. I told them I hit a deer, and they said there should have been a lot more damage." She remembered something else. "David ..."

"Yes?"

"Cristina, my secretary. I told her the same thing. I could see that she didn't believe me either. So it had to be one of the three of them."

"No," David said slowly.

She stared at him. "What do you mean?"

"Sit down, Carmen, and listen to me. If any of them was suspicious of you, they could have told your story to a dozen people. The report of the accident has been in all the newspapers. Someone has put two and two together. I think the letter was a bluff, testing you. It was a terrible mistake to send that money."

"But why?"

"Because now they know you're guilty, don't you see? You've given them the proof they needed."

"Oh, God! What should I do?" Carmen asked.

David Renaux was thoughtful for a moment. "I have an idea how we can find out who these bastards are."

At ten o'clock the following morning, Carmen and David were seated in the office of Richard Ginsburg, vice president of the Manhattan First Security Bank.

"And what can I do for you, today?" Mr. Ginsburg asked.

David said, "We would like to check on a numbered bank account in Zurich."

"Yes?"

"We want to know whose account it is."

Ginsburg rubbed his hands across his chin. "Is there a crime involved?"

David said quickly, "No! Why do you ask?"

"Well, unless there's some kind of criminal activity, such as laundering money or breaking the laws of Switzerland or the United States, Switzerland will not violate the secrecy of its numbered bank accounts. Their reputation is built on confidentiality."

"Surely, there's some way to ...?"

"I'm sorry. I'm afraid not."

Carmen and David looked at each other. Carmen's face was filled with despair.

David rose. "Thank you for your time."

"I'm sorry I couldn't help you." He escorted them out of his office.

When Carmen drove into the garage that evening, neither Scott nor Red was around. Carmen parked her car, and as she passed the little office, through the window she saw a typewriter on a stand. She stopped, staring at it, wondering if it had a broken letter E. I have to find out, she thought.

She walked over to the office, hesitated a moment, then opened the door and stepped inside ...As she moved toward the typewriter, Scott suddenly appeared out of nowhere.

"Evenin', Mrs. Renaux," he said. "Can I help you?"

She spun around, startled. "No. I ... I just left my car. Good night." She hurried toward the door.

"Good night, Mrs. Renaux."

In the morning, when Carmen passed the garage office, the typewriter was gone. In its place was a personal computer.

Scott saw her staring at it. "Nice, huh? I decided to bring this place into the twentieth century."

Now that he can afford it?

When Carmen told David about it that evening, he said thoughtfully, "It's a possibility, but we need proof."

Monday morning, when Carmen went to her office, Cristina was waiting for her.

"Are you feeling better, Mrs. Renaux?"

"Yes. Thank you."

"Yesterday was my birthday. Look what my husband got me!" She walked over to a closet and pulled out a luxurious mink coat. "Isn't it beautiful?"

18

Jennifer Stanley enjoyed having Susan as a roommate. She was always upbeat and fun and cheerful. She had had a bad marriage and had sworn never to get involved with a man again. Jennifer wasn't sure what Susan's definition of never was, because she seemed to be out with a different man every week.

"Married men are the best." Susan philosophized.

"They feel guilty, so they're always buying you presents. With a single man, you have to ask yourself, Why is he still single?"

She said to Jennifer, "You aren't dating anyone, are you?"

"No." Jennifer thought of the men who had wanted to take her out. "I don't want to go out just for the sake of going out, Susan. I have to be with someone I really care about."

"Well, have I got a man for you!" Susan said.

"You're going to love him! His name is Tom Vogel. I told him all about you, and he's dying to meet you."

"I really don't think..."

"He'll pick you up tomorrow night at eight o'clock."

Tom Vogel was tall, very tall, in an appealing, ungainly way. His hair was thick and dark, and his smile exploded disarmingly as he looked at Jennifer.

"Susan wasn't exaggerating. You're a knockout!"

"Thank you," Jennifer said. She felt a little shiver of pleasure.

"Have you ever been to Houston's?"

It was one of the finest restaurants in Miami.

"No." The truth was that she could not afford to eat at Houston's. Not even with the raise she had been given.

"Well, that's where we have a reservation."

At dinner, Tony talked mostly about himself, but Jennifer did not mind. He was entertaining and charming. "He's drop-dead gorgeous," Susan had said. And he was.

The dinner was delicious. For dessert, Jennifer had ordered chocolate souffle and Tom had ice cream. As they were lingering over coffee, Jennifer thought, Is he going to ask me to his apartment, and if he does, will I go? No.

I can't do that. Not on the first date. He'll think I'm cheap. When we go out the next time...

The check arrived. Tony scanned it and said, "It looks right." He ticked off the items on the check. "You had the pate and the lobster ..."

"Yes."

"And you had the French fries and salad, and the souffle, right?"

She looked at him, puzzled. "That's right…"

"Okay." He did some quick addition. "Your share of the bill is fifty dollars and forty cents."

Jennifer sat there in shock. "I beg your pardon?"

Tom grinned. "I know how independent you women are today. You won't let guys do anything for you, will you? There," he said magnanimously, "I'll take care of your share of the tip."

"I'm sorry it didn't work out." Susan apologized. "He's really a honey. Are you going to see him again?"

"I can't afford him," Jennifer said bitterly.

"Well, I have someone else for you. You'll love..."

"No. Susan, I really don't want ..."

"Trust me."

Paul Raley was a man in his late thirties and, Jennifer had to admit, quite attractive. He took her to Jennie's Restaurant on Historic Strawberry Hill, famous for its authentic Croatian food.

"Susan really did me a favor," Raley said. "You're very lovely."

"Thank you."

"Did Susan tell you I have an advertising agency?"

"No. She didn't."

"Oh, yes. I have one of the biggest firms in Florida City. Everybody knows me."

"That's nice. I..."

"We handle some of the biggest clients in the country."

"You do? I'm not..."

"Oh, yes. We handle celebrities, banks, big businesses, chain stores ..."

"Well, I..."

"... supermarkets. You name it, we represent them all."

"That's..."

"Let me tell you how I got started ..."

He never stopped talking during dinner, and the only subject was Paul Raley.

"He was probably just nervous." Susan apologized.

"Well, I can tell you, he made me nervous. If there's anything you want to know about the life of Paul Raley since the day he was born, just ask me!"

"Jim Miles."

"What?"

"Jim Miles. I just remembered. He used to date a girlfriend of mine. She was absolutely crazy about him."

"Thanks, Susan, but no."

"I'm going to call him."

The following night, Jim Miles appeared. He was nice-looking, and he had a sweet and engaging personality. When he walked in the door and looked at Jennifer, he said, "I know blind dates are always difficult. I'm rather shy myself, so I know how you must feel, Jennifer."

She liked him immediately.

They went to the Evergreen Chinese Restaurant on State Avenue for dinner.

"You work for an architectural firm. That must be exciting. I don't think people realize how important architects are."

He's sensitive, Jennifer thought happily. She smiled. "I couldn't agree with you more."

The evening was delightful, and the more they talked, the more Jennifer liked him. She decided to be bold.

"Would you like to come back to my apartment for a nightcap?" she asked.

"No. Let's go back to my place."

"Your place?"

He leaned forward and squeezed her hand. "That's where I keep the whips and chains."

Alan Walker owned an accounting firm in the building where John, Mark & Thomson was quartered. Two or three mornings a week, Jennifer would find herself in the elevator with him. He seemed a pleasant-enough man. He was in his thirties, quietly intelligent-looking, sandy haired, and he wore black rimmed glasses.

The acquaintance began with polite nods, then "Good morning," then "You're looking very well today," and after a few months, "I wonder if you'd like to have dinner with me some evening?" He was watching her passionately, waiting for an answer.

Jennifer smiled. "All right."

It was instant love on Alan's part. On their first date, he took Jennifer to EBT, one of the top restaurants in Miami. He was obviously thrilled to be out with her.

He told her a little about himself. "I was born right here in good old Miami. My father was born here, too. The acorn doesn't fall far from the oak. You know what I mean?"

Jennifer knew what he meant.

"I always knew I wanted to be an accountant. When I got out of school, I went to work for the Biden & Benson Financial Corporation. Now I have my own firm."

"That's nice," Jennifer said.

"That's about all there is to tell about me. Tell me about you."

Jennifer was silent for a moment. I'm the illegitimate daughter of one of the richest men in the world. You've probably heard of him. He just die in an accident. I'm an heiress to his estate. She looked around the elegant room. I could buy this restaurant, if I wanted to. I could probably buy this whole town, if I wanted to.

Henry was staring at her. "Jennifer?"

"Oh! I ...I'm sorry. I was born in Milwaukee. My ... my father died when I was young. My mother and I traveled around the country a great deal. When she passed away, I decided to stay here and get a job." I hope my nose isn't growing.

Alan Walker put a hand over hers. "So you've never had a man to take care of you." He leaned forward and said earnestly, "I would like to take care of you for the rest of your life."

Jennifer looked at him in surprise. "I don't mean to sound like Doris Day, but we hardly know each other."

"I want to change that."
When Jennifer got home, Susan was waiting for her.

"Well?" she asked. "How did your date go?" Jennifer said, thoughtfully, "He's very sweet, and ..."

"He's crazy about you!"

Jennifer smiled. "I think he proposed."

Susan's eyes widened. "You think he proposed? My God! Don't you know if the man proposed or not?"

"Well, he said he wanted to take care of me for the rest of my life."

"That's a proposal!" Susan exclaimed. "That's a proposal! Marry him! Quick! Marry him before he changes his mind!"

Jennifer laughed. "What's the hurry?"

"Listen to me. Invite him over here for dinner. I'll cook it, and you tell him you made it."

Jennifer laughed. "Thank you. No. When I find the man I want to marry, we may be eating Chinese food out of cartons, but believe me, the dinner table will be beautifully set with flowers and candlelight."

On their next date, Alan said, "You know, Miami is a great place to bring up kids."

"Yes, it is." Jennifer's only problem was that she wasn't sure that she wanted to bring up his children. He was reliable, decent, sober, but...

She discussed it with Susan.

"He keeps asking me to marry him," Jennifer said.

"What's he like?"

She thought for a moment, trying to think of the most romantic and exciting things she could say about Alan Walker. "He's reliable, sober, decent ..."

Susan looked at her a moment. "In other words, he's dull."

Jennifer said defensively, "He isn't exactly dull ..." Susan nodded, knowingly. "He's dull. Marry him."

"What?"

"Marry him. Good dull husbands are hard to find."

Getting from one payday to the next was a financial minefield. There were paycheck deductions, and rent, and automobile expenses, and groceries, and clothes to buy. Jennifer owned a Toyota, and it seemed to her that she spent more on it than she did on herself. She was constantly borrowing money from Susan.

One evening, when Jennifer was getting dressed, Susan said,

"It's another big Alan night, huh? Where's he taking you tonight?"

"We're going to Symphony Hall. Cleo Laine is performing."

"Has old Alan proposed again?"

Jennifer hesitated. The truth was that Alan proposed every time they were together. She felt pressured, but she could not bring herself to say yes.

"Don't lose him," Susan warned.

Susan is probably right, Jennifer thought. Alan Walker would make a good husband. He's ... She hesitated. He's reliable, sober, decent ...Is that enough?

As Jennifer was going out the door, Susan called, "Can I borrow your black shoes?"

"Sure." And Jennifer was gone.

Susan went into Jennifer's bedroom and opened the closet door. The pair of shoes she wanted was on the top shelf. As she reached for them, a cardboard box that was sitting precariously on the shelf fell down, and its contents spilled out all over the floor.

"Damn!" Susan bent down to gather up the papers.

They consisted of dozens of newspaper clippings, photographs, and articles, and they were all about the Robert Stanley family. There seemed to be hundreds of them.

Suddenly, Jennifer came hurrying back into the room. "I forgot my..." She stopped as she saw the papers on the floor. "What are you doing?"

"I'm sorry." Susan apologized. "The box fell down." Blushing, Jennifer bent down and started putting the papers back in the box.

"I had no idea you were so interested in the rich and famous," Susan said.

Silently, Jennifer kept shoving the papers into the box.

As she gathered a handful of photographs, she came across a small gold heart-shaped locket that her mother had given her before she died. Jennifer put the locket aside.

Susan was studying her, puzzled. "Jennifer?"

"Yes."

"Why are you so interested in Robert Stanley?"

"I'm not. I ... This was my mother's."

Susan shrugged. "Okay." She reached for a paper. It was from a scandal magazine, and the headline caught her eye: TYCOON GETS CHILDREN'S GOVERNESS PREGNANT-BABY BORN OUT-OF-WEDLOCK-MOTHER AND BABY DISAPPEAR!
Susan was staring at Jennifer, openmouthed. "My God! You're Robert Stanley's daughter!"

Jennifer's mouth tightened. She shook her head and continued putting the papers back.

"Aren't you?"

Jennifer stopped. "Please, I'd rather not talk about it, if you don't mind."

Susan jumped to her feet. "You'd rather not talk about it? You're the daughter of one of the richest men in the world, and you'd rather not talk about it? Are you insane?"

"Susan ..."

"Do you know how much he was worth? Billions."

"That has nothing to do with me."

"If you're his daughter, it has everything to do with you. You're an heiress! All you have to do is tell the family who you are, and..."

"No."

"No ... what?"

"You don't understand." Jennifer rose and then sank down on the bed. "Robert Stanley was an awful man. He abandoned my mother, she hated him, and I hate him."

"You don't hate anyone with that much money. You understand them."

Jennifer shook her head. "I don't want any part of them."

"Jennifer, heiresses don't live in crummy apartments and buy clothes at discount, and borrow to pay the rent. Your family would hate knowing you live like this. They'd be humiliated."

"They don't even know I'm alive."

"Then you've got to tell them." "Susan

..."

"Yes?"

"Drop the subject." Susan looked at her for a long time. "Sure. By the way, you couldn't loan me a million or two till payday, could you?"

19

Thomas continued to be desperate. His mood drive was out of control. For the last twenty-four hours, he had been dialing Connie's home number, and there had been no answer. Who is she with? Thomas agonized. What is she doing?

He picked up the telephone and dialed once again.

The phone rang for a long time, and just as Thomas was about to hang up, he heard Connie's voice.

"Hello."

"Connie! How are you?"

"Who the hell is this?"

"It's Thomas."

"Thomas?" There was a pause. "Oh, yes."

Thomas felt a twinge of disappointment. "How are you?"

"Fine," Connie said.

"I told you I was going to have a wonderful surprise for you."

"Yes?" She sounded bored.

"Do you remember what you said to me about going to St.-Tropez on a beautiful white yacht?"

"What about it?"

"How would you like to leave next month?"

"Are you serious?"

"You bet I am."

"Well, I don't know. You've got a friend with a yacht?"

"I'm about to buy a yacht."

"You're not on something, are you, Judge?"

"On ...? No, no! I've just come into some money. A lot of money."

"St.-Tropez, huh? Yeah, that sounds great. Sure, I'd love to go with you."

Thomas felt a deep sense of relief. "Wonderful! Meanwhile, don't ..."He couldn't bring himself even to think about it. "I'll be in touch with you, Connie." He replaced the receiver and sat on the edge of his bed. "I'd love to go with you." He could visualize the two of them on a beautiful yacht, cruising around the world together. Together.

Thomas picked up the phone book and turned to the yellow pages.

The offices of John Alden Yachts, Inc., are located on Los Angeles Commercial Wharf. The sales manager came up to Thomas as he entered.

"What can I do for you today, sir?"

Thomas looked at him, and said casually, "I'd like to buy a yacht." The words rolled off his tongue.

His father's yacht would probably be part of the estate, but Thomas had no intention of sharing a ship with his brother and sister.

"Motor or sail?"

"I ... er ... I'm not sure. I want to be able to go around the world in it."

"We're probably talking motor."

"It must be white."

The sales manager looked at him strangely. "Yes, of course. How large a boat did you have in mind?"

Blue Skies is one hundred and eighty feet.

"Two hundred feet."

The sales manager blinked. "Ah. I see. Of course, a yacht like that would be very expensive, Mr. .... er ... "

"Judge Stanley. My father was Robert Stanley."

The man's face lit up.

"Money is no object," Thomas said.

"Certainly not! Well, Judge Stanley, we're going to find you a yacht that everyone will envy. White, of course. Meanwhile, here is a portfolio of some available yachts. Call me when you decide which ones you're interested in."

Billy Stanley was thinking about polo ponies. All his life he had had to ride his friends' ponies, but now he could afford to buy the finest string in the world. He was on the phone, talking to Nicole Carson.

"I want to buy your ponies," Billy said. His voice was filled with excitement. He listened a moment. "That's right, the whole stable. I'm very serious. Right… "

The conversation lasted half an hour, and when Billy replaced the receiver, he was grinning. He went to find Anita. She was seated alone on the veranda. Billy could still see the bruises on her face where he had hit her.

"Anita ..."

She looked up, confused. "Yes?"

"I have to talk to you. I ... I don't know where to begin."

She sat there, waiting. He took a deep breath.

"I know I've been a rotten husband. Some of the things I've done are inexcusable. But, darling, all that is going to change now. Don't you see? We're rich. Really rich. I want to make everything up to you." He took her hand. "I'm going to get off drugs this time. I really am. We're going to have a whole different life."

She looked into his eyes, and said tonelessly, "Are we, Billy?"

"Yes. I promise. I know I've said it before, but this time it's really going to work. I've made up my mind. I'm going to a clinic somewhere where they can cure me. I want to get out of this hell I've been in. Anita..." There was desperation in his voice. "I can't do it without you. You know I can't... "

She looked at him a long time, and then cradled him in her arms. "Poor baby. I know," she whispered. "I know. I'll help you ..."

It was time for Mary Perkins to leave.

Thomas found her in the study. He closed the door. "I just wanted to thank you again, Mary."

She smiled. "It's been fun. I really had a good time."

She looked up at him archly. "Maybe I should become an actress."

He smiled. "You'd be good at it. You certainly fooled this audience."

"I did, didn't I?"

"Here's the rest of your money." He took an envelope out of his pocket. "And your plane ticket back to San Francisco."

"Thank you."

He looked at his watch. "You'd better get going."

"Right. I just want you to know that I appreciate everything. I mean, you're getting me out of prison and all."

He smiled. "That's all right. Have a good trip."

"Thanks."

He watched her go upstairs to pack. The game was over.

Check and checkmate.

Mary Perkins was in her bedroom finishing packing when Carmen walked in.

"Hi, Jennifer. I just wanted to..." She stopped. "What are you doing?"

"I'm going home."

Carmen looked at her in surprise. "So soon? Why? I was hoping we might spend some time together and get acquainted. We have so many years to catch up on."

"Sure. Well, some other time."

Carmen sat on the edge of the bed. "It's like a miracle, isn't it? Finding each other after all these years?"

Mary went on with her packing. "Yeah. It's a miracle, all right."

"You must feel like Cinderella. I mean, one minute you're living a perfectly average life and the next minute someone hands you a billion dollars."

Mary stopped her packing. "What?"

"I said ..."

"A billion dollars?"

"Yes. According to Father's will, that's what we each inherit."

Mary was looking at Carmen, stunned. "We each get a billion dollars?"

"Didn't they tell you?"

"No," Mary said slowly. "They didn't tell me." There was a thoughtful expression on her face. "You know, Carmen, you're right. Maybe we should get better acquainted."

Thomas was in the solarium, looking at photographs of yachts, when Damon approached him.

"Excuse me, Judge Stanley. There's a phone call for you."

"I'll take it in here."

It was Lynda Powell in San Francisco.

"Thomas?"

"Yes."

"I have some really great news for you!"

"Oh?"

"Now that I'm retiring early, how would you like to be appointed chief judge?"

It was all Thomas could do to keep from giggling. "That would be wonderful, Lynda."

"Well, it's yours!"

"I ... I don't know what to say." What should I say?

"Billionaires don't sit on the bench in a dirty little courtroom in San Francisco, handing out sentences to the misfits of the world"? Or "I'll be too busy sailing around the world on my yacht"?

"How soon can you get back to San Francisco?"

"It will be a while," Thomas said. "I have a lot to do here."

"Well, we'll all be waiting for you."

Don't hold your breath. "Good-bye." He replaced the receiver and glanced at his watch. It was time for Mary to be leaving for the airport. Thomas went upstairs to see if she was ready.

When he walked into Mary's bedroom, she was unpacking her suitcase.

He looked at her in surprise. "You're not ready."

She looked up at him and smiled. "No. I'm unpacking. I've been thinking, I like it here. Maybe I should stay awhile."

He frowned. "What are you talking about? You're catching a plane to San Francisco."

"There'll be another plane along, Judge." She grinned. "Maybe I'll even buy my own."

"What are you saying?"

"You told me you wanted me to help you play a little joke on someone."

"Yes?"

"Well, the joke seems to be on me. I'm worth a billion dollars."

Thomas's expression hardened. "I want you to get out of here. Now!"

"Do you? I think I'll go when I'm ready," Mary said. "And I'm not ready."

Thomas stood there, studying her. "What ... what is it you want?"

She nodded: "That's better. The billion dollars I'm supposed to get. You were planning to keep it for yourself, right? I figured you were pulling a little scam to pick up some extra money, but a billion dollars! That's a different ball game. I think I deserve a share of that."

There was a knock at the bedroom door. "Excuse me,"

Damon said. "Luncheon is served." Mary turned to Thomas.

"You go along. I won't be joining you. I have some important errands to run."

Later that afternoon, packages began to arrive at Rose Hill. There were boxes of dresses from Armani, sportswear from Stacy Boutique, lingerie from Jordan Marsh, a sable coat from Neiman Davidus, and a diamond bracelet from Cartier. All the packages were addressed to Miss Jennifer Stanley.

When Mary walked in the door at four-thirty, Thomas was waiting to confront her, furious.

"What do you think you're doing?" he demanded. She smiled. "I needed a few things. After all, your sister has to be well dressed, doesn't she? It's amazing how much credit a store will give you when you're a Stanley. You will take care of the bills, won't you?"

"Jennifer ..."

"Mary." She reminded him. "By the way, I saw the pictures of yachts on the table. Are you planning to buy one?"

"That's none of your business."

"Don't be too sure. Maybe you and I will take a cruise. We'll name the yacht Mary. Or should we name it Jennifer? We can go around the world together. I don't like being alone."

Thomas thought for a moment. "It seems that I underestimated you. You're a very clever young woman."

"Coming from you, that's a big compliment."

"I hope that you're also a reasonable young woman."

"That depends. What do you call reasonable?"

"One million dollars. Cash."

Her heart began to beat faster. "And I can keep the things I bought today?"

"All of them."

She took a deep breath. "You have a deal."

"Good. I'll get the money to you as quickly as I can. I'll be going back to San Francisco in the next few days." He took a key from his pocket and handed it to her. "Here's the key to my house. I want you to stay there and wait for me. And don't talk: to anyone."

"All right." She tried to hide her excitement. Maybe I should have asked for more, she thought.

"I'll book you on the next plane out of here."

"What about the things I bought ...?"

"I'll have them sent on to you."

"Good. Hey, we both came out of this great, didn't we?"

He nodded. "Yes. We did."

Thomas took Mary to International Airport to see her off

.

At the airport, she said, "What are you going to tell the others? About my leaving, I mean."

"I'll tell them that you had to go visit a very good friend who became ill, a friend in South America."

She looked at him wistfully. "Do you want to know something, Judge? That yachting trip would have been fun."

Over the loudspeaker, her flight was being called.

"That's me, I guess."

"Have a nice flight."

"Thanks. I'll see you in San Francisco."

Thomas watched her go into the departures terminal and stood there, waiting until the plane took off. Then he went back to the limousine and said to the chauffeur, "Bell Air."

When Thomas arrived back at the house, he went directly to his room and called Chief Judge Lynda Powell.

"We're all waiting for you, Thomas. When are you coming back? We're planning a little celebration in your honor."

"Very soon, Lyn," Thomas said. "Meanwhile, I could use your help with a problem I've run into."

"Certainly. What can I do for you?"

"It's about a felon I tried to help. Mary Perkins. I believe I told you about her."

"I remember. What's the problem?"

"The poor woman has deluded herself into believing she's my sister. She followed me to Los Angeles and tried to murder me."

"My God! That's terrible!"

"She's on her way back to San Francisco now, Lyn. She stole the key to my house, and I don't know what she plans to do next. The woman is a dangerous lunatic. She's threatened to kill my whole family. I want her committed to the San Francisco Mental Health Facility. If you'll fax me the commitment papers, I'll sign it. I'll arrange for her psychiatric examinations myself."

"Of course. I'll take care of it immediately, Thomas."

"I'll appreciate it. She's on United Airlines Flight 307. It arrives at eight-fifteen tonight. I suggest that you have people there at the airport to pick her up. Tell them to be careful. She should be put in maximum security at San Francisco, and not allowed any visitors."

"I'll see to it. I'm sorry you had to go through this, Thomas."

There was a shrug in Thomas's voice. "You know what they say, Lyn: 'No good deed, no matter how small, goes unpunished.' "

At dinner that evening, Carmen asked, "Isn't Jennifer joining us tonight?"

Thomas said regretfully, "Unfortunately, no. She asked me to say good-bye to all of you. She's gone to take care of a friend in South America who's had a stroke. It was rather sudden."

"But the will has not been ..."

"Jennifer has given me her power of attorney and wants me to arrange for her share to go into a trust fund."

A servant placed a bowl of Los Angeles clam chowder in front of Thomas.

"Ab," he said. "That looks delicious! I'm hungry tonight."

United Airlines Flight 307 was making its final approach to LAX International Airport on schedule. A metallic voice came over the loudspeaker. "Ladies and gentlemen, would you fasten your seat belts, please?"

Mary Perkins had enjoyed the flight tremendously. She had spent most of the time dreaming about what she was going to do with the million dollars and all the clothes and jewelry she had bought. And all because I was busted! Isn't that a kick!

When the plane landed, Mary gathered the things she had carried on board and started to walk down the ramp. A flight attendant stayed directly behind her. Near the plane was an ambulance, flanked by two paramedics in white jackets, and a doctor. The flight attendant saw them and pointed to Mary. As Mary stepped off the ramp, one of the men approached her.

"Excuse me," he said.

Mary looked up at him. "Yes?"

"Are you Mary Perkins?"

"Why, yes. What's ...?"

"I'm Dr. Zimmerman." He took her arm. "We'd like you to come with us, please." He started leading her toward the ambulance.

Mary tried to jerk away. "Wait a minute! What are you doing?"

The other two men had moved to either side of her to hold her arms.

"Just come along quietly, Miss Perkins," the doctor said.

"Help!" Mary screamed. "Help me!"

The other passengers were standing there, gaping.

"What's the matter with all of you?" Mary yelled.

"Are you blind? I'm being kidnapped! I'm Jennifer Stanley!

I'm Robert Stanley's daughter!"

"Of course, you are," Dr. Zimmerman said soothingly. "Just calm down."

The observers watched in astonishment as Mary was carried into the back of the ambulance, kicking and screaming.

Inside the ambulance, the doctor took out a syringe and pressed the needle into Mary's arm. "Relax," he said. "Everything is going to be all right."

"You must be crazy!" Mary said. "You must be ..." Her eyes began to droop.

The ambulance doors closed, and the ambulance sped away.

When Thomas got the report, he laughed out loud. He could visualize the sonofabitch being carried off. He would arrange for her to be kept in a mental health facility for the rest of her life.

Now the game is really over, he thought. I've done it!

The old man would turn over in his grave if he still had one, if he knew that I was getting control of Stanley Enterprises. I'll give Connie everything she's ever dreamed of. Perfect. Everything was perfect. The events of the day had filled Thomas with a sexual excitement. I need some relief. He opened his suitcase and, from the back of it, took out a copy of the Damson Address Book. There were many bars listed in Los Angeles. He chose the Sunset Strip. I'll skip dinner. I'll go straight to the club. And then he thought What a surprise!

Jennifer and Susan were getting dressed to go to work. Susan asked,

"How was your date with Henry last night?"

"The Scott."

"That bad, huh? Have the marriage banns been posted yet?"

"God, forbid!" Jennifer said. "Henry is sweet, but ..."

She sighed. "He isn't for me."

"He might not be," Susan said, "but these are for you." She handed Jennifer five envelopes.

They were all bills. Jennifer opened them. Three of them were Divided OVERDUE and another was Divided THIRD NOTICE. Jennifer studied them a moment.

"Susan, I wonder if you could lend me ..."

Susan looked at her in amazement. "I don't understand you."

"What do you mean?"

"You're working like 'a galley slave, you can't pay your bills, and all you have to do is lift your little finger and you could come up with a few million dollars, give or take some change."

"It's not my money."

"Of course it's your money!" Susan snapped. "Robert Stanley was your father, wasn't he? Ergo, you're entitled to a share of his estate. And I don't use the word ergo very often."

"Forget it. I told you how he treated my mother. He wouldn't have left me a dime."

Susan sighed. "Damn! And I was looking forward to living with a millionaire!"

They walked down to the parking lot where they kept their cars. Jennifer's space was empty. She stared at it in shock. "It's gone!"

"Are you sure you parked your car here last night?" Susan asked.

"Yes."

"Someone stole it!"

Jennifer shook her head. "No," she said slowly.

"What do you mean?"

She turned to look at Susan. "They must have repossessed it. I'm three payments behind."

"Wonderful," Susan said tonelessly. "That's just wonderful."

Susan was unable to get her roommate's situation out of her mind. It's like a fairy tale, Susan thought. A princess who doesn't know she's a princess. Only in this case, she knows it, but she's too proud to do anything about it. It's not fair! The family has all that money, and she has nothing. Well, if she won't do something about it, I damn well will. She'll thank me for it.

That evening, after Jennifer went out, Susan examined the box of clippings again. She took out a recent newspaper article mentioning that the Stanley heirs had gone back to Bell Air for the funeral services.

If the princess won't go to them, Susan thought, they're going to come to the princess.

She sat down and began to write a letter. It was addressed to Judge Thomas Stanley.

20

Thomas Stanley signed the commitment papers putting Mary Perkins in San Francisco Mental Health Facility. Three psychiatrists were required to agree to the commitment, but Thomas knew that that would be easy for him to handle.

He reviewed everything he had done from the very beginning, and decided that there had been no flaws in his game plan. Donald had disappeared in Australia, and Mary Perkins had been disposed of. That left Henry Brooks, but he would be no problem. Everyone had an Achilles' heel, and his was his stupid family. No, Brooks will never talk because he couldn't bear the thought of spending his life in prison, away from his dear ones.

The minute the will is probated, I'll return to San Francisco and pick up Connie. Maybe we'll even buy a house in St.- Tropez. He began to get aroused at the thought. We'll sail around the world in my yacht. I've always wanted to see Venice ... and Positano ... and Capri... We'll go on safari in Kenya, and see the Taj Mahal together in the moonlight. And who do I owe all this to? To Daddy. Dear old Daddy.

"You're a sonofabitch, Thomas, and you'll always be. I don't know how the hell anything like you came from my loins ..."

Well, who has the last laugh now, Father?

Thomas went downstairs to join his brother and sister for lunch. He was hungry again.

"It's really a pity that Jennifer had to leave so quickly," Carmen said. "I would have liked to have gotten to know her better."

"I'm sure she plans to return as soon as she can," David said.

That's certainly true, Thomas thought. He would make sure she never got out.

The talk turned to the future.

Anita said, cautiously, "Billy is going to buy a group of polo ponies."

"It's not a group!" Billy snapped. "It's a string. A string of polo ponies."

"I'm sorry, darling. I just..."

"Forget it!"

Thomas said to Carmen, "What are your plans?"

"... we are counting on your further support ... We would appreciate it if you would deposit 1 million U.S. dollars ... within the next ten days."

"Carmen?"

"Oh. I'm going to ... to expand the business. I'll open shops in London and in Paris."

"That sounds exciting," Anita said.

"I have a show in New York in two weeks. I have to run down there and get it ready."

Carmen looked over at Thomas. "What are you going to do with your share of the estate?"

Thomas said piously, "Charity, mostly. There are so many worthy organizations that need help."

He was only half listening to the conversation at the table. He looked around the table at his brother and sister. If it weren't for me, you'd be getting nothing. Nothing!

He turned to look at Billy. His brother had become a dope addict, throwing his life away. Money won't help him, Thomas thought. It will only buy him more dope. He wondered where Billy was getting the stuff.

Thomas turned to his sister. Carmen was bright and successful, and she had made the most of her talents. David was seated next to her, telling an amusing anecdote to Anita. He's attractive and charming. And then there was Anita. He thought of her as Poor Anita. Why she put up with Billy was beyond him. She must love him very much. She certainly hasn't gotten anything out of her marriage. He wondered what the expressions on their faces would be if he stood up and said, "I control Stanley Enterprises. I had our father murdered, his body dug up, and I hired someone to impersonate our half-sister. "He smiled at the thought. It was difficult holding a secret as delicious as the one he had.

After lunch, Thomas went to his room to call Connie again. There was no answer. She's out with someone, Thomas thought, despairingly. She doesn't believe me about the yacht. Well, I'll prove it to her! When is that damn will going to be probated? I'll have to call Harold, or that young lawyer, George Brown.

There was a knock at the door. Damon stood there.

"Excuse me, Judge Stanley. A letter arrived for you."

Probably from Lynda Powell, congratulating me.

"Thank you, Damon." He took the envelope. It had a Miami return address. He stared at it a moment, puzzled, then opened it and began to read the letter.

Dear Judge Stanley:

I think you should know that you have a half-sister named Jennifer. She is the daughter of Rosa Newman and your father. She lives here in Miami. Her address is 45Nw 25th Ave, Apt # 3A, Miami, Florida.

I'm sure Jennifer would be most happy to hear from you.

Sincerely,

A Friend

Thomas stared at the letter disbelievingly, and he felt a cold chill. "No!" he cried aloud. "No!" I won't have it! Not now! Maybe she's a fake. But he had a terrible feeling that this Jennifer was genuine. And now the bitch is coming forward to claim her share of the estate! My share. Thomas corrected himself. It doesn't belong to her. I can't let her come here. It would ruin everything. I would have to explain the other Jennifer, and ... He shuddered. "No!" I have to have her taken care of. Fast. He reached for the telephone and dialed Henry Brooks' number.

21

He'd kept the curious out while the doctor made his examination. Now he looks at the doctor. The dermatologist shook his head. "I've seen cases similar to yours, but never one this bad."

Henry Brooks scratched his hand and nodded.

"You see, Mr. Brooks, we were confronted with three possibilities. Your itching could have been caused by a fungus, an allergy, or it could be neurodermatitis. The skin scraping I took from your hand and put under the microscope showed me that it wasn't a fungus. And you said you didn't handle chemicals on the job ..."

"That's right."

"So, we've narrowed it down. What you have is lichen simplex chronicus, or localized neurodermatitis."

"That sounds awful. Is there something you can do about it?"

"Fortunately, there is." The doctor took a tube from a cabinet in a corner of the office and opened it. "Is your hand itching now?"

Henry Brooks scratched again. "Yes. It feels like it's on fire."

"I want you to rub some of this cream on your hand."

Henry Brooks squeezed out some of the cream and began to rub it into his hand. It was like a miracle.

"The itching has stopped!" Brooks said.

"Good. Use that, and you won't have any more problems."

"Thank you, Doctor. I can't tell you what a relief this is."

"I'll give you a prescription. You can take the tube with you."

"Thank you."

Driving home, Henry Brooks was singing aloud. It was the first time since he had met Judge Thomas Stanley that his hand had not itched. It was a wonderful feeling of freedom. Still whistling, he pulled into the garage and walked into the kitchen. Helen was waiting for him.

"You had a telephone call," she said." A Mr. Jones.

He said it was urgent."

His hand began itching.

He had hurt some people, but he had done it for the love of his kids. He had committed some crimes, but it was for the family. Henry Brooks did not believe he really had been at fault. This was different. This was a cold blooded murder.

When he had returned the phone call, he had protested. "I can't do that, Judge. You'll have to find someone else."

There had been a silence. And then, "How's the family?"

The flight to Miami was uneventful. Judge Stanley had given him detailed instructions. "Her name is Jennifer Stanley. You have her address and apartment number. She won't be expecting you. All you have to do is to go there and handle her. "

He took a taxi from the Miami Airport to downtown Miami.

"Beautiful day," the taxi driver said.

"Yep."

"Where did you come in from?"

"New York. I live here."

"Nice place to live."

"Sure is. I have a little repair work to do around the house. Would you drop me off at a hardware store?"

"Right."

Five minutes later, Henry Brooks was saying to a clerk in the store, "I need a hunting knife."

"We have just the thing, sir. Would you come this way, please?"

The knife was a thing of beauty, about six inches long, with a sharp pointed end and serrated edges.

"Will this do?"

"I'm sure it will," Henry Brooks said.

"Will that be cash or charge?"

"Cash."

His next stop was at a stationery store. Henry Brooks studied the apartment building at 45 Nw 25th Ave, Apt # 3A in Miami for five minutes, examining exits and entrances. He left and returned at eight P.M., when it began to get dark. He wanted to make sure that if Jennifer Stanley had a job, she would be home from work. He had noted that the apartment building had no doorman. There was an elevator, but he took the stairs. It was not smart to be in small enclosed places. They were traps. He reached the third floor. Apartment 3B was down the hall on the left. The knife was taped to the inside pocket of his jacket. He rang the doorbell. A moment later, the door opened, and he found himself facing an attractive woman.

"Hello." She had a nice smile. "Can I help you?"

She was younger than he had expected, and he wondered why Judge Stanley wanted her killed.

Well, that's none of my business. He took out a card and handed it to her.

"I'm with the A C. Nielsen Company," he said smoothly. "We don't have any of the Nielsen family in this area, and we're looking for people who might be interested."

She shook her head. "No, thanks." She started to close the door.

"We pay one hundred dollars a week." The door stayed half open.

"A hundred dollars a week?"

"Yes, ma'am."

The door was wide open now.

"All you have to do is record the names of the programs you watch. We'll give you a contract for one year."

Five thousand dollars! "Come in," she said. He walked into the apartment.

"Sit down, Mr..."

"John. John Kimbal."

"Mr. John. How did you happen to select me?"

"Our company does random checking. We have to make sure that none of the people is involved in television in any way, so we can keep our survey accurate. You don't have any connection with any television production programs or networks, do you?"

She laughed. "Gosh, no. What would I have to do exactly?"

"It's really very simple. We'll give you a chart with all the television programs listed on it, and all you have to do is make a check every time you watch a program. That way our computer can figure out how many viewers each program has. The Nielsen family is scattered around the United States, so we get a clear picture of which shows are popular in which areas and with whom. Would you be interested?"

"Oh, yes."

He took out some printed forms and a pen. "How many hours a day do you watch television?"

"Not very many. I work all day."

"But you do watch some television?"

"Oh, certainly. I watch the news at night, and sometimes an old movie. I like Larry King."

He made a note. "Do you watch much educational television?"

"I watch PBS on Sundays."

"By the way, do you live alone here?"

"I have a roommate, but she's not here."

So they were alone.

His hand began to itch. He started to reach into his inside pocket to untapped the knife. He heard footsteps in the hall outside. He stopped.

"Did you say I get five thousand dollars a year just for doing this?"

"That's right. Oh, I forgot to mention. We also give you a new color TV set."

"That's fantastic!"

The footsteps were gone. He reached inside his pocket again and felt the handle of the knife. "Could I have a glass of water, please? It's been a long day."

"Certainly." He watched her get up and goes over to the small bar in the comer. He slipped the knife out of its sheath and moved up behind her.

She was saying, "My roommate watches PBS more than I do."

He lifted the knife, ready to strike.

"But Jennifer's more intellectual than I am."

Baker's hand froze in midair. "Jennifer?"

"My roommate. Or she was. She's gone. I found a note when I got home saying she had left and didn't know when she'd be ... "She turned around, holding the glass of water, and saw the upraised knife in his hand. "What ...?"

She screamed.

Henry Brooks turned and fled. Henry Brooks telephoned Thomas Stanley.

"I'm in Florida City, but the girl is gone."

"What do you mean, gone?"

"Her roommate says she left."

He was silent for a moment. "I have a feeling she's headed for Los Angeles. I want you to get up here right away."

"Yes, sir."

Thomas Stanley slammed down the receiver and began to pace. Everything had been going so perfectly! The girl had to be found and disposed of. She was a loose cannon. Even after he received control of the estate, Thomas knew he would not rest easy as long as she was alive. I've got to find her, Thomas thought. I've got to! But where?

Damon came into the room. He looked puzzled. "Excuse me, Judge Stanley. There is a Miss Jennifer Stanley here to see you."

22

It was because of Carmen that Jennifer decided to go to Los Angeles. Returning from lunch one day, Jennifer passed an exclusive dress shop, and in the window was an original design by Carmen. Jennifer looked at it for a long time. That's my sister, Jennifer thought. I can't blame her for what happened to my mother. And I can't blame my brothers. And suddenly she was filled with an overpowering desire to see them, to meet them, to talk to them, to have a family at last.

When Jennifer returned to the office, she told Thomson that she would be gone for a few days. Embarrassed, she said, "I wonder if I could have an advance on my salary?"

Thomson smiled. "Sure. You have a vacation coming. Here. Have a good time."

Will I have a good time? Jennifer wondered. Or am I making a terrible mistake?

When Jennifer returned home, Susan had not arrived yet. I can't wait for her, Jennifer decided. If I don't go now, I'll never go. She packed her suitcase and left a note. On the way to the bus terminal, Jennifer had second thoughts. What am I doing? Why did I make this sudden decision? Then she thought ironically, sudden? It's taken me fourteen years! She was filled with an enormous sense of excitement. What was her family going to be like? She knew that one of her brothers was a judge, the other was a famous polo player, and her sister was a famous designer. It's a family of achievers, Jennifer thought, and who am I? I hope they don't look down on me. Merely thinking about what lay ahead made Jennifer's heart skip a beat. She boarded a Greyhound bus and was on her way.

When the bus arrived at South Station in Los Angeles, Jennifer found a taxi.

"Where to, lady?" the driver asked.

And Jennifer completely lost her nerve. She had intended to say, "Bell Air." Instead, she said, "I don't know."

The taxi driver turned around to look at her. "Gee, I don't know, either."

"Could you just drive around? I've never been to Los Angeles before."

He nodded. "Sure."

They drove west along Main Street until they reached the Los Angeles downtown.

The driver said, "This is the oldest public park in the United States. They used to use it for hangings."

And Jennifer could hear her mother's voice. "I used to take the children to the park in the winter to ice skate. Billy was a natural athlete. I wish you could have met him, Jennifer. He was such a handsome boy. I always thought he was going to be the successful one in the family." It was as though her mother were with her, sharing this moment.

They had reached Charles Street, the entrance to the Public Garden. The driver said, "See those bronze ducklings? Believe it or not, they've all got names."

"We used to have picnics in the Public Garden. There are cute bronze ducklings at the entrance. They're named Jack, Kack, Lack, Mack, Nack, Ouack, Pack, and Quack. "Jennifer had thought that was so funny that she had made her mother repeat the names over and over again.

Jennifer looked at the meter. The drive was getting expensive. "Could you recommend an inexpensive hotel?"

"Sure. How about the Grand Hotel?"

"Would you take me there, please?"

"Right."

Five minutes later, they pulled up in front of the hotel.

"Enjoy Los Angeles, lady."

"Thank you." Am I going to enjoy it, or will it be a disaster? Jennifer paid the driver and went into the hotel. She approached the young clerk behind the desk.

"Hello," he said. "May I help you?"

"I'd like a room, please."

"Single?"

"Yes."

"How long will you be staying?"

She hesitated. An hour? Ten years? "I don't know."

"Right." He checked the key rack. "I have a nice single for you on the fourth floor."

"Thank you." She signed the register in a neat hand. Jennifer Stanley.

The clerk handed her a key. "There you are. Enjoy your stay."

The room was small, but neat and clean. As soon as Jennifer unpacked, she telephoned Susan.

"Jennifer? My God! Where are you?"

"I'm in Los Angeles."

"Are you all right?" She sounded hysterical.

"Yes. Why?"

"Someone came to the apartment, looking for you, and I think he wanted to kill you!"

"What are you talking about?"

"He had a knife and ... you should have seen the look on his face..." She was gasping for breath.

"When he found out I wasn't you, he ran!"

"I don't believe it!"

"He said he was with A C. Nielsen, but I called their office, and they never heard of him! Do you know anyone who would want to harm you?"

"Of course not, Susan! Don't be ridiculous! Did you call the police?"

"I did. But there wasn't much they could do except to tell me to be more careful."

"Well, I'm just fine, so don't worry."

She heard Susan take a deep breath. "All right. As long as you're okay. Jennifer?"

"Yes."

"Be careful, will you?"

"Of course." Susan and her imagination! Who in the world would want to kill me?

"Do you know when you're coming back?"

The kind of question the clerk had asked her.

"No."

"You're there to see your family, aren't you?"

"Yes."

"Good luck."

"Thanks, Susan."

"Keep in touch."

"I will."

Jennifer replaced the receiver. She stood there, wondering what to do next. If I had any brains, I would get back on the bus and go home. I've been stalling. Did I come to Los Angeles to see the sights? No. I came here to meet my family. Am I going to meet them? No ... Yes.... She sat on the edge of the bed, her mind in turmoil.

What if they hate me? I must not think that. They're going to love me, and I'm going to love them. She looked at the telephone and thought, maybe it would be better if I called them. No. Then they might not want to see me. She went to the closet and selected her best dress. If I don't do it now, I'll never do it, Jennifer decided. Thirty minutes later, she was in a taxi on her way to Bell Air to meet her family.

23

Thomas was staring at Damon in disbelief. "Jennifer Stanley ... is here?"

"Yes, sir." There was a puzzled tone in the butler's voice. "But it isn't the Miss Stanley who was here earlier."

Thomas forced a smile. "Of course not. I'm afraid it's an impostor."

"An impostor, sir?"

"Yes. They'll be coming out of the woodwork, Damon, all claiming a right to the family fortune."

"That's terrible, sir. Shall I call the police?"

"No," Thomas said quickly. That was the last thing he wanted. "I'll handle it. Send her into the library."

"Yes, sir."

Thomas's mind was racing. So the real Jennifer Stanley had finally showed up. It was fortunate that none of the other members of the family was home at the moment. He would have to get rid of her immediately.

Thomas walked into the library. Jennifer was standing in the middle of the room, looking at a portrait of Robert Stanley. Thomas stood there a moment, studying the woman. She was beautiful. It was too bad that...

Jennifer turned around and saw him. "Hello."

"Hello."

"You're Thomas."

"That's right. Who are you?"

Her smile faded. "Didn't ...? I'm Jennifer Stanley."

"Really? You'll forgive my asking, but do you have any proof of that?"

"Proof? Well, yes.... I ... that is ... no proof I just assumed..."

He moved closer to her. "How did you happen to come here?"

"I decided that it was time to meet my family."

"After twenty-six years?"

"Yes."

Looking at her, listening to her speak, there was no question in Thomas's mind. She was genuine, dangerous, and would have to be disposed of quickly.

Thomas forced a smile. "Well, you can imagine what a shock this is to me. I mean, for you to appear here out of the blue and ..."

"I know. I'm sorry. I probably should have called first. "

Thomas asked casually, "You came to Los Angeles alone?"

"Yes."

His mind was racing. "Does anyone else know you're here?"

"No. Well, my roommate, Susan, in Miami..."

"Where are you staying?"

"At the Grand Hotel."

"That's a nice hotel. What room are you in?"

"Four fifteen."

"All right. Why don't you go back to your hotel and wait there for us? I want to prepare Billy and Carmen for this. They're going to be as surprised as I was."

"I'm sorry. I should have..."

"No problem. Now that we've met, I know that everything is going to be just fine."

"Thank you, Thomas."

"You're welcome!" He almost choked on the word Jennifer. "Let me call a taxi for you."

Five minutes later, she was gone.

Henry Brooks had just returned to his hotel room in downtown Los Angeles when the telephone call came. He picked it up.

"Henry?"

"I'm sorry. I have no news yet, Judge. I've combed this whole town. I went to the airport and..."

"She's here, stupid!"

"What?"

"She's here in Los Angeles. She's staying at the Grand Hotel, room four fifteen. I want her taken care of tonight. And I don't want any more bungling, do you understand?"

"What happened was not my..."

"Do you understand?"

"Yes, sir."

"Then do it!" Thomas slammed down the receiver. He went to find Damon.

"Damon, about that young woman who was here pretending she was my sister?"

"Yes, sir?"

"I wouldn't say anything about it to the other members of the family. It would just upset them."

"I understand, sir. You're very thoughtful."

Jennifer walked over to The Ritz-Carlton for dinner. The hotel was beautiful, just as her mother had described it. On Sunday, I used to take the children there for brunch. Jennifer sat in the dining room and visualized her mother there at a table with young Thomas, Billy, and Carmen. I wish I could have grown up with them, Jennifer thought. But at least I'm going to meet them now. She wondered whether her mother would have approved of what she was doing. Jennifer had been taken aback by Thomas's reception. He had seemed ... cold. But that's only natural, Jennifer thought. A stranger walks in and says, "I'm your sister." Of course he would be suspicious. But I'm sure I can convince them.

When the check came, Jennifer stared at it in shock. I have to be careful, she thought. I have to have enough money left to take the bus back to Florida.

As she stepped outside The Ritz-Carlton, a tour bus was getting ready to leave. On an impulse, she boarded it. She wanted to see as much of her mother's city as she could.

Henry Brooks strode into the lobby of the Grand Hotel as though he belonged there and took the stairs to the fourth floor. This time there would be no mistake. Room 415 was in the middle of the corridor. Henry Brooks scanned the hallway to make sure no one was around, and knocked on the door. There was no answer. He knocked again. "Miss Stanley?" Still no answer.

He took a small case from his pocket and selected a pick. It took him only seconds to open the door. Henry Brooks stepped inside, closing the door behind him. The room was empty.

"Miss Stanley?"

He walked into the bathroom. Empty. He went back into the bedroom. He took a knife out of his pocket, moved a chair in back of the door, and sat in the dark, waiting. It was one hour later when he heard someone approaching.

Henry Brooks rose quickly and stood behind the door, the knife in his hands. He heard the key turn in the lock, and the door started to swing open. He raised the knife high over his head, ready to strike. Jennifer Stanley stepped in and pressed the light switch on. He heard her say, "Very well. Come in."

A crowd of reporters poured into the room.

24

It was Robert Sanders, the night manager at the Grand Hotel, who inadvertently saved Jennifer's life. He had come on duty at six o'clock that evening, and had automatically checked the hotel register. When he came across the name of Jennifer Stanley, he stared at it in surprise. Ever since Robert Stanley had died, the newspapers had been full of stories about the Stanley family. They had dredged up the ancient scandal of Stanley's affair with the children's governess and the suicide of Stanley's wife. Robert Stanley had an illegitimate daughter named Jennifer. There were rumors that she had come to Los Angeles in secret. Shortly after going on a shopping spree, she had reportedly left for South America. Now, it seemed that she was back. And she's staying at my hotel! Robert Sanders thought excitedly.

He turned to the front-desk clerk. "Do you know how much publicity this could mean for the hotel?"

A minute later, he was on the telephone to the press.

When Jennifer arrived back at the hotel after her sightseeing tour, the lobby was filled with reporters, eagerly awaiting her. As soon as she walked into the lobby, they pounced.

"Miss Stanley! I'm from The Los Angeles Globe. We've been looking for you, but we heard that you had left town. Could you tell us ...?"

A television camera was pointed at her. "Miss Stanley, I'm with WCVB-TV. We would like to get a statement from you... "

"Miss Stanley, I'm from The Los Angeles Phoenix. We want to know your reaction to ..."

"Look this way, Miss Stanley! Smile! Thank you."

Flashes were popping.

Jennifer stood there, filled with confusion. Oh, my God, she thought. The family is going to think that I'm some kind of publicity hound. She turned to the reporters.

"I'm sorry. I have nothing to say."

She fled into the elevator. They piled in after her. "People magazine wants to do a story on your life, and what it feels like to be estranged from your family for over twenty-five years ..."

"We heard you had gone to South America ..."

"Are you planning to live in Los Angeles?"

"Why aren't you staying at Bell Air?"

She got out of the elevator at the fourth floor and hurried down the corridor. They were at her heels. There was no way to escape them.

Jennifer took out her key and opened the door to her room. She stepped inside and turned on the light. "Very well. Come in."

Hidden behind the door, Henry Brooks was caught by surprise, the knife in his raised hand. As the reporters shoved past him, he quickly put the knife back in his pocket and mingled with the group.

Jennifer turned to the reporters. "All right. One question at a time, please."

Frustrated, Brooks backed toward the door and slipped out. Judge Stanley was not going to be pleased.

For the next thirty minutes, Jennifer answered questions as best she could. Finally, they were gone.

Jennifer locked the door and went to bed. In the morning, the television stations and newspapers featured stories about Jennifer Stanley. Thomas read the papers and was furious. Billy and Carmen joined him at the breakfast table.

"What's all this nonsense about some woman calling herself Jennifer Stanley?" Billy asked.

"She's a phony," Thomas said glibly. "She came to the door yesterday, demanding money, and I sent her away. I didn't expect her to pull a cheap publicity stunt like this. Don't worry. I'll take care of her."

He put in a call to Frank Harold. "Have you seen the morning papers?"

"Yes."

"This con artist is going around town claiming that she's our sister."

Harold said, "Do you want me to have her arrested?"

"No! That would only create more publicity. I want you to get her out of town."

"All right. I'll take care of it, Judge Stanley."

"Thank you."

Frank Harold sent for George Brown.

"There's a problem," he said.

George nodded. "I know. I've heard the morning news and seen the papers. Who is she?"

"Obviously someone who thinks she can horn in on the family fortune. Judge Stanley suggested we get her out of town. Will you handle her?"

"My pleasure," George said grimly.

One hour later, George was knocking on Jennifer's hotel room door.

When Jennifer opened the door and saw him standing there, she said, "I'm sorry. I'm not talking to any more reporters. I ..."

"I'm not a reporter. May I come in?"

"Who are you?"

"My name is George Brown. I'm with the law firm representing the Robert Stanley estate."

"Oh. I see. Yes. Come in."

George walked into the room.

"Did you tell the press that you are Jennifer Stanley?"

"I'm afraid I was caught off guard. I didn't expect them, you see, and ..."

"But you did claim to be Robert Stanley's daughter?"

"Yes. I am his daughter."

He looked at her and said cynically, "Of course, you have proof of that."

"Well, no," Jennifer said slowly. "I don't."

"Come on," George insisted. "You must have some proof." He intended to nail her with her own lies.

"I have nothing," she said.

He studied her, surprised. She was not what he had expected. There was a disarming frankness about her. She seems intelligent. How could she have been stupid enough to come here claiming to be Robert Stanley's daughter without any proof?

"That's too bad," George said. "Judge Stanley wants you to get out of town."

Jennifer's eyes widened. "What?"

"That's right."

"But ... I don't understand. I haven't even met my other brother or sister."

So she's determined to keep up the bluff, George thought. "Look, I don't know who you are, or what your game is, but you could go to jail for this. We're giving you a break. What you're doing is against the law. You have a choice. You either can get out of town and stop bothering the family, or we can have you arrested."

Jennifer stood there in shock. "Arrested? I ... I don't know what to say."

"It's your decision."

"They don't even want to see me?" Jennifer asked without any feeling.

"That's putting it mildly."

She took a deep breath. "All right. If that's what they want, I'll go back to Florida. I promise you, they'll never hear from me again."

"You came a long way to pull your little scam."

"That's very wise." He stood there a moment, watching her, puzzled. "Well, good-bye."

She did not reply.

George was in Frank Harold's office.

"Did you see the woman, George?"

"Yes. She's going back home." He seemed distracted.

"Good. I'll tell Judge Stanley. He'll be pleased."

"Do you know what's bugging me, Frank?"

"What?"

"The dog didn't bark."

"I beg your pardon?"

"The Sherlock Holmes story. The clue was in what didn't happen."

"George, what does that have to do with...?"

"She came here without any proof."

Harold looked at him, puzzled. "I don't understand. That should have convinced you."

"On the contrary. Why would she come here, all the way from Florida, claiming to be Robert Stanley's daughter, and not have a single thing to back it up?"

"There are a lot of weirdoes out there, George."

"She's not a weirdo. You should have seen her. And there are a couple of other things that bother me, Frank."

"Yes?"

"Robert Stanley's body disappeared ... When I went to talk to Donald Herman, the only witness to Stanley's accident, he had disappeared... And no one seems to know where the first Jennifer Stanley suddenly disappeared too."

Frank Harold was frowning. "What are you saying?"

George said, slowly, "There's something going on that needs to be explained. I'm going to have another talk with the lady."

George Brown walked into the lobby of the Grand Hotel and approached the desk clerk. "Would you ring Miss Jennifer Stanley, please?"

The clerk looked up. "Oh, I'm sorry. Miss Stanley has checked out."

"Did she leave a forwarding address?"

"No, sir. I'm afraid not."

George stood there, frustrated. There was nothing more he could do. Well, maybe I was wrong, he thought philosophically. Maybe she really is an impostor. Now we'll never know. He turned and went out into the street. The doorman was ushering a couple into a taxi.

"Excuse me," George said.

The doorman turned. "Taxi, sir?"

"No. I want to ask you a question. Did you see Miss Stanley come out of the hotel this morning?"

"I certainly did. Everybody was staring at her. She's quite a celebrity. I got a taxi for her."

"I don't suppose you know where she went?" He found that he was holding his breath.

"Sure. I told the cab driver where to take her."

"And where was that?" George asked impatiently.

"To the Greyhound bus terminal at South Station. I thought it was strange that someone as rich as that would..."

"I do want a taxi."

George walked into the crowded Greyhound bus terminal and looked around. Jennifer was nowhere to be seen. She's gone, George thought despairingly. A voice on a loud speaker was calling out the departing buses. He heard the voice say, " ... and Miami," and George hurried out to the loading platform.

Jennifer was just starting to get on the bus.

"Hold it!" he called.

She turned, startled.

George hurried up to her. "I want to talk to you."

She looked at him, angry. "I have nothing more to say to you." She turned to go.

He grabbed her arm. "Wait a minute! We really have to talk."

"My bus is leaving."

"There'll be another one."

"My suitcase is on it."

George turned to a porter. "This woman is about to have a baby. Get her suitcase out of there. Quick!"

The porter looked at Jennifer in surprise. "Right." He hurriedly opened the luggage compartment. "Which is yours, lady?"

Jennifer turned to George, puzzled. "Do you know what you're doing?"

"No," George said.

She studied him a moment, then made a decision. She pointed to her suitcase. "That one."

The porter pulled it out. "Do you want me to get you an ambulance or anything?"

"Thank you. I'll be fine."

George picked up the suitcase, and they headed for the exit. "Have you had breakfast?"

"I'm not hungry," she said coldly.

"You'd better have something. You're eating for two now, you know."

They had breakfast at Julien. She sat across from George, her body rigid with anger.

When they had ordered, George said, "I'm curious about something. What made you think you could claim part of the Stanley estate without any proof at all of your identity?"

Jennifer looked at him indignantly. "I didn't go there to claim part of the Stanley estate. My father wouldn't have left anything to me. I wanted to meet my family. Obviously they didn't want to meet me."

"Do you have any documents ... any kind of proof at all of who you are?"

She thought of all the clippings piled up in her apartment and shook her head. "No. Nothing."

"There's someone I want you to talk to."

"This is Frank Harold." George hesitated. "Er ..."

"Jennifer Stanley."

Harold said skeptically, "Sit down, miss."

Jennifer sat on the edge of a chair, ready to get up and walk out.

Harold was studying her. She had the Stanley deep gray eyes, but so did lots of other people. "You claim you're Rosa Newman's daughter."

"I don't claim anything. I am Rosa Newman's daughter."

"And where is your mother?"

"She died a number of years ago."

"Oh, I'm sorry to hear that. Could you tell us about her?"

"No," Jennifer said. "I really would rather not." She stood up. "I want to get out of here."

"Look, we're trying to help you," George said.

She turned to him. "Are you? My family doesn't want to see me. You want to turn me over to the police. I don't need that kind of help." She started toward the door.

George said, "Wait! If you are who you say you are, you must have something that will prove you're Robert Stanley's daughter."

"I told you, I don't," Jennifer said. "My mother and I shut Robert Stanley out of our lives."

"What did your mother look like?" Frank Harold asked.

"She was beautiful," Jennifer said. Her voice softened.

"She was the loveliest ..." She remembered something.

"I have a picture of her." She took the small gold heart shaped locket from around her neck and handed it to Harold.

He looked up at her a moment, then opened the locket. On one side was a picture of Robert Stanley, and on the other side a picture of Rosa Newman. The inscription read TO R.N. WITH LOVE, R.S. The date was 1969.

Frank Harold stared at the locket for a long time.

When he looked up, his voice was husky.

"We owe you an apology, my dear." He turned to George. "This is Jennifer Stanley."

25

Carmen had been unable to get the conversation with Anita out of her mind. Anita seemed incapable of coping with the situation by herself. "Billy's trying hard. He really is... Oh, I love him so much!" He needs a lot of help, Carmen thought. I have to do something. He's my brother. I must talk to him. Carmen went to find Damon.

"Is Mr. William at home?"

"Yes, ma'am. I believe he's in his room."

"Thank you."

She thought of the scene at the table, with Anita's bruised face. "What happened?"

"I bumped into a door ..." How could she have put up with it all this time? Carmen went upstairs and knocked on the door to Billy's room. There was no answer. "Billy?"

She opened the door and stepped inside. A bitter-almond smell permeated the room. Carmen stood there a moment, and then moved toward the bathroom. She could see Billy through the open door. He was heating heroin on a piece of aluminum foil. As it began to liquefy and evaporate, she watched Billy inhale the smoke from a rolled up straw he held in his mouth. Carmen stepped into the bathroom. "Billy ...?"

He looked around and grinned. "Hi, Sis!" He turned and inhaled deeply again.

"For God's sake! Stop that!"

"Hey, relax. You know what this is called? Chasing the dragon. See the little dragon curling up in the smoke?" He was smiling happily.

"Billy, please let me talk to you."

"Sure, Sis. What can I do for you? I know it's not a money problem. We're billionaires! What are you looking so depressed about? The sun is out, and it's a beautiful day!" His eyes were glistening.

Carmen stood there looking at him, filled with compassion. "Billy, I had a talk with Anita. She told me how you got started on drugs at the hospital."

He nodded. "Yeah. Best thing that ever happened to me."

"No. It's the most terrible thing that ever happened to you. Do you have any idea what you're doing with your life?"

"Sure I do. It's called living it up, Sis!"

She took his hand and said, earnestly, "You need help."

"Me? I don't need any help. I'm fine!"

"No, you aren't. Listen to me, Billy. This is your life we're talking about, and it's not only your life. Think of Anita. For years you've put her through a living hell, and she stood for it because she loves you so much. You're not only destroying your life, you're destroying hers. You've got to do something about this now, before it's too late. It's not important how you got started on drugs. The important thing is that you get off them."

Billy's smile faded. He looked into Carmen's eyes and started to say, something, then stopped. "Carmen ... "

"Yes?"

He licked his lips. "I ... I know you're right. I want to stop. I've tried. God, how I've tried. But I can't."

"Of course, you can," she said fiercely. "You can do it. We're going to beat this together. Anita and I are behind you. Who supplies you with heroin, Billy?"

He stood there, looking at her in astonishment.

"My God! You don't know?"

Carmen shook her head. "No."
"Anita."

26

Frank Harold looked at the gold locket for a long time. "I knew your mother, Jennifer, and I liked her. She was wonderful with the Stanley children, and they adored her."

"She adored them, too," Jennifer said. "She used to talk to me about them all the time."

"What happened to your mother was terrible. You can't imagine what a scandal it created. Los Angeles can be a very small town. Robert Stanley behaved very badly. Your mother had no choice but to leave." He shook his head. "Life must have been very difficult for the two of you."

"Mother had a hard time. The awful thing was that I think she still loved Robert Stanley, in spite of everything." She looked at George. "I don't understand what's happening. Why doesn't my family want to see me?"

The two men exchanged a look. "Let me explain," George said. He hesitated, choosing his words carefully. "A short time ago, a woman showed up here, claiming to be Jennifer Stanley."

"But that's impossible!" Jennifer said. "I'm ..."

George held up a hand. "I know. The family hired a private detective to make sure she was authentic."

"And they found out that she wasn't."

"No. They found out that she was."

Jennifer looked at him, bewildered. "What?"

"This detective said he found fingerprints that the woman had taken when she got a driver's license in San Francisco when she was seventeen and they matched the prints of the woman calling herself Jennifer Stanley."

Jennifer was more puzzled than ever. "But I ... I've never been in California."

Harold said, "Jennifer, there may be an elaborate conspiracy going on to get part of the Stanley estate. I'm afraid you're caught in the middle of it."

"I can't believe it!"

"Whoever is behind this can't afford to have two Jennifer Stanley's around."

George added, "The only way the plan can work successfully is to get you out of the way."

"When you say 'out of the way' ..." She stopped, remembering something. "Oh, no!"

"What is it?" Harold asked.

"Two nights ago I talked to my roommate, and she was hysterical. She said a man came to our apartment with a knife and tried to attack her. He thought she was me!" It was difficult for Jennifer to find her voice. "Who ... who's doing this?"

"If I had to guess, I'd say it's probably a member of the family," George told her.

"But ... why?"

"There's a large fortune at stake, and the will is going to be probated in a few days."

"What does that have to do with me? My father never even acknowledged me. He wouldn't have left me anything."

Harold said, "As a matter of fact, if we can prove your identity, your share of the overall estate is more than a billion dollars."

She sat, shocked. When she found her voice, she said, "A billion dollars?"

"That's right. But someone else is after that money. That's why you're in danger."

"I see." She stood there looking at them, feeling a rising panic. "What am I going to do?"

"I'll tell you what you're not going to do," George told her. "You're not going back to a hotel. I want you to stay out of sight until we find out what's going on."

"I could go back to Florida until ..."

Harold said, "I think it would be better if you stayed here, Jennifer. We'll find a place to hide you."

"She could stay at my house," George suggested. "No one will think of looking for her there."

The two men turned to Jennifer.

She hesitated. "Well ... yes. That will be fine."

"Good."

Jennifer said slowly, "None of this would be happening if my father was alive."

"Oh, I don't like all of it," George told her. "I think he has an auto accident."

They took the service elevator to the office building garage and got into George's car.

"I don't want anyone to see you," George said. "We have to keep you out of sight for the next few days."

They started driving down State Street.

"How about some lunch?"

Jennifer looked over at him and smiled. "You always seem to be feeding me."

"I know a restaurant that's off the beaten path. It's in an old house on Gloucester Street. I don't think anyone will see us there."

L'Espalier was an elegant nineteenth-century town house with one of the finest views in Los Angeles. As George and Jennifer walked in, they were greeted by the captain.

"Good afternoon," he said. "Will you come this way, please? I have a nice table for you by the window."

"If you don't mind," George said, "we'd prefer something against the wall."

The captain blinked. "Against the wall?"

"Yes. We like privacy."

"Of course." He led them to a table in a comer. "I'll send your waiter right over." He was staring at Jennifer, and his face suddenly lit up. "Ah! Miss Stanley. It's a pleasure to have you here. I saw your picture in the newspaper. "

Jennifer looked at George, not knowing what to say. George exclaimed, "My God! We left the children in the car! Let's go get them!" And to the captain, "We'd like two martinis, very dry. Hold the olives. We'll be right back."

"Yes, sir." The captain watched the two of them hurry out of the restaurant.

"What are you doing?" Jennifer asked.

"Getting out of here. All he has to do is call the press, and we're in trouble. We'll go somewhere else."

They found a little restaurant on Dalton Street and ordered lunch.

George sat there, studying her. "How does it feel to be a celebrity?" he asked.

"Please don't joke about that. I feel terrible."

"I know," he said contritely. "I'm sorry." He was finding it very easy to be with her. He thought about how rude he had been when they first met.

"Do you ... do you really think I'm in danger, Mr. Brown?" Jennifer asked.

"Call me George. Yes. I'm afraid you are. But it will be for only a little while. By the time the will is probated, we'll know who's behind this. In the meantime, I'm going to see to it that you're safe."

"Thank you. I ... I appreciate it."

They were staring at each other, and when an approaching waiter saw the looks on their faces, he decided not to interrupt them.

In the car, George asked, "Is this your first time in Los Angeles?"

"Yes."

"It's an interesting city." They were passing the old John Hancock Building. George pointed to the tower.
"You see that beacon?".

"Yes."

"It broadcasts the weather."

"How can a beacon ...?"

"I'm glad you asked. When the light is a steady blue, it means the weather is clear. If it's a flashing blue, you can expect clouds to be near. A steady red means rain ahead, and flashing red, snow instead."

Jennifer laughed. George slowed down.

"This is a small bridge in Los Angeles."

Jennifer turned to stare at him. "I beg your pardon?"

George grinned. "It's true."

"What's a Smoot?"

"A Smoot is a measurement using the body of Oliver San Francisco Smoot, who was five feet seven inches. It started as a joke, but when the city rebuilt the bridge, they kept the David. The Smoot became a standard of length in 1958."

She laughed. "That's incredible!"

As they passed the Bunker Hill Monument, Jennifer exclaimed, "Oh! That's where the Battle of Bunker Hill took place, isn't it?"
"No," George said.

"What do you mean?"

"The Battle of Bunker Hill was fought on San Francisco's Hill."

George's home was in the Newbury Street area of Los Angeles, a charming two-story house with comfortable furniture and colorful prints hanging on the walls.

"Do you live here alone?" Jennifer asked.

"Yes. I have a housekeeper who comes in twice a week. I'm going to tell her not to come in for the next few days. I don't want anyone to know you're here."

Jennifer looked at George and said warmly, "I want you to know I really appreciate what you're doing for me."

"My pleasure. Come on, I'll show you your bedroom."

He led her upstairs to the guest room. "This is it. I hope you'll be comfortable."

"Oh, yes. It's lovely," Jennifer said.

"I'll bring in some groceries. I usually eat out."

"I could..." She stopped. "On second thought, I'd better not. My roommate says my cooking is lethal."

"I think I'm a fair... hand at a stove," George said. "I'll do some cooking for us." He looked at her and said slowly. "I haven't had anyone to cook for a while."

Back off, he told himself. You're way off base. You couldn't keep her in handkerchiefs.

"I want you to make yourself at home. You'll be completely safe here."

She looked at him a long time, and then smiled. "Thank you."

They went back downstairs. George pointed out the amenities. "Television; VCR, radio, CD player... You'll be comfortable."

"It's wonderful." She wanted to say, "Just like I feel with you."

"Well, if there's nothing else," he said awkwardly. Jennifer gave him a warm smile. "I can't think of anything."

"Then I'll be getting back to the office. I have a lot of questions without answers."

She watched him walk toward the door.

"George?"

He turned around. "Yes?"

"Is it all right if I call my roommate? She'll be worried about me."

He shook his head. "Absolutely not. I don't want you to make any telephone calls or leave this house. Your life may depend on it."

27

"I'm Dr. Weissman. Do you understand that this conversation is going to be tape-recorded?"

"Yes, Doctor."

"Are you feeling calmer now?"

"I'm calm, but I'm angry."

"What are you angry about?"

"I shouldn't be in this place. I'm not crazy. I've been framed."

"Oh? Who framed you?"

"Thomas Stanley."

"Judge Thomas Stanley?"

"That's right."

"Why would he want to do that?"

"For money."

"Do you have money?"

"No. I mean, yes ... that is ... I could have had it.

He promised me a million dollars, and a sable coat, and jewelry."

"Why would Judge Stanley promise you that?"

"Let me start at the beginning. I'm not really Jennifer Stanley. My name is Mary Perkins."

"When you came in here, you insisted you were Jennifer Stanley."

"Forget that. I'm really not. Look ... here's what happened. Judge Stanley hired me to pose as his sister. "

"Why did he do that?"

"So I could get a share of the Stanley estate and turn it over to him."

"And for doing that he promised you a million dollars, a sable coat; and some jewelry?"

"You don't believe me, do you? Well, I can prove it. He took me to Bell Air. That's where the Stanley family lives in Los Angeles. I can describe the house to you, and I can tell you all about the family."

"You're aware that these are very serious charges you're making?"

"You bet I am. But I suppose you won't do anything about it because he happens to be a judge."

"You're quite wrong. I assure you that your charges will be very thoroughly investigated."

"Good! I want the bastard locked away the way he has me locked away. I want out of here!"

"You understand that besides my examination, two of my colleagues also will have to evaluate your mental state?"

"Let them. I'm as sane as you are."

"Dr. Clifton will be in this afternoon, and then we'll decide how we're going to proceed."

"The sooner, the better. I can't stand this damned place!"

When the matron brought Mary her lunch, the matron said, "I just talked to Dr. Clifton. He'll be here in an hour."

"Thank you." Mary was ready for him. She was ready for all of them. She was going to tell them everything she knew, from the very beginning. And when I'm through, Mary thought, they're going to lock him up and let me go. The thought filled her with satisfaction. I'll be free! And then Mary thought, Free to do what? I'll be out on the streets again. Maybe they'll even revoke my parole and put me back in the joint!

She threw her lunch tray against the wall. Damn them!

They can't do this to me! Yesterday I was worth a million dollars, and today... Wait! Wait! An idea flashed through Mary's mind that was so exciting that it sent a chill through her. Holy God! What am I doing? I've already proved that I'm Jennifer Stanley. I have witnesses. The whole family heard Fredy Tillman say that my fingerprints showed that I was Jennifer Stanley. Why the hell would I ever want to be Mary Perkins when I can be Jennifer Stanley? No wonder they have me locked up in here. I must have been out of my mind! She rang the bell for the matron.

When the matron came in, Mary said excitedly, "I want to see the doctor right away!"

"I know. You have an appointment with him in..."

"Now. Right now!"

The matron took one look at Mary's expression and said, "Calm down. I'll get him."

Ten minutes later, Dr. Frank Clifton walked into Mary's room. "You asked to see me?"

"Yes." She smiled apologetically. "I'm afraid I've been playing a little game, Doctor."

"Really?"

"Yes. It's very embarrassing. You see, the truth is that I was very upset with my brother, Thomas, and I wanted to punish him. But I realize now that that was wrong. I'm not upset anymore, and I want to go home to Rose Hill."

"I read the transcript of your interview this morning.You said that your name was Mary Perkins and that you were framed... "

Mary laughed. "That was naughty of me. I just said that to upset Thomas. No. I'm Jennifer Stanley." He looked at her. "Can you prove that?"

This was the moment Mary had been waiting for.

"Oh, yes!" she said triumphantly. "Thomas proved it himself. He hired a private detective named Fredy Tillman, who matched my fingerprints with prints I had made for a driver's license when I was younger. They're real. There's no question about it."

"Detective Fredy Tillman, you say?"

"That's right. He does work for the district attorney's office here in San Francisco."

He studied her a moment. "Now, you're certain of this?' You're not, Mary Perkins-you're Jennifer Stanley?"

"Absolutely."

"And this private detective, Fredy Tillman, can verify that?"

She smiled. "He already has. All you have to do is call the district attorney's office and get hold of him."

Dr. Clifton nodded. "All right. I'll do that."

At ten o'clock the following morning, Dr. Clifton, accompanied by the matron, returned to Mary's room.

"Good morning."

"Good morning, Doctor." She looked at him eagerly.

"Did you talk to Fredy Tillman?"

"Yes. I want to be sure that I understand this. Your story about Judge Stanley's involving you in some kind of conspiracy was false?"

"Completely. I said that because I wanted to punish for my brother. But everything is all right now. I'm ready to go home."

"Fredy Tillman can prove that you're Jennifer Stanley?"

"Absolutely."

Dr. Clifton turned to the matron and nodded. She signaled to someone. A tall, lean black man walked into the room.

He looked at Mary and said, "I'm Fredy Tillman. Can I help you?"

He was a complete stranger.

28

And at least she was in New York, center of the American fashion industry. The showroom was decorated in muted shades of aubergine which would not detract from the clothes. The fashion show was going well. The models moved gracefully along the runway, and each new design received enthusiastic applause. The ballroom was packed. Every seat was occupied, and there were standees in the rear.

Backstage there was a stir, and Carmen turned to see what was happening. Two uniformed policemen were making their way toward her.

Carmen's heart began to race.

One of the policemen said, "Are you Carmen Stanley Renaux?"

"Yes."

"I'm placing you under arrest for the murder of Amy Nelson."

"No!" she screamed. "I didn't mean to do it! It was an accident! Please! Please! Please ...!"

She woke up in a panic, her body trembling.

It was a recurring nightmare. I can't go on like this, Carmen thought. I can't! I have to do something.

She wanted desperately to talk to David. He had reluctantly returned to New York. "I have a job to do, darling. They won't let me take any more time off."

"I understand, David. I'll be back there in a few days. I have to get a show ready."

Carmen was leaving for New York that afternoon, but before she went, there was something she felt she had to do. The conversation with Billy had been very disturbing. He's blaming his problems on Anita.

Carmen found Anita on the veranda.

"Good morning," Carmen said.

"Good morning."

Carmen took a seat opposite her. "I have to talk to you."

"Yes?"

It was awkward. "I had a talk with Billy. He's in bad shape. He ... he thinks that you're the one who's been supplying him with heroin."

"He told you that?"

"Yes."

There was a long pause. "Well, it's true."

Carmen stared at her in disbelief. "What? I ... I don't understand. You told me you were trying to get him off drugs. Why would you want to keep him addicted?"

"You really don't understand, do you?" Her tone was bitter. "You live in your own little goddamned world. Well, let me tell you something, Miss Famous Designer! I was a waitress when Billy got me pregnant. I never expected William Stanley to marry me. And do you know why he did? So he could feel he was better than his father. Well, Billy married me, all right. And everybody treated me like dirt. When my brother, Harold, came down for the wedding, they acted like he was some kind of trash."

"Anita ..."

"To tell you the truth, I was dumbfounded when your brother said he wanted to marry me. I didn't even know if it was his baby. I could have been a good wife to Billy, but no one even gave me a chance. To them I was still a waitress. I didn't lose the baby, I had an abortion. I thought maybe Billy would divorce me, but he didn't. I was his token symbol of how democratic he was. Well, let me tell you something, lady. I don't need that. I'm as good as you or anyone else."

Each word was a blow. "Did you ever love Billy?"

Anita shrugged. "He was good-looking and fun, but then he had that bad fall during the polo game, and everything changed. The hospital gave him drugs, and when he got out, they expected him to stop taking them. One night, he was

341

in pain, and I said, 'I have a little treat for you.' And after that, whenever he was in pain, I gave him his little treat. Pretty soon he needed it, whether he was in pain or not. My brother is a pusher, and I was able to get the entire heroin I needed. I made Billy beg me for it. And sometimes I'd tell him I was out of it just to watch him sweat and cry-oh, how Mr. William Stanley needed me! He wasn't so high and mighty then! I goaded him into hitting me, and then he'd feel terrible about what he had done, and he'd come crawling back to me with gifts. You see, when Billy is off dope, I'm nothing. When he's on it, I'm the one who has the power. He may be a Stanley, and maybe I was only a waitress, but I control him."

Carmen was staring at her in horror.

"Your brother's tried to quit, all right. When it got real bad, his friends would get him into a detox center, and I'd go visit him and watch the great Stanley suffer the agonies of hell. And each time he came out, I'd be waiting for him with my little treat. It was payback time."

Carmen was finding it hard to breathe. "You're a monster," she said slowly. "I want you to leave."

"You bet! I can't wait to get out of this place." She grinned. "Of course, I'm not leaving for nothing. How much of a settlement will I get?"

"Whatever it is," Carmen said, "it will be too much. Now get out of here."

"Right." Then she added with an affected tone, "I'll have my lawyer call your lawyer."

"She's really leaving me?"

"Yes."

"That means ..."

"I know what it means, Billy. Can you handle it?" He looked at his sister and smiled. "I think so. Yes. I think I can."

"I'm sure of it."

He took a deep breath. "Thanks, Carmen. I would never have had the courage to get rid of her."

She smiled. "What are sisters for?"

That afternoon, Carmen left for New York. The fashion showing would be in one week.

Clothing is the single biggest business in New York.

A successful fashion designer can have an effect on the economy all around the world. A designer's whim has a far-flung impact on everyone from Blackburn pickers in India to Scottish weavers to silkworms in China and Japan. It has an effect on the wool industry and the silk industry. The Donna Karan and Calvin Klein's and Ralph Laurens are a major economic influence, and Carmen had arrived in that category. It was rumored that she was about to be named the Women's Wear Designer of the Year by the Council of

Fashion Designers of America, the most prestigious award a designer could receive.

Carmen Stanley Renaux led a busy life. In September, she looked at large assortments of fabrics, and in October, she selected the ones she wanted for her new designs. December and January were devoted to designing the new fashions, and in February, to refining them. In April, she was ready to show her fall collection.

Carmen Stanley Designs was, located at 550 Seventh Avenue, sharing the building with Bill Blass and Oscar de la Renta. Her next showing was going to be at the Bryant Park tent, which could seat up to a thousand people.

When Carmen arrived at her office, Cristina said, "I've got good news. The showing is completely booked!"

"Thank you," Carmen said absently. Her mind was on other things.

"By the way, there's a letter marked URGENT for you on your desk. It was just delivered by messenger."

The words sent a jolt through Carmen's body. She walked over to her desk and looked at the envelope. The return address was Wild Animal Protection Association, 3000 Park Avenue,

New York, New York. She stared at it for a long time. There was no 3000 Park Avenue. Carmen opened the letter with trembling fingers.

Dear Mrs. Renaux,

My Swiss banker informs me that he has not yet received the million dollars that my association requested. In view of your delinquency, I must inform you that our needs have been increased to 5 million dollars. If this payment is made, I promise we will not bother you again. You have fifteen days to deposit the money in our account. If you fail to do so, I regret that we shall have to communicate with the appropriate authorities.

It was unsigned.

Carmen stood there in a panic, reading it over and over, again and again. Five million dollars! It's impossible, she thought. I can never raise that kind of money that quickly. What a fool I was!

When David came home that night, Carmen showed him the letter.

"Five million dollars!" he exploded. "That's ridiculous! Who do they think you are?"

"They know who I am," Carmen said. "That's the problem. I've got to get hold of some money quickly. But how?"

"I don't know ... I suppose a bank would loan you money against your inheritance, but I don't like the idea of… "

"David, it's my life I'm talking about. Our lives. I'm going to see about getting that loan."

Greg Coleman was the vice president in charge of the New York Union Bank. He was in his forties and had worked his way up from a junior teller. He was an ambitious man. One day I'll be on the board of directors, he thought, and after that ... who knows? His thoughts were interrupted by his secretary.

"Miss Carmen Stanley is here to see you."

He felt a small frisson of pleasure. She had been a good customer as a successful designer, but now she was one of the wealthiest women in the world. He had tried for several years to get Robert Stanley's account, without success. And now...

"Show her in," Coleman told his secretary.

When Carmen walked into his office, Coleman rose and greeted her with a smile and a warm handshake.
"I'm so pleased to see you," he said. "Do sit down. Some coffee or something stronger?"

"No, thanks," Carmen said.

"I want to offer my condolences on the death of your father." His voice was suitably grave.

"Thank you."

"What can I do for you?" He knew what she was going to say. She was going to turn her billions over to him to invest...

"I want to borrow some money."

He blinked. "I beg your pardon?"

"I need five million dollars.".

He thought rapidly. According to the newspapers, her share of the estate should be more than a billion dollars. Even with taxes... He smiled. "Well, I don't think there will be any problem. You've always been one of our favorite customers, you know. What security would you like to put up?"

"I'm an heir in my father's will."

He nodded. "Yes. I read that."

"I'd like to borrow the money against my share of the estate."

"I see. Has your father's will been probated yet?"

"No, but it will be soon."

"That's fine." He leaned forward. "Of course, we'd have to see a copy of the will."

"Yes," Carmen said eagerly. "I can arrange that."

"And we would have to know the exact amount of your share of the inheritance."

"I don't know the exact amount," Carmen said. "Well, the banking laws are quite strict, you know. Probates can take some time. Why don't you come back after the probate, and I'll be happy to ..."

"I need the money now," Carmen said desperately.

She wanted to scream.

"Oh, dear. Naturally, we want to do everything we can to accommodate you." He raised his hands in a helpless gesture. "But unfortunately, our hands are tied until..."

Carmen rose to her feet. "Thank you."

"As soon as ..."

She was gone.

When Carmen returned to the office, Cristina said excitedly, "I have to talk to you."

She was in no mood to hear Cristina's problems.

"What is it?" Carmen asked.

"My husband called me a few minutes ago. His company is transferring him to Paris. So, I'll be leaving."

"You're going ... going to Paris?"

Cristina beamed. "Yes! Isn't that wonderful? I'll be sorry to leave you. But don't worry. I'll stay in touch."

So it was Cristina. But there's no way to prove it. First the mink coat and now Paris. With five million dollars, she can afford to live anywhere in the world. How do I handle this? If I tell her that I know, she'll deny it. Maybe she'll demand more. David will know what to do.

"Cristina ..."

One of Carmen's assistants came in. "Carmen! I have to talk to you about the bridge collection. I don't think we have enough designs for..."

Carmen could bear no more. "Excuse me. I don't feel well. I'm going home."

Her assistant looked at her in amazement. "But we're in the middle of!"

"I'm sorry."

And Carmen was gone.

When Carmen walked into her apartment, it was empty.

David was working late. She looked around at all the beautiful things in the room, and thought, They'll never stop until they take everything. They're going to blinded me dry. David was right. I should have gone to the police that night. Now I'm a criminal. I've got to confess. Now, while I have the courage. She sat there, thinking about what this was going to do to her, to David, and to her family. There would be lurid headlines, and a trial, and probably prison. It would be the end of her career. But I can't go on like this, Carmen thought. I'll go crazy.

Almost in a daze, she got up and walked into David's den. She remembered that he kept his typewriter on a shelf in the closet. She took it down and put it on the desk. She rolled a sheet of paper into the platen and began to type.

To Whom It May Concern:

My name is Carmen

She stopped. The letter E was broken.

"Why, David? For God's sake, why?" Carmen's voice was filled with anguish.

"It was your fault."

"No! I told you...It was an accident! I ..."

"I'm not talking about the accident. I'm talking about you! The big successful wife who was too busy to find time for her husband."

It was as though he had slapped her. "That's not true. I..."

"All you ever thought about was yourself, Carmen. Everywhere we went, you were always the star. You let me tag along like a pet poodle."

"That's not fair!" she said.

"Isn't it? You go off to your fashion shows all over the world so you can get your picture in the papers, and I'm sitting here alone, waiting for you to return. Do you think I liked being 'Mr. Carmen'? I wanted a wife. Don't worry, my darling Carmen. I make comfortable myself with other women while you were gone."

Her face was pale.

"They were real flesh-and-blood women, who had time for me. Not some damned made-upempty shell."

"Stop it!" Carmen cried.

"When you told me about the accident, I saw a way to become free of you. Do you want to know something, my dear? I enjoyed watching you squirm when you read those letters. It paid me back a little for all the humiliation I've gone through."

"That's enough! Pack your bags and get out of here. I never want to see you again!"

David smile broadly. "There's very little chance of that. By the way, do you still plan to go to the police?"

"Get out!" Carmen said. "Now!"

"I'm leaving. I think I'll go back to Paris. And, darling, I won't tell if you won't. You're safe."

An hour later, he was gone.

At nine o'clock in the morning, Carmen put in a call to George Brown.

"Good morning, Mrs. Renaux. What can I do for you?"

"I'm returning to Los Angeles this afternoon," Carmen said. "I have a confession to make."

She was seated across from George, looking pale and drawn. She sat there frozen, unable to begin.

George prompted her. "You said you had a confession to make."

"Yes. I ... I killed someone." She began to cry. "It was an accident, but ... I ran away." Her face was a mask of anguish. "I ran away ... and left her there."

"Take it easy," George said. "Start at the beginning."

She began to talk.

Thirty minutes later, George looked out his window, thinking about what he had just heard.

"And you want to go to the police?"

"Yes. It was what I should have done in the first place. I ... I don't care what they do to me anymore."

George said thoughtfully, "Since you're giving yourself up voluntarily and it was an accident, I think the court will be lenient."

She was trying to control herself. "I just want it over with."

"What about your husband?"

She looked up. "What about him?"

"Blackmail is against the law. You have the number of the account in Switzerland where you sent the money he stole from you. All you have to do is press charges and..."

"No!" Her tone was fierce. "I don't want anything more to do with him. Let him go on with his life. I want to get on with mine."

George nodded. "Whatever you say. I'm going to take you down to police headquarters. You may have to spend the night in jail, but I'll have you bailed out very quickly."

Carmen smiled in a weak and tired manner. "Now I can do something I've never done before."

"What's that?"

"Design a dress in stripes."

That evening, when he got home, George told Jennifer what had happened.

Jennifer was horrified. "Her own husband was black-mailing her? That's terrible." She studied him for a long time. "I think it's wonderful that you spend your life helping people in trouble."

George looked at her and thought, I'm the one in trouble. George Brown was awakened by the aroma of fresh coffee and the smell of cooking bacon. He sat up in bed, startled. Had the housekeeper come in today? He had told her not to. George put on his robe and slippers, and hurried down to the kitchen. Jennifer was in there, preparing breakfast. She looked up as George entered.

"Good morning," she said cheerfully. "How do you like your eggs?"

"Uh ... scrambled."

"Right. Scrambled eggs and bacon are my specialty. As a matter of fact, my one specialty. I told you, I'm a terrible cook."

George smiled. "You don't have to cook. If you wanted to, you could hire a few hundred chefs."

"Am I really going to get that much money, George?"

"That's right. Your share of the estate will be over a billion dollars."

She found it difficult to swallow. "A billion ...? I don't believe it."

"It's true."

"There's not that much money in the world, George."

"Well, your father had most of what there was."

"I ... I don't know what to say."

"Then may I say something?"

"Of course."

"The eggs are burning."

"Oh, Sorry." She quickly took them off the stove.

"I'll make another batch."

"Don't bother. The burned bacon will be enough." She laughed. "I'm sorry."

George walked over to the cabinet and took out a box of cereal. "How about a nice cold breakfast?"

"Perfect," Jennifer said.

He poured some cereal into a bowl for each of them, took the milk out of the refrigerator, and they sat down at the kitchen table.

"Don't you have someone to cook for you?" Jennifer asked.

"You mean, am I involved with anyone?"

She blushed. "Something like that."

"No. I was in a relationship for two years, but it didn't work out."

"I'm sorry."

"What about you?" George asked.

She thought of Alan Walker. "I don't think so."

He looked at her, curious. "You aren't sure?"

"It's difficult to explain. One of us wants to get married," she said tactfully, "and one of us doesn't."

"I see. When this is over, will you be going back to Miami?"

"I honestly don't know. It seems so strange, being here. My mother talked to me so often about Los Angeles. She was born here, and loved it. In a way, it's like coming home. I wish I could have known my father."

No, you don't, George thought.

"Did you know him?"

"No. He dealt only with Frank Harold."

They sat there talking for more than an hour, and there was an easy camaraderie between them. George filled Jennifer in on what had happened earlier-the arrival of the stranger who called herself Jennifer Stanley, the empty grave, and Donald Herman's 'disappearance.

"That's incredible!" Jennifer said. "Who could be behind this?"

"I don't know, but I'm trying to find out," George assured her. "In the meantime, you'll be safe here. Very safe."

She smiled, and said, "I feel safe here. Thank you." He started to say something, and then stopped. He looked at his watch. "I'd better get dressed and get down to the office. I have a lot to do."

George was meeting with Harold.

"Any progress yet?" Harold asked.

George shook his head. "It's all smoke. Whoever planned this is a genius. I'm trying to trace Donald Herman. He flew from Corsica to Paris to Australia. I spoke to the Sydney police. They were stunned to learn that Herman is in their country. There's a circular out from Interpol, and they're looking for him. I think Robert Stanley signed his own death warrant when he called here and said he wanted to change his will. Someone decided to stop him. The only witness to what happened that night is Donald Herman. When we find him, we'll know a lot more."

"I wonder if we should bring our police in on this." Harold suggested.

George shook his head "What we know is all circumstantial, Frank. The only crime we can prove is that someone dug up a body-and we don't even know who did that."

"What about the detective they hired, who verified the woman's fingerprints?"

"Fredy Tillman. I've left three messages for him. If I don't hear back from him by six o'clock tonight, I'm going to fly to San Francisco. I believe he's deeply involved."

"What do you suppose was meant to happen to the shares of the estate that the impostor was going to get?"

"My hunch is that whoever planned this had her sign her share over to them. The person probably used some dummy trusts to hide it. I'm convinced that we're looking for a member of the family ...I think we can eliminate Carmen as a suspect." He told Harold about the conversation he had had with her. "If she were behind this, she wouldn't have come forth with a confession, not at this time, anyway. She would have waited until the estate was settled and she had the money. As far as her husband is concerned, I think we can eliminate David. He's a small-time blackmailer. He isn't capable of setting up anything like this."

"What about the others?"

"Judge Stanley. I talked to a friend of mine with the San Francisco Bar Association. My friend says everyone thinks very highly of Stanley. In fact, he's just been appointed chief judge. Another thing in his favor: Judge Stanley was the one who said that the first Jennifer who appeared was a fraud, and he was the one who insisted on a DNA test. I doubt he'd do something like this. Billy interests me. I'm pretty sure he's on drugs, and that's an expensive habit. I checked on his wife, Anita. She isn't smart enough to be behind this scheme. But there's a rumor she has a brother who's bad business. I'm going to look into it."

George spoke to his secretary on the intercom. "Please get me Lieutenant Michael Kennedy of the Los Angeles police."

A few minutes later, she buzzed George. "Lieutenant Kennedy is on line one."

George picked up the phone.

"Lieutenant. Thank you for taking my call. I'm George Brown with REYNOLDS & FRANK HAROLD ATTORNEYS AT LAW. We're trying to locate a relative in the matter of the Robert Stanley estate."

"Mr. Brown, I'd be glad to help if I can."

"Would you please check with the New York City police to see if they have any files on Mrs. William Stanley's brother-in-law? His name is Harold King, He works in the Bronx."

"No problem. I'll get back to you."

"Thanks."

After lunch, Frank Harold stopped by George's office.

"How's the investigation going?" he asked.

"Too slow to suit me. Whoever planned this covered his or her tracks pretty thoroughly."

"How is Jennifer holding up?"

George smiled. "She's wonderful."

There was something in the tone of his voice that made Frank Harold take a closer look at him.

"She's a very attractive young lady."

"I know," George said wistfully. "I know."

An hour later, the call came in from Australia.

"Mr. Brown?"

"Yes."

"Chief Inspector McFarlin here from Sydney."

"Yes, Chief Inspector."

"We found your man."

George felt his heart jump. "That's wonderful! I'd like to arrange immediate extradition to bring him ..."

"Oh, I don't think there's any hurry. Donald Herman is dead."

George felt his heart sink. "What?"

"We found his body a little while ago. His right hand had been cut off, and he had been shot several times."

"The Russian gangs have a quaint custom. First they cut off your hand, then they let you to be blind, and then they shoot you. "

"I see. Thank you, Inspector."

Dead end. George sat there, staring at the wall. All his leads were disappearing. He realized how heavily he had been counting on Donald Herman's testimony.

George's secretary interrupted his thoughts. "There's a Mr. Tillman for you on line three."

George looked at his watch. It was 5:55 P.M. He picked up the telephone. "Mr. Tillman?"

"Yes ... I'm sorry I couldn't return your calls earlier. I've been out of town for the past two days. What can I do for you?"

A lot, George thought. You can tell me how you faked those fingerprints. George chose his words carefully. "I'm calling about Jennifer Stanley. When you were in Los Angeles recently, you checked out her fingerprints and ..."

"Mr.Brown..."

"Yes?"

"I've never been in Los Angeles."

George took a deep breath. "Mr. Tillman, according to the register at the Holiday Inn, you were here on ..."

"Someone has been using my name."

George listened, stunned. It was the final dead end, the last lead. "I don't suppose you have any idea who it is?"

"Well, it's very strange, Mr. Brown. A woman claimed that I was in Los Angeles and that I could identify her as Jennifer Stanley I'd never seen her before in my life."

George felt a surge of hope. "Do you know who she is?"

"Yes. Her name is Perkins. Mary Perkins."

George picked up a pen. "Where can I reach her?"

"She's in San Francisco Mental Health Facility."

"Thanks a lot. I really appreciate this."

"Let's keep in touch. I'd like to know what's going on. I don't like people going around impersonating me."

"Right." George replaced the receiver. Mary Perkins.

When George got home that evening, Jennifer was waiting to greet him.

I fixed dinner," she told him. "Well, I didn't exactly fix it. Do you like Chinese food?"

He smiled. "Love it!"

"Good. We have eight cartons of it."

When George walked into the dining room, the table was set with flowers and candles.

"Is there any news?" Jennifer asked.

George said cautiously, "We may have gotten our first break. I have the name of a woman who seems to be involved in this. I'm flying to San Francisco in the morning to talk with her. I have a feeling we may have all the answers tomorrow."

"That would be wonderful!" Jennifer said excitedly.

"I'll be so glad when this is over."

"So will I," George told her. Or will I? She'll be a real part of the Stanley family-way out of my reach. Dinner lasted two hours, and they were not even aware of what they were eating. They talked about everything and they talked about nothing, and it was as though they had known each other forever. They discussed the past and the present, and they carefully avoided talking about the future. There is no future for us, George thought unhappily.

Finally, reluctantly, George said, "Well, we'd better go to bed."

She looked at him with raised eyebrows, and they both burst out laughing.

"What I meant ..."

"I know what you meant. Good night, George."

"Good night, Jennifer."

29

Early the following morning, George boarded a United flight for San Francisco. From San Francisco's Airport he took a taxi.

"Where to?" the driver asked.

"San Francisco Mental Health Facility."

The driver turned around and looked at George. "Are you okay?"

"Yes. Why?"

"Just asking."

At the Facility, George approached the uniformed security guard at the front desk.

The guard looked up. "Can I help you?"

"Yes. I'd like to see Mary Perkins."

"Is she an employee?"

That had not occurred to George. "I'm not sure."

The guard took a closer look at him. "You're not sure?"

"All I know is that she's here."

The guard reached in a drawer and took out a roster with a list of names. After a moment, he said, "She doesn't work here. Could she be a patient?"

"I ... I don't know. It's possible."

The guard gave George another look, then reached into a different drawer and pulled out a computer printout. He scanned it, and in the middle, he stopped. "Perkins. Mary."

"That's right." He was surprised. "Is she a patient here?"

"Uh-huh. Are you a relative?"

"No ..."

"Then I'm afraid you can't see her."

"I have to see her," George said. "It's very important."

"Sorry. I have my orders. Unless you've been cleared before hand, you can't visit any of the patients."

"Who's in charge here?" George asked.

"I am."

"I mean, in charge of the hospital."

"Dr. Kimbal."

"I want to see him."

"Right." The guard picked up the telephone and dialed a number. "Dr. Kimbal, this is Joe at the front desk. There's a gentleman here who wants to see you."

He looked up at George. "Your name?"

"George Brown. I'm an attorney."

"George Brown. He's an attorney ... right." He replaced the receiver and turned to George. "Someone will be along to take you to his office."

Five minutes later, George was escorted into the office of Dr. Gary Kimbal. Kimbal was a man in his fifties, but he looked older and careworn.

"What can I do for you, Mr. Brown?"

"I need to see a patient you have here. Mary Perkins."

"Ab, yes. Interesting case. Are you related to her?"

"No, but I'm investigating a possible murder, and it's very important that I talk to her. I think she may be a key to it."

"I'm sorry. I can't help you."

"You have to," George said. "It's ..."

"Mr. Brown, I couldn't help you even if I wanted to."

"Why not?"

"Because Mary Perkins is in a padded cell. She attacks everyone who goes near her. This morning, she tried to kill a matron and two doctors."

"What?"

"She keeps changing her identity and screaming for her brother, Thomas, and the crew of her yacht. The only way we can quiet her is to keep her heavily sedated."

"Oh, my God," George said. "Do you have any idea when she might come out of it?"

Dr. Kimbal shook his head. "She's under close observation. Perhaps in time she'll calm down, and we can reevaluate her condition. Until then ..."

30

At six A.M., a harbor patrol boat was cruising along the Newport Beach close to Santa Ana River, when one of the policemen aboard spotted an object floating in the water ahead.

"Off the starboard bow!" he called. "It looks like a log. Let's pick it up before it sinks something."

The log turned out to be a body, and even more startling, a body that had been embalmed.

The policeman stared down at it and said, "How the hell did an embalmed body get into Santa Ana River?"

Lieutenant Michael Kennedy was talking to the coroner.

"Are you sure of that?"

The coroner replied, "Absolutely. It's Robert Stanley.

I embalmed him myself. Later, we had an exhumation order, and when we dug up the coffin ... Well, you know, we reported it to the police."

"Who asked to have the body exhumed?"

"The family. They handled it through their attorney, Frank Harold."

"I think I'll have a talk with Mr. Frank Harold."

When George returned to Los Angeles from San Francisco, he went directly to Frank Harold's office.

"You look beat," Harold said.

"Not beat-beaten. The whole thing is falling apart, Frank. We had three possible leads: Donald Herman, Fredy Tillman, and Mary Perkins. Well, Herman is dead, it's the wrong Tillman, and Mary Perkins is locked away in an asylum. We have nothing...!"

The voice of Harold's secretary came over the intercom. "Excuse me. There's a Lieutenant Kennedy here to see you, Mr. Frank Harold."

"Send him in."

Michael Kennedy was a rugged-looking man with eyes that had seen everything.

"Mr. Frank Harold?"

"Yes. This is my associate George Brown. I believe you two have spoken on the phone. Sit down. What can we do for you?"

"We just found the body of Robert Stanley."

"What? Where?"

"Swimming in the Pacific Ocean close to Santa Ana River. You ordered his body dug up, didn't you?"

"Yes."

"May I ask why?" Harold told him.

When Harold was finished, Kennedy said, "You have no idea who it was that posed as this investigator, Tillman?"

"No. I talked to Tillman." George answered. "He has no idea, either."

Kennedy sighed. "It gets 'curiouser and curiouser.' "Where is Robert Stanley's body now?" George asked. "They're keeping him at the morgue for the present.

I hope he doesn't disappear again."

"I do, too," George said. "We'll have Paul Weissman run a DNA test on Jennifer."

When George called Thomas to tell him that his father's body had been found, Thomas was genuinely shocked.

"That's terrible!" he said. "Who could have done a thing like that?"

"That's what we're trying to find out," George told him.

Thomas was furious. That incompetent idiot, Brooks. He's going to pay for this. I have to get this settled before it gets out of hand. "Mr. Brown, as you may be aware, I've been appointed chief judge of San Francisco. I have a very heavy caseload, and they're pressuring me to return. I can't delay much longer. I'd appreciate it if you could do something to get the probate finished quickly."

"I put in a call this morning," George told him. "It should be closed within the next three days."

"That will be fine. Keep me informed, please."

"I'll do that, Judge."

George sat in his office reviewing the events of the past few weeks. He recalled the conversation he had had with Chief Inspector McFarlin.

"We found his body a little while ago. His right hand had been cut off, and he had been shot several times. "But wait, George thought. There's something he didn't tell me. He picked up the telephone and put in another call to Australia.

The voice on the other end of the telephone said,

"This is Chief Inspector McFarlin."

"Yes, Inspector. This is George Brown. I forgot to ask you a question. When you found Donald Herman's body, were there any papers on him? ... I see ... that's fine... Thank you very much."

When George hung up the phone, his secretary's voice came over the intercom. "Lieutenant Kennedy is holding on line two."

George punched the phone button.

"Lieutenant. Sorry to keep you waiting. I was on an overseas call."

"The NYPD gave me some interesting information on Harold King. He seems to be quite a slippery character."

George picked up a pen. "Go ahead."

"The police believe that the Brooksy he works for is a front for a drug ring." The lieutenant paused, then continued. "King is probably a drug pusher. But he's clever. They haven't been able to nail him yet."

"Anything else?" George asked.

"The police believe the operation is tied into the French mafia with a connection through Marseilles. If I learn anything else, I'll call."

"Thanks, lieutenant. That's very helpful."

George put down the phone and headed out the office door.

When George arrived home, filled with anticipation, he called, "Jennifer?"

There was no answer.

He began to panic. "Jennifer!" She's been kidnapped or killed, he thought, and he felt a sudden sense of alarm. Jennifer appeared at the top of the stairs. "George?"

He took a deep breath. "I thought ..." He was pale.

"Are you all right?"

"Yes."

She came down the stairs. "Did things go well in San Francisco?"

He shook his head. "I'm afraid not." He told her what had happened. "We're going to have a reading of the will on Thursday, Jennifer. That's only three days from now. Whoever is behind this has to get rid of you by then or his--or her-plan can't work."

She swallowed. "I see. Do you have any idea who it is?"

"As a matter of fact ..." The telephone rang. "Excuse me." George picked up the telephone. "Hello?"

"This is Dr. Thompson in Florida. Sorry I didn't call earlier, but I've been away."

"Dr. Thompson. Thank you for returning my call. Our firm represents the Stanley estate."

"What can I do for you?"

"I'm calling about William Stanley. I believe he's a patient of yours."

"Yes."

"Does he have a drug problem, Doctor?"

"Mr. Brown, I'm not at liberty to discuss any of my patients."

I understand. I'm not asking this out of curiosity. It's very important"

"I'm afraid I can't."

"You did have him admitted to the Harbor Group Clinic in Jupiter, didn't you?"

There was a long hesitation. "Yes. That's a matter of record."

"Thank you, Doctor. That's all I needed to know." George replaced the receiver and stood there a moment.
"It's unbelievable!"

"What?" Jennifer asked.

"Sit down ..."

Thirty minutes later, George was in his car headed for Bell Air. All the pieces had finally feet into place. He's brilliant. It almost worked. It could still work if anything happened to Jennifer, George thought. At Bell Air, Damon answered the door. "Good evening, Mr. Brown."

"Good evening, Damon. Is Judge Stanley in?"

"He's in the library. I'll tell him you're here."

"Thank you." He watched Damon walk off.

A minute later, the butler returned. "Judge Stanley will see you now."

"Thank you."

George walked into the library. Thomas was sitting in front of a chess board, concentrating. He looked up as George walked in.

"You wanted to see me?"

"Yes. I believe the young woman who came to see you several days ago is the real Jennifer. The other Jennifer was a fake."

"But that's not possible."

"I'm afraid it's true, and I've found out who's behind all this."

There was a momentary silence. Then Thomas said slowly, "You have?"

"Yes. I'm afraid this is going to shock you. It's your brother, Billy."

Thomas was looking up at George in amazement. "Are you saying that Billy is responsible for what's been happening?"

"That's right."

"I ... I can't believe it."

"Neither could I, but it all checks out. I talked to his doctor in Bell Air. Did you know your brother is on drugs?"

"I ... I've suspected it."

"Drugs are expensive. Billy isn't working. He needs money, and he was obviously looking for a bigger share of the estate. He's the one who hired the fake Jennifer, but when you came to us and asked for a DNA test, he panicked and had your father's body removed from the coffin because he couldn't afford to have that test made. That's what tipped me off. And I suspect that he sent someone to Miami to have the real Jennifer killed. Did you know that Anita has a brother who's tied into the mob? As long as Jennifer's alive and there are two Jennifer's around, his plan can't work."

"Are you sure of all this?"

"Absolutely. There's something else, Judge."

"Yes?"

"I don't think your father die in auto accident. I believe that Billy had your father murdered. Anita's brother could have arranged that too. I'm told he has connections with the Marseilles mafia. They could easily have paid a crew member to do it. I'm flying to Italy tonight to have a talk with the local authority."

Thomas was listening intently. When he spoke, he said approvingly, "That's a good idea." Captain Bargas knows nothing.

"I'll try to be back by Thursday for the reading of the will."

Thomas said, "What about the real Jennifer? ... Are you sure she's safe?"

"Oh, yes," George said. "She's staying where no one can find her. She's at my house."

31

The extraordinary piece of good fortune that I had been given was the opportunity to fight it my way. The gods are on my side. He could not believe his good fortune. It was an incredible stroke of luck. Last night, George Brown had delivered Jennifer into his hands. Henry Brooks is an incompetent fool; Thomas thought. I'll take care of Jennifer myself this time.

He looked up as Damon came into the room.

"Excuse me, Judge Stanley. There's a telephone call for you."

It was Lynda Powell. "Thomas?"

"Yes, Lyn."

"I just wanted to bring you up to date on the Mary Perkins matter."

"Yes?"

"Dr. Clifton just called me. The woman is insane. She's carrying on so badly that they have to have her locked away in the violent ward."

Thomas felt a sharp sense of relief. "I'm sorry to hear that."

"Anyway, I wanted to ease your mind and let you know that she's no longer any danger to you or your family."

"I appreciate that," Thomas said. And he did.

Thomas went to his room and telephoned Connie. There was a long delay before Connie answered.

"Hello?" Thomas could hear voices in the background.

"Connie?"

"Who is this?"

"It's Thomas."

"Oh, yeah. Thomas."

He could hear the tinkling of glasses. "Are you having a party, Connie?"

"Uh-huh, Do you want to join us?"

Thomas wondered who was at the party. "I wish I could. I'm calling to tell you to get ready to go on that trip we talked about."

Connie laughed. "You mean on that great big white yacht to St.-Tropez?"

"That's right."

"Sure. I can be ready anytime," she said mockingly.

"Connie, I'm serious."

"Oh, come off it, Thomas. Judges don't have yachts. I have to go now. My guests are calling me."

"Wait a minute!" Thomas said desperately. "Do you know who I am?"

"Sure, you're..."

"I'm Thomas Stanley. My father was Robert Stanley."

There was a moment of silence. "Are you kidding me?"

"No. I'm in Los Angeles now, settling up the estate."

"My God! You're that Stanley. I didn't know. I'm sorry. I ... I've been hearing stuff on the news, but I didn't pay much attention. I never figured it was you."

"That's all right."

"You really meant it about taking me to St-Tropez, didn't you?"

"Of course I did. We're going to do a lot of things together," Thomas said. "That is, if you want to."

"I certainly do!" Connie's voice was suddenly filled with enthusiasm. "Gee, Thomas, this is really great news ..." When Thomas replaced the receiver, he was smiling. Connie was taken care of. Now, he thought, it's time to take care of my half-sister.

Thomas went into the library where Robert Stanley's gun collection was kept, opened the case, and removed a mahogany box. From a drawer below the case, he took out some ammunition. He put the ammunition in his pocket and carried the wooden box upstairs to his bedroom, locked the door behind him, and opened the box. Inside were two matching Rugger revolvers, Robert Stanley's favorites. Thomas removed one, carefully loaded it, and then placed the extra ammunition and the box containing the other revolver in his bureau drawer. One shot will do it, he thought. They had taught him to shoot well at the military school his father had sent him to. Thank you, Father.

Next, Thomas picked up a telephone directory and looked for George Brown's home address: 280 Newbury Street, Los Angeles.

Thomas made his way to the garage, where there were half a dozen cars. He chose the black Mercedes as being the least conspicuous. He opened the garage door and listened to see if the noise had disturbed anyone. There was only silence. On the drive to George Brown's house, Thomas thought about what he was about to do. He had never physically committed a murder before. But this time he had no choice. Jennifer Stanley was the last obstacle between him and his dreams. With her gone, his problems would be over. Forever, Thomas thought.

He drove slowly, careful not to attract attention. When he reached Newbury Street, Thomas cruised past George's address. A few cars were parked on the street, but no pedestrians were around.

He parked the car a block away and walked back to the house. He rang the doorbell and waited.

Jennifer's voice came through the door. "Who is it?"

"It's Judge Stanley."

Jennifer opened the door. She looked at him in surprise.

"What are you doing here? Is anything wrong?"

"No, not at all," he said easily. "George Brown asked me to have a talk with you. He told me you were here. May I come in?"

"Yes, of course."

Thomas walked into the hall and watched Jennifer close the door behind him. She led the way into the living room.

"George isn't here," she said. "He's on his way to San Francisco."

"I know." He looked around. "Are you alone? Isn't there a housekeeper or someone to stay with you?"

"No. I'm safe here. May I offer you something?"

"No, thanks."

"What did you want to talk to me about?"

"I came to talk about you, Jennifer. I'm disappointed in you."

"Disappointed ...?"

"You should never have come here. Did you really think you could walk in and try to collect a fortune that doesn't belong to you?"

She looked at him a moment. "But I have a right to..."

"You have a right to nothing!" Thomas snapped. "Where were you all those years when we were being humiliated and punished by our father? He went out of his way to hurt us every chance he got. He put us through hell. You didn't have to go through any of that. Well, we did, and we deserve the money. Not you."

"I ... what do you want me to do?"

Thomas gave a short laugh. "What do I want you to do? Nothing. You've done it already. You damned near spoiled everything, do you know that?"

"I don't understand."

"It's really quite simple." He took out the revolver.

"You're going to disappear."

She took a step back. "But I ..."

"Don't say anything. Let's not waste time. You and I are going on a little trip."

She stiffened. "What if I won't go?"

"Oh, you'll be going. Dead or alive. Suit yourself."

In the moment of silence that followed, Thomas heard his voice boom out from the next room. "Oh, you'll be going. Dead or alive. Suit yourself" He whirled around.

"What ... ?"

George Brown, Frank Harold, Lieutenant Kennedy, and two uniformed policemen stepped into the living room. George was holding a tape recorder.

Lieutenant Kennedy said, "Give me the gun, Judge."

Thomas froze for an instant, and then he forced a smile. "Of course. I was just trying to scare this woman into getting out of here. She's a fraud, you know." He put the gun in the detective's outstretched hand. "She tried to claim part of the Stanley estate. Well, I wasn't about to let her get away with it. So I ..."

"It's over, Judge," George said.

"What are you talking about? You said Billy was responsible for ..."

"Billy wasn't up to planning anything as clever as this, and Carmen was already very successful. So I started checking up on you. Donald Herman was killed in Australia, but the Australian police found your telephone number in his pocket. You used him to murder your father. You're the one who brought in Mary Perkins and then insisted she was an impostor to throw suspicion off yourself. You're the one who insisted on the DNA test and arranged to have the body removed. And you're the one who put in the phony call to Tillman.

You hired Mary Perkins to impersonate Jennifer, and then had her committed to a psychiatric ward."

Thomas looked around the room, and when he spoke, his voice was dangerously calm. "And a phone number on a dead man is your evidence? I can't believe this! You set up your pitiful little trap based on that? You don't have a shred of proof. My telephone number was in Donald's pocket because I thought my father might be in danger. I told Donald to be careful. Obviously, he wasn't careful enough. Whoever killed my father probably killed Donald. That's who the police should be looking for. I called Tillman because I wanted him to find out the truth. Someone impersonated him. I have no idea who. And unless you can find him and tie him to me, you have nothing. As far as Mary Perkins is concerned, I really believed that she was our sister. When she suddenly went crazy, going on a buying spree and threatening to kill us all, I persuaded her to go to San Francisco. Then I arranged to have her picked up and committed. I wanted to keep all this out of the press to protect the family."

Jennifer said, "But you came here to kill me."

Thomas shook his head. "I had no intention of killing you. You're an impostor. I just wanted to scare you away."

"You're lying."

He turned to the others. "There's something else you might consider. It's possible that none of the family is involved. It could be some insider who's manipulating this, someone who put in an impostor and planned to convince the family she was genuine and then split a share of the estate with her. That didn't occur to any of you, did it?"

He turned to Frank Harold. "I'm going to sue you both for slander, and I'm going to take away everything you've got. These are my witnesses. Before I'm through with you, you'll wish you had never heard of me. I control billions, and I'm going to use them to destroy you."

He looked at George. "I promise you that your last act as a lawyer will be the reading of the Stanley will. Now, unless you want to charge me with carrying an unlicensed weapon, I'll be leaving."

The group looked at one another uncertainly.

"No? Well, good evening, then."

They watched helplessly as he walked out the door.

Lieutenant Kennedy was the first one to find his voice.

"My God!" he said. "Do you believe that?"

"He's bluffing," George said slowly. "But we can't prove it. He's right. We need proof. I thought he would crack, but I underestimated him."

Frank Harold spoke. "It looks like our little plan backfired. Without Donald Herman or the testimony of the Perkins woman, we have nothing but suspicions."

"What about the threat on my life?" Jennifer protested.

George said, "You heard what he said. He was just trying to scare you because he thought you were an impostor."

"He wasn't just trying to scare me," Jennifer said. "He intended to kill me."

"I know. But there isn't a thing we can do. Dickens had it right: 'The law is an ass ...' We're right back where we started."

Harold frowned. "It's worse than that, George. Thomas meant what he said about suing us. Unless we can prove our charges, we're in trouble."

When the others had left, Jennifer said to George, "I'm so sorry about all this. I feel responsible in away. If I hadn't come ..."

"Don't be silly," George said.

"But he said he's going to ruin you. Can he do that?" George shrugged. "We'll have to see."

Jennifer hesitated. "George, I'd like to help you."

He looked at her, puzzled. "What do you mean?"

"Well, I'm going to have a lot of money. I'd like to give you enough so you can..."

He put his hands on her shoulders. "Thank you, Jennifer. I can't take your money. I'll be fine."

"But ..."

"Don't worry about it."

She shuddered. "He's an evil man."

"It was very brave of you to do what you did."

"You said there was no way to get him, so I thought if you sent him here, that could be the way to trap him."

"It looks as though we're the ones who fell into the trap, doesn't it?"

That night, Jennifer lay in her bed, thinking about George and wondering how she could protect him. I shouldn't have come, she thought, but if I hadn't come, I wouldn't have met him.

In the next room, George lay in bed, thinking about Jennifer. It was frustrating to think that she was lying in her bed with only a thin wall between them. What am I talking about? That wall is a billion dollars thick.

Thomas was in his bad mood. On the way home, he thought about what had just taken place, and how he had outwitted them. They're pygmies trying to fell a giant, he thought. And he had no idea that that was once his father's thought. Thomas has a very bad mood drive.

When Thomas reached Bell Air, Damon greeted him.

"Good evening, Judge Thomas. I hope you're well this evening."

"Never better, Damon. Never better."

"Can I get you anything?"

"Yes. I think I'd like a glass of champagne."

"Of course, sir."

It was a celebration, the celebration of his victory.

Tomorrow I'll be worth over two billion dollars. He said the phrase lovingly over and over. "Two billion dollars ... two billion dollars ..." He decided to call Connie.

This time Connie recognized his voice immediately.

"Thomas! How are you?" Her voice was warm.

"Fine, Connie."

"I've been waiting to hear from you."

Thomas felt a little thrill. "Have you? How would you like to come to Los Angeles tomorrow?"

"Sure ... but what for?"

"For the reading of the will. I'm going to inherit over two billion dollars."

"Two ... that's fantastic!"

"I want you here at my side. We're going to pick out that yacht together."

"Oh, Thomas! That sounds wonderful!"

"Then you'll come?"

"Of course, I will."

When Connie replaced the receiver, she sat there saying lovingly over and over, "Two billion dollars ... two billion dollars... "

32

The will of Robert Stanley was in the center of discussion not only in the media, but also between his inheritants and lawyers. The day before the reading of the will, Carmen and Billy were seated in George's office.

"I don't understand why we're here," Billy said.

"The reading is supposed to be tomorrow."

"There's someone I want you to meet," George told them.

"Who?"

"Your sister."

They were both staring at him. "We've already met her," Carmen said.

George pressed a button on the intercom. "Would you ask her to come in, please?"

Carmen and Billy looked at each other, puzzled.

The door opened, and Jennifer Stanley walked into the office.

George stood up. "This is your sister, Jennifer."

"What the hell are you talking about?" Billy exploded. "What are you trying to pull?"

"Let me explain," George said quietly. He spoke for fifteen minutes, and finished by saying, "Paul Weissman confirms that her DNA matches your father's."

When George was through, Billy said, "Thomas! I can't believe it!"

"Believe it."

"I don't understand. The other woman's fingerprints prove that she is Jennifer," Billy said. "I still have the fingerprint card."

George felt his pulse pounding. "You do?"

"Yeah. I kept it as kind of a joke."

"I want you to do me a favor," George said.

At ten o'clock the next morning, a large group was gathered in the conference room of Reynolds & Frank Harold Attorney at law. Frank Harold sat at the head of a table. In the room were Carmen, Thomas, Billy, George, and Jennifer. In addition, there were several strangers present.

Harold introduced two of them. "This is Bryant Watkins and Gerald Walton. They're with the law firms that represent Stanley Enterprises. They've brought with them the financial report on the company. I'll discuss the will first, then they can take over the meeting."

"Let's get on with it," Thomas said impatiently. He was sitting apart from the others. I'm not only going to get the money, but I'm going to destroy you bastards.

Frank Harold nodded. "Very well."

In front of Harold was a large file divided Robert Stanley-LAST WILL AND TESTAMENT. "I'm going to give each of you a copy of the will so it won't be necessary to wade through all the technicalities. I've already told you that Robert Stanley's children will equally inherit the estate."

Jennifer glanced over at George, a look of bemusement on her face.

I'm glad for her, George thought. Even though it puts her way out of my reach.

Frank Harold was going on. "There are a dozen or so bequests, but they're all minor."

Thomas was thinking, Connie will be here this afternoon. I want to be at the airport to meet him.

"As you were told earlier, Stanley Enterprises has assets of approximately six billion dollars." Harold nodded toward Bryant Watkins. "I'll let Mr. Watkins take it from here."

Bryant Watkins opened a briefcase and spread some papers out on the conference table. "As Mr. Frank Harold said, there are six billion dollars in assets. However ..."

There was a pregnant pause. He looked around the room.

"Stanley Enterprises is in debt in excess of fifteen billion dollars."

Billy was on his feet. "What the hell are you saying?"

Thomas's face turned pale. "Is this some kind of joke?"

"It has to be!" Carmen said hoarsely.

Mr. Watkins turned to one of the men in the room. "Mr. Scott Richter is with the Securities and Exchange Commission. I'll let him explain."

Richter nodded. "For the last two years, Robert Stanley was convinced that interest rates were going to fall. In the past, he had made millions by betting on that. When interest rates started to rise, he was still convinced they would drop again, and he kept leveraging his bets. He did massive borrowing to buy long-term bonds, but the interest rates went up and his borrowing costs jumped, while the value of the bonds tumbled. The banks were willing to do business with him because of his reputation and his vast fortune, but when he tried to recoup his losses by starting to invest in high-risk securities, they began to get worried. He made a series of disastrous investments. Some of the money he borrowed was pledged by securities he had bought with borrowed money as collateral for further borrowing."

"In other words," Gerald Walton interjected, "he was pyramiding his debts, operating illegally."

"That is correct. Unfortunately for him, interest rates underwent one of the steepest climbs in financial history. He had to keep borrowing money to cover the money he had already borrowed. It was a vicious circle."

They sat there, hanging on Richter's every word. "Your father gave his personal guarantee to the company's pension plan and illegally used that money to buy more stock. When the banks began to question what he was doing, he set up decoy companies and provided false records of solvency and fake sales of his properties to drive up the value of his paper. He was committing fraud. In the end, he was counting on a consortium of banks to bail him out of trouble. They refused. When they told the Securities and Exchange Commission what was happening, Interpol was brought into the picture."

Richter indicated the man seated next to him. "This is Inspector Patel, with the French Surety. Inspector, would you explain the rest of it, please?"

Inspector Patel spoke English with a slight French accent. "At the request of Interpol, we traced Robert Stanley to Monte Carlo, and I sent three detectives there to follow him. He managed to elude them. Interpol had put out a green code to all police departments that Robert

Stanley was under suspicion and should be watched. If they had known the extent of his crimes, they would have circulated a red code, or top priority, and we would have apprehended him."

Billy was in a state of shock. "That's why he left us his estate. Because there was nothing in it!"

Bryant Watkins said, "You're right about that. You were all in your father's will because the banks refused to go along with him and he knew that, in essence, he was leaving you nothing. But he spoke to Ben Ginsburg at Credit Lyonnais, who promised to help him. The moment Robert Stanley thought that he was solvent again, he planned to change his will to cut you out of it."

"But what about the yacht, and the plane, and the houses?" Carmen asked.

"I'm sorry," Watkins said. "Everything will be sold to payoff part of the debt."

Thomas sat there, like dead. It was a nightmare beyond his imagination. He was no longer Thomas Stanley, Multibillionaire. He was only a judge.

Thomas got up to leave, shaken. "I don't know what to say. If there's nothing else "He had to get to the airport quickly to meet Connie and try to explain what had happened.

George spoke up. "There is something else."

He turned. "Yes?"

George nodded to a man standing at the door. The door opened, and Henry Brooks walked in.

"Hi, Judge."

The breakthrough had come when Billy told George that he had the fingerprint card.

"I'd like to see it," George told him.

Billy had been puzzled. "Why? It just has the woman's two sets of fingerprints on it, and they matched. We all checked it."

"But the man who called himself Fredy Tillman took the fingerprints, right?"

"Yes."

"Then if he touched the card, his fingerprints will be on it."

George's hunch had proved to be right. Henry Brooks' prints were all over the card, and it had taken less than thirty minutes for the computers to reveal his identity. George had telephoned the district attorney in San Francisco. A warrant was issued, and two detectives had appeared at Henry Brooks' house.

He was in the yard playing catch with Bob.

"Mr. Brooks?"

"Yes."

The detectives showed their badges. "The district attorney would like to talk to you."

"No. I can't." He was indignant.

"May I ask why?" one of the detectives asked.

"You can see why, can't you? I'm playing ball with my son!"

The district attorney had read the transcript of Henry Brooks' trial. He looked at the man seated in front of him and said, "I understand you're a family man."

"That's right," Henry Brooks said proudly. "That's what this country is all about. If every family could..."

"Mr. Brooks." He leaned forward. "You've been working with Judge Stanley."

"I don't know any Judge Stanley."

"Let me refresh your memory. He put you on parole. He used you to impersonate a private detective named Fredy Tillman, and we have reason to believe he also asked you to kill a Jennifer Stanley."

"I don't know what you're talking about."

"What I'm talking about is a sentence of ten to twenty years. I'm going to push for the twenty."

Henry Brooks turned pale. "You can't do that! Why, my wife and kids would ..."

"Exactly. On the other hand," the district attorney said, "if you're willing to turn state's evidence, I'm prepared to arrange for you to get off very lightly."

Henry Brooks was beginning to perspire. "What ... what do I have to do?"

"Talk to me ..."

Now, in the conference room of Reynolds & Frank Harold Attorney at law, Henry Brooks looked at Thomas, and said, "How are you, Judge?"

Billy looked up and exclaimed, "Hey! It's Frank Tillman!"

George said to Thomas, "This is the man you ordered to break into our offices, to get you a copy of your father's will, to dig up your father's body, and to kill Jennifer Stanley."

It took a moment for Thomas to find his voice. "You're crazy! He's a convicted felon. No one is going to take his word against mine!"

"No one has to take his word," George said. "Have you seen this man before?"

"Of course. He was tried in my court."

"What's his name?"

"His name is ..." Thomas saw the trap. "I mean ... he probably has a lot of aliases."

"When you tried him in your courtroom, his name was Henry Brooks."

"That ... that's right."

"But when he came to Los Angeles, you introduced him as Fredy Tillman."

Thomas was floundering. "Well, I ... I ..."

"You had him released into your custody, and you used him to try to prove that Mary Perkins was the real Jennifer."

"No! I had nothing to do with that. I never met that woman until she showed up here."

George turned to Lieutenant Kennedy. "Did you get that, Lieutenant?"

"Yes."

George turned back to Thomas. "We checked on Mary Perkins. She was also tried in your courtroom and released into your custody. The district attorney in San Francisco issued a search warrant this morning for your safe-deposit box. He called a little while ago to tell me that they found a document giving you Jennifer Stanley's share of your father's estate. The document was signed five days before the supposed Jennifer Stanley arrived in Los Angeles."

Thomas was breathing hard, trying to regain his wits.

"I... I ... This is preposterous!"

Lieutenant Kennedy said, "I'm placing you under arrest, Judge Stanley, for conspiracy to commit murder. We'll arrange for extradition papers. You'll be sent back to San Francisco."

Thomas stood there, his world collapsing around him.

"You have the right to remain" silent. If you choose to give up this right, anything you say can and will be used against you in a court of law. You have the right to talk to a lawyer and have him present with you while you are being questioned. If you cannot afford to hire a lawyer, one will be appointed to represent you before any questioning, if you wish one. Do you understand?"

Lieutenant Kennedy asked.

"Yes." And then a slow triumphant smile lit his face.

I know how to beat them! he thought happily.

"Are you ready, Judge?"

He nodded and said calmly, "Yes. I'm ready. I'd like to go back to Bell Air to pick up my things."

"That's fine. We'll have these two policemen   accompany you."

Thomas turned to look at Jennifer, and there was so much hatred in his eyes that it made her shudder.

Thirty minutes later, Thomas and the two policemen reached Bell Air. They walked into the front hall.

"It will take me only a few minutes to pack," Thomas said.

They watched as Thomas went up the staircase to his room. In his room, Thomas walked over to the bureau containing the revolver and loaded it.

The sound of the shot seemed to reverberate.

Billy and Carmen were seated in the drawing room at Bell Air. Half a dozen men in white overalls were taking down paintings from the walls and starting to dismantle the furnishings.

"It's the end of an era." Carmen sighed.

"It's the beginning," Billy said. He smiled. "I wish I could see Anita's face when she finds out what her half of my fortune is!" He took his sister's hand. "Are you okay? About David, I mean."

She nodded. "I'll get over it. Anyhow, I'm going to be very busy. I have a preliminary hearing in two weeks. After that, I'll see what happens."

"I'm sure everything will be all right." He rose. "I have an important telephone call to make," Billy told her. He had to break the news to Nicole Carson.

"Nicole," Billy said apologetically, "I'm afraid I'm going to have to go back on our deal. Things haven't worked out as I had hoped they would."

"Are you all right, Billy?"

"Yes. A lot has been going on here. Anita and I are finished."

There was a long pause. "Oh? Are you coming back to Bell Air?"

"Frankly, I don't know what I'm going to do."

"Billy?"

"Yes?"

Her voice was soft. "Come back, please."

Jennifer and George were out on the patio.

"I'm sorry about the way things turned out," George said. "About you not getting the money, I mean."

Jennifer smiled at him. "I don't really need a hundred chefs."

"You're not disappointed that your trip here was wasted?"

She looked up at him. "Was it wasted, George?" They never knew who made the first move, but she was in his arms, and he was holding her, and they were kissing.

"I've wanted to do this since the first time I saw you."

Jennifer shook her head. "The first time you saw me, you told me to get out of town!"

He grinned. "I did, didn't I? I don't ever want you to leave."

And she thought of Susan's words. "Don't you know if the man proposed?"

"Is that a proposal?" Jennifer asked.

He held her tighter. "You bet it is. Will you marry me?"

"Oh, yes!"

Carmen came out to the patio. She was holding a piece of paper in her hand.

"I ... I just got this in the mail."

George looked at her, worried. "Not another ...?"

"No. I've been voted Women's Wear Designer of the Year."

Billy and Carmen and Jennifer and George were seated at the dining-room table. All around them workmen were moving chairs and couches, and carrying them off.

George turned to Billy. "What are you going to do now?"

"I'm going back to Bell Air. First, I'm going to check in with Dr. Thompson. Then a friend of mine has a string of ponies that I'm going to ride."

Carmen looked at Jennifer. "Are you going back to Miami?"

When I was a little girl, Jennifer thought, I wished that someone would take me out of Florida and bring me to a magical place where I would find my prince. She took George's hand. "No," Jennifer said. "I'm not going back to Miami."

They watched two men take down the huge portrait of Robert Stanley.

"I never like that picture," Billy said.

END

BAD MOOD DRIVE

BAD MOOD DRIVE is a Crime Fiction, created on November 21, 2010 for entertainment purposes only. The main idea is that wealthy man Robert Stanley is driven by his "bad mood," which create frustration. He treats his family members and friends with no respect whatsoever. The story involves crime based on family problems. The book is highly recommended for people, whose English is a second language. It's not recommended for children at age 18 and below, because of bad behaviors and mild form of violence.

ISBN: 978 - 1- 6140000 - 3 – 7

LCCN: 2014916291

BOOK DESCRIPTION

Millionaire Robert Stanley is in Monte Carlo—his yacht Blue Skies in port, a beautiful woman on his lap, and his bodyguard Donald Herman standing nearby, ever vigilant. Stanley's enjoying all the benefits of wealth, little knowing he's about to die.

Stanley's death behind the wheel of his blue Mercedes seems like an accident, but there's no denying many people wanted the man dead. As a businessman, Stanley had been ruthless, gleefully driving competitors into bankruptcy and—it's rumored—suicide. He gained control of his company by turning the board of directors against his own father, an act that cemented his reputation as a merciless egomaniac.

Stanley's behavior at home mirrored his business dealings. Cruel and lascivious, his infidelity drove his wife to suicide. Blamed for her death by his children, Stanley worked to isolate them from each other, leaving them only a small trust from their mother for expenses.

No, Robert Stanley will not be mourned, but was his death murder? And, if so, was he the target of a family plot or organized crime?

A tense thriller from the mind of Alan Douglas, Bad Mood Drive will keep you guessing until its shocking conclusion.

Alan Douglas
List of his Book (Paperback) set up as POD (Print on Demand)
with Create Space (Amazon.com Company)USA

1. Bad Mood Drive: American English Edition
ISBN-13: 978-1614000037
ISBN-10: 1614000034
LCCN: 2014916291
Create Space Title ID # 4979997

2. Bad Mood Drive: Spanish-English Double Edition
ISBN-13: 978-1614000020
ISBN-10: 1614000026
LCCN: 2014953099
Create Space Title ID # 4967359

3. Guia De Humor Mala
Bad Mood Drive: Spanish Edition
ISBN-13: 978-0983180913
ISBN-10: 0983180911
Create Space Title ID # 4967359

4. Bad Mood: English Edition
ISBN-13: 978-1503001299 (CreateSpace-Assigned)
ISBN-10: 1503001296
BISAC: Fiction / Crime
Create Space Title ID # 5073664

5. MAUVAISE COMMANDE d'HUMEUR
Bad Mood Drive French Edition
ISBN-13: 978-1614000051
ISBN-10: 1614000050
BISAC: Fiction / Crime
Create Space Title ID # 5069020

6. Bad Mood Drive
French-English Double Edition
ISBN-13: 978-1614000044
ISBN-10: 1614000042
BISAC: Fiction / Crime
Create Space Title ID # 4989961

7. Movimentacao Ma Do Modo
Bad Mood Drive Portuguese (Brazil) Edition
ISBN-13: 978-1614000006
ISBN-10: 161400000X
BISAC: Fiction / General
Create Space Title ID # 3572061

8. Bad Mood Drive
Portuguese (Brazil) - English Double Edition
ISBN-13: 978-1614000105
ISBN-10: 1614000107
BISAC: Fiction / Crime
Create Space Title ID # 5167586

9. Bad Mood Drive: German Edition
ISBN-13: 978-1614000136
ISBN-10: 1614000131
BISAC: Fiction / Crime
Create Space Title ID # 5225599

10. Bad Mood Drive: German - English Double Edition
ISBN-13: 978-1614000143
ISBN-10: 161400014X
BISAC: Fiction / Crime
Create Space Title ID # 5225622

11. Bad Mood Drive: Polish Edition
ISBN-13: 978-1614000174
ISBN-10: 1614000174
BISAC: Fiction / Crime
Create Space Title ID # 5249511

12. Bad Mood Drive: Polish-English Double Edition
ISBN-13: 978-1614000181
ISBN-10: 1614000182
BISAC: Fiction / Crime
Create Space Title ID # 5249544

13. Bad Mood Drive: Italian Edition
ISBN-13: 978-1614000198
ISBN-10: 1614000190
BISAC: Fiction / Crime
Create Space Title ID # 5253420

14. Bad Mood Drive: Italian - English Double Edition
ISBN-13: 978-1614000204
ISBN-10: 1614000204
BISAC: Fiction / Crime
Create Space Title ID # 5253634

15. Bad Mood Drive: Bulgarian Edition
ISBN-13: 978-1614000235
ISBN-10: 1614000239
BISAC: Fiction / Crime
Create Space Title ID # 5330553

16. Bad Mood Drive: Bulgarian-English Double Edition
ISBN-13: 978-1614000242
ISBN-10: 1614000247
BISAC: Fiction / Crime
Create Space Title ID # 5330601

17. Bad Mood Drive: Russian Edition
ISBN-13: 978-1614000211
ISBN-10: 1614000212
BISAC: Fiction / Crime
Create Space Title ID # 5267174

18. Bad Mood Drive: Russian - English Double Edition
ISBN-13: 978-1614000228
ISBN-10: 1614000220
BISAC: Fiction / Crime
Create Space Title ID # 5267250

19. Bad Mood Drive: Arabic Edition
ISBN-13: 978-1614000112
ISBN-10: 1614000115
BISAC: Fiction / Crime
Create Space Title ID # 5190152

20. Bad Mood Drive: Arabic-English Double Edition
ISBN-13: 978-1614000129
ISBN-10: 1614000123
BISAC: Fiction / Crime
Create Space Title ID # 5190446

21. Bad Mood Drive: Hindi Edition
ISBN-13: 978-1614000150
ISBN-10: 1614000158
BISAC: Fiction / Crime
Create Space Title ID # 5233401

22. Bad Mood Drive: Hindi-English Double Edition
ISBN-13: 978-1614000167
ISBN-10: 1614000166
BISAC: Fiction / Crime
Create Space Title ID # 5233880

23. Bad Mood Drive: Japanese Edition
ISBN-13: 978-1614000068
ISBN-10: 1614000069
BISAC: True Crime / General
Create Space Title ID # 5094820

24. Bad Mood Drive: Japanese - English Double Edition
ISBN-13: 978-1614000082
ISBN-10: 1614000085
BISAC: Fiction / Crime
Create Space Title ID # 5097840

25. Bad Mood Drive: Chinese (Simplified) Edition
ISBN-13: 978-1614000075
ISBN-10: 1614000077
BISAC: Fiction / Crime
Create Space Title ID # 5112746

26. Bad Mood Drive: Chinese (Simplified)-English Double Edition
ISBN-13: 978-1614000099
ISBN-10: 1614000093
BISAC: Fiction / Crime
Create Space Title ID # 5115013

27. Bad Mood Drive: Chinese (Traditional) Edition
ISBN-13: 978-1614000266
ISBN-10: 1614000263
BISAC: Fiction / Crime
Create Space Title ID # 5333954

28. Bad Mood Drive: Chinese (Traditional)-English Double Edition
ISBN-13: 978-1614000273
ISBN-10: 1614000271
BISAC: Fiction / Crime
Create Space Title ID # 5333980

AUTHOR BIOGRAPHY

Alan Douglas is an American writer with a strong academic background who graduated from Bernard Baruch College, New York. He has lived on the East Coast, Chicago, and Milwaukee, and currently resides in Los Angeles, California.

Douglas has four screenplays registered with the Writers Guild of America and the Library of Congress. Bad Mood Drive is available in multiple languages, including an English/French double edition to promote American English internationally. His next project, Charming Lady, is currently under development.

www.ingramcontent.com/pod-product-compliance
Lightning Source LLC
Chambersburg PA
CBHW070752280626
47162CB00016B/166